NOT FAIR

By the same author

MOTHER LOVE
GEMINI
SUFFER LITTLE CHILDREN
PRAYING MANTIS
SIEGE

NOT FAIR

Domini Taylor

LITTLE, BROWN AND COMPANY

A *Little, Brown* Book

First published in Great Britain in 1992
by Little, Brown and Company

Copyright © 1992 by Domini Taylor

The moral right of the author has been asserted.

All rights reserved.
No part of this publication may be reproduced,
stored in a retrieval system, or transmitted, in any
form or by any means, without the prior
permission in writing of the publisher, nor be
otherwise circulated in any form of binding or
cover other than that in which it is published and
without a similar condition including this
condition being imposed on the subsequent purchaser.

*All characters in this publication are fictitious
and any resemblance to real persons, living or dead,
is purely coincidental.*

A CIP catalogue record for this book is available
from the British Library.

ISBN 0 316 90359 0

Typeset by Leaper & Gard Ltd, Bristol
Printed in England by Clays Ltd, St Ives plc

Little, Brown and Company (UK) Limited
165 Great Dover Street
London SE1 4YA

CHAPTER ONE

'I'M TOO SELFISH TO SAY NO,' said Nicola Maude. 'But I'm too careful to say yes.'

'Too scared?'

'All right. I'm scared to say yes.'

'I'll settle for maybe,' said David Parkinson. 'But not for ever.'

He held her hand. Her fingers returned the pressure of his. A splash of sunlight, filtered and animated by the leaves of the walnut tree, slid over her hair, which was the strange silvery-tawny colour of old polished pewter in firelight. She smiled. It was a warm and real smile, careful perhaps but not scared, a wide, childish smile which spread like a blessing all over her face.

They sat on the edge of a lawn by a small house outside a small city. It was mid-afternoon in mid-May, the weather brilliant, the garden with an air of astonishment at finding itself so full of colours. Down the fitful West wind came the bongs of the Cathedral clock striking four; overlapping but late, as always, sounded the other clocks in the other towers – the parish church of All Saints, the Collegiate Church of St Stephen, the Chapel of the Hospital of the Holy Cross.

Nico was approaching her twenty-second birthday. This was her fifth serious proposal of marriage, not counting childish outbursts (one of these last, indeed, sulkily out of her life, but the others remained friends). She was a girl who kept her friends – a girl who had been amazed the year before to find how many friends she had, to discover how much she was loved.

Her eyes were grey, her face heart-shaped, her nose impertinent, her mouth too generous for classic beauty. Her brow and cheeks were already tinted to pink-gold by the sun, the season being in the new style of English summers, in which asparagus was cut in the kitchen gardens in early April, and freckles dusted the noses of the girls a full month earlier than usual.

Nico's voice, when she spoke, sounded as though she might easily decide to sing. She often did sing. As a very young child she had first sung in the choir of her father's church; she did so for a short time until his death, when she was six. She had been singing ever since, alone and in groups and in other churches; she had sung in the cathedral and thereabouts, and in the homes of friends in distant places. David had grown up to the sound of Nico's voice, in anthems and ballads and snatches from Fred Astaire movies, and to him it had the colour of her hair – warmer than silver, cooler than gold. David held that Nico's voice was the most beautiful sound in the world; but he knew that he was prejudiced, because he had been in love with her since he was ten years old.

'You're scared to say yes,' said David, 'because—'

'You know why.'

'Because you have the idiotic idea I'm asking out of pity.'

'Not exactly. Not quite idiotic. I think you *think*

you're not. But I'm not sure you can be *sure* you're not.'

'You're getting in a muddle with double negatives.'

She laughed.

David said, 'Look at that. You're as tough as an old boot. I could strike a match on any bit of you. Fancy *laughing* while you're refusing the offer of a tender and adoring heart.'

'I'm not really in a muddle. I know what I mean, and you know what I mean. You could easily be fooling yourself. It's all precisely because you're sweet, because you're a sweet, kind man.'

'That's a bloody funny reason for turning me down.'

'I admit it's ironic. But you do see. How could anyone as nice as you not feel pity? And do something about it? And pretend it wasn't pity? Pretend even to yourself it wasn't?'

'Of course it's pity,' said David. 'You're stupid and ugly and unmusical, you can't draw and nobody's ever wanted to draw you. Of course I wouldn't be asking you except out of pity.'

She laughed again, gently. She was a clever girl, too clever not to know that she was lovely and beloved, that she was gifted and admired. Her laugh had in it a note of justified confidence; a note of surprise, as though she had not yet got used to awareness of beauty and talent; and a note of bitterness.

'I'd wake up in the morning,' she said, 'and see your face, and never be quite sure why you were there.'

'My darling love, can't you get it through your thick head that you are quite simply the person I want to spend the rest of my life with?'

She raised his hand with her hand, and leaned her cheek against it. It was a gesture of trust and friendship, of gratitude and deep affection; perhaps not of passion, physical commitment, overpowering love.

3

They sat in silence for a little, David on a rustic bench, his elbow on the arm, Nico in a chair. He was wearing khaki cotton pants and a faded blue shirt, short-sleeved, open-necked. He was neat; his clothes were clean and well pressed; his hands and fingernails were spotless. Nico wore jeans and a pink shirt. Her hair, with a natural wave, hung to her shoulders; it was not very tidy, but it gave back the splashes of sunlight with the brilliance of polished metal.

David was twenty-six. He seemed to strangers medium in every way – of medium height and build, medium mousy colouring with medium hazel eyes, of medium academic achievement and medium sporting prowess, sprung of middle people with middle incomes and middling homes: a young man, strangers would have said, who would never sniff disgrace or glory, who would live a moderate life undefiled by pitch, unsanctified by the divine fire. But this view of David left out of account some qualities that did not show, and one central fact about him which showed, from time to time, all too clearly: his absorbing and abiding love for Nico.

She did not perfectly trust his love, because there might be pity mixed into it. She did not perfectly trust her own love, because, fifteen months before, she had believed herself in love with somebody else.

The walnut tree spread its dappled shade over a third of the lawn. This was bounded on one side by an old brick wall with a border in front; on the next side by an untidy and charming colony of shrubs and old-fashioned roses; on the third side by the rough grass of an orchard. Beyond the orchard ran a small road, one of those which looped out of the town to the villages, langs running between high banks crowned with hawthorn and sweetbriar, little-used thoroughfares on the way to nowhere important.

On the fourth side of the lawn was a paved terrace, and behind that the house. The house was the decent indestructible Victorian cottage found for Nico's mother after the father died. It had been the house of the head keeper of an estate broken up between the wars. Head keepers were important men in pheasant-shooting country in 1880. This one's house was built of local stone, with a stone roof pitched between massive chimneys. The small upstairs windows peeped through a vertical jungle of roses, clematis and honeysuckle; in the cracks between the flagstones of the terrace grew pinks and lavender and lilies-of-the-valley.

The house contained no inherited treasures, and few which had been wedding presents. In the summer it smelled of roses and beeswax polish; in the winter it smelled of paraffin heaters, wet dog and apple-wood on the open fire. These things were more widely known, the house more often visited, than anybody would have guessed who drove by and saw the roof over the fruit trees.

Nico sat with David's knuckles against her cheek. Between their faces hung eighteen inches of scented air: love spoken and unspoken, memory shared and solitary. Between them hung, for Nico, the crash and scream and terror, the agony and horror of that dark winter corner under the trees, the car skidding on the black ice and hitting the horses ...

The memory was there because it was always there, unexorcized after fifteen months of gradual and partial recovery, after such kindness and goodwill as Nico would not have believed.

In the ordinary face close to hers, Nico saw nothing ordinary. It would have been impossible for her to have looked at that face and seen nothing behind it, so long and so well had she known him. His family had lived, lived still, in her father's parish. They were churchgoers, neighbours, friends. A big, kind boy with mouse-coloured hair inhabited the misty country of Nico's earliest memories (he had seemed big to her then, being four years older): a boy who left a gap in her life when he went away to boarding school, in spite of the difference in their ages: a boy who was always risking his neck climbing his father's elm trees, and jumping hairy fences on hairy ponies, but who always, unreasonably, tried to prevent Nico from risking hers...

Bees swung amongst the fruit blossom; over the nearby fields, under a few small, comfortable clouds, the skylarks quivered and vibrated in the middle air with the passion of their music.

Nico suddenly began to cry, but she could not tell David why, because she did not know why.

David went away a little before five; he had an hour's work to do in the estate office of his father's property, which he managed: he had to busy himself with wages, invoices and the VAT returns. He kissed Nico on the forehead after he had risen to his feet; he might have kissed her cheek, but her cheek was wet with tears.

Nico watched him go, round the corner of the house and out of sight. She heard the starter of his car, the buzz of the engine, the crunch of the tyres on the gravel.

The garden was empty without him. The afternoon was suddenly empty.

Across the lawn fell the shadow of Hugh, who was dead.

Nico sighed. She propelled herself in her wheelchair across the lawn to the terrace, and into the house by the door where they had taken away the step.

It had cost a surprising amount of money to make the house suitable for someone in a wheelchair. Steps had to become ramps; a ground-floor bedroom had to be improvised out of the dining room, and a bath put into the little brick-floored room where Nico's mother had arranged flowers and scrubbed vegetables. It would not have been worth such expense, such effort and inconvenience, if the wheelchair had been temporary – if there had been any serious hope that the wheelchair might be temporary. Since there was no such hope, Nico's Aunt Viola had provided the money – more exactly, her husband Hilary, a man of bottomless generosity. He gave Nico and her mother as much as they would let him give them.

Nico's mother Alice spent part of that afternoon at Hilary and Vi's house. She was keeping an eye on things while they were in America. It was only five miles away; she went over two or three times a week, to make sure that the birds were being fed and the house-plants watered. It was not quite unnecessary. The Cavenhams had an excellent Portuguese couple, butler and cook, but they sometimes forgot the special rearing food for the canary chicks, and they were apt, in their anxiety, to overwater the jasmine. Alice had at one time been afraid of upsetting them, an outsider horning in and supervising, but she had found that it was not so. They seemed pleased to see her whenever she appeared: they seemed to like her. She realized also that they were glad to be relieved of responsibility. If anything looked like going wrong, they asked her what to do, so that nothing could be their fault.

Many things could go wrong, because the house was large and full of luxuries and treasures. The pool could turn green, or the lawns brown; bills could be unpaid or paid twice.

It was a small enough return for Alice to make, for the generosity of her sister and brother-in-law. They had always been good; since the 'accident' they had been magnificent. It was not only money which Vi had so prodigally given – she had given courage, gaiety, support, amusement, hope. Her strength had been amazing, unceasing. Alice was not exactly weak, Nicola not weak at all, but the double blow, Nicola and Hugh, would have been heavy indeed without Vi.

Alice did her usual quick spin through the lovely rooms of the house, those on the south side shuttered and in semi-darkness, to protect Persian carpets and Georgian furniture from the sun. Where there were bare floorboards, her feet clattered intrusively in the big silence. The rooms had a faint, pleasant smell, quite unlike the smell of Alice's cottage.

It was the smell of wealth.

Alice noted that Maria and the two daily women had been keeping everything dusted and polished.

In Vi's little morning room, on a piecrust table covered with bric-a-brac, stood a familiar photograph in a silver frame: Nicola at the age of sixteen, playing tennis on the court of this house – Nicola running along the baseline with her racquet outstretched, with her pale hair streaming, with her beautiful long legs in very short shorts, the photograph taken by Hilary on a well-remembered August afternoon ...

Originally, Hilary and Vi living so close had not been Alice's favourite thing. The contrast was too blatant, too gross and cruel – the wife of a very rich baronet, and the wife and widow of a country parson. Hilary could have chosen to live anywhere in the world (his awful inherited

Derbyshire mansion having been a boys' prep school since 1938) but Vi had wanted to be near Alice. Reasonable. On the face of it, very nice. Everybody who thought about it approved and understood the decision. And when March Court came unexpectedly on the market ...

Alice was ever thereafter a battleground, struggling not to show envy, struggling not even to feel envy. She found envy, in herself as in others, the most tawdry and squalid of the deadly sins. She herself had so much to be thankful for. A roof over one's head need be no more than that, and hers was far more than that. And then she looked at the rococo garlands on the ceiling of the library, the Gainsborough portrait and the Rex Whistler painting of the house: she looked at the view over the terrace from the French windows of the drawing room ...

Self-pity was a sin against the Holy Ghost, and *Nicola never felt it.* Mother was rebuked by daughter. Alice must *not* feel sorry for herself. And yet, and yet, Alice thought that only a monstrous prig could have failed to covet some of Vi's and Hilary's things. Moral rules forbidding a little covetousness were simply too tough to observe. Therefore there was always a kind of toothache twinge when Alice visited the house, and most of all when she was acting as a caretaker, when she was temporary mistress of all she surveyed.

It was not that Alice regretted having married Barney. It was not that she regretted his being a country parson, with a stipend less than the wages of a teenage typist. Alice and Vi had each chosen as they had chosen.

What if it had been the other way round? Alice hoped she would have been as generous as Vi, as good and thoughtful and loyal. That camel was sure enough going through the eye of that needle. And they were giving Nicola a car, expensively adapted for the disabled. It was due any time. Nicola was mad for it. Vi would probably insure it and license it and have it serviced.

Vi would have done the same for Alice, all those years, if Alice had let her. Vi knew that Alice had to have a car and could hardly afford one. Why not let her? Because Alice was not prepared to be in all ways her sister's pensioner. She could not fool herself that she was financially independent, but she could cling to shreds of self-respect.

Nicola would soon start to earn her own living. She could do that all right. Who needed legs to sit at a desk?

Alice had a cup of tea with Pedro and Maria, and drove home in the late afternoon through gold light and green shade, through birdsong and the bells of the Cathedral calling the people to Evensong.

David heard the bells through the open window of the estate office. If he faced the window he saw his father's wheat, the cattle in the pasture beyond which sloped down to the river, more water-meadows across the river, the oak wood, and then the swell of downland speckled with sheep. To the north were the fringes of the town, and crowning them the spire of the Cathedral. The whole scene basked in the golden light of late afternoon, giving a sense of having been there for a very long time, of intending to stay there for ever. It was impossible to work with such a prospect.

If he turned away he saw his photograph of Nico, taken two years before at a picnic on the river-bank. There were other people in the picture – Hugh Jarvis, Felicity Peacock, David himself, a laughing group boiling a kettle on a campfire – but the reason for having it was Nico. She looked so happy. They were all happy that day. David had not discovered that Nico was falling for Hugh, Flickie had not discovered that Hugh was falling for Nico, and Nico and Hugh were only then discovering that they were falling for one another. It was impossible to work under the eyes of the people in the photograph.

David's father came in, Jack Parkinson, dapper as always, wearing a collar and tie, knife-edge creases in his trousers. He was trying to retire, for David's sake, and finding it impossible. The farm could do without him, but not he without the farm.

'Where were you this afternoon?'

'Proposing to Nico Maude.'

'Oh.'

Jack went to the window and looked out, as though to check that the countryside was still there. It was obvious that he did not know what to say, because he did not know what to think. He and David had not precisely discussed the matter, because it was all too obvious to need discussion: Nico was beautiful and in all ways excellent, well educated and of good family. She could not have children or do housework. She would always need looking after, almost nursing. She was a hopelessly impractical choice of wife for a working farmer. She was irresistible. They both knew all this, and so did everybody else.

Jack said, for something to say, 'What about Hugh?'

'I don't know.'

'A dead rival might be tougher than a living one.'

'Maybe. But if Hugh was alive I wouldn't have a chance.'

Jack walked round the office, and went back to the window. He frowned at the distant Cathedral.

David said, 'I suppose one might adopt.'

'I suppose so.'

Between them, over the happy photograph, hung the unspoken thought: best of a bad job.

'Adoption,' said Jack at last. 'Have you discussed that with Nico?'

'No, of course not.'

Each waited for the other to say something, but there was nothing to say, until the subject was changed.

'Did you want me this afternoon?' said David.

'Oh yes. The fellow came about the fencing. He left some bumph. I think he's too expensive. I said you'd ring him in the morning.'

David knew that his father was making a deliberate and sustained effort not to come to a decision about the fencing, to leave it to David. David was grateful, but his mind was too full of Nico to weigh the claims of the various contractors. He knew that he had to think about the farm a good deal of the time, but for the moment he could only think about Nico.

To see her sitting there, you'd never guess there was anything wrong with her. There wasn't anything wrong with her, except that some of her didn't work.

'It's not fair, is it?' said David's father suddenly.

'It makes you doubt the goodness of God.'

'Nicola doesn't feel like that, does she?'

'I don't see how she could fail to.'

'Please don't say any of that in front of your mother.'

'No, of course not, nor her mother.'

'Nothing would ever make Alice doubt the goodness of God.'

'Alice isn't crippled.'

'She'd rather be,' said David's father. 'She'd much rather be crippled than have Nico crippled. You of all people ought to be clear about that, if you're joining that family. Alice'd infinitely rather sacrifice herself. She's been living entirely for the child since her husband was killed.'

'Yes. Why did he fall off that train? Nobody's talked about that for years. I remember when nobody talked about anything else, unless you thought we were listening. *Pas devant les enfants.* Heavens, you were bad at that. Why *did* it happen? Was he tight?'

'He'd been to an Old Boys' dinner. They had port and so forth. He was quite unused to alcohol. Somebody put him on the train at Waterloo. There was a suggestion that he was a bit woozy.'

'I hope he was plastered, that he never knew what happened, that he died happy. Isn't that the best thing to wish?'

'I suppose so, as the alternatives are unthinkable.'

David nodded. The single logical alternative was that Nico's father had jumped. Nobody had thought that likely, but nobody could deny that it was possible. It was terrible to think of possible reasons. This was what David remembered, from the murmured, unhappy, ghoulish conversations when he was ten.

Alice had been distraught — David could remember that, too — but she had had to pull herself together, get on with her life, because she had Nico. Nico had saved Alice. Alice had been repaying the debt ever since. This was evident to David's family and to all their neighbours; David had been brought up to it, as received wisdom.

Why was Nico not overprotected and spoilt? She just wasn't. Alice was wiser than people thought, or Nico even more remarkable, or both.

★

It was always a little startling, to jump straight from March Court into Turner's Cottage.

There were an awful lot of differences. There was a different smell. But the biggest difference was one of space.

Alice had recently been talking (at a reception at the Deanery in Milchester) to a man who worked for the United Nations in Namibia. He was English, but he had become African. He would not sever his roots, but he would not live in Britain, either. The country was cramped. He had come to value elbow-room, to need solitude and empty horizons. That was the feeling you had at March Court. You could swing a cat. You could breathe. You could get away from people. In the cottage, Alice and Nicola had to be careful about gesturing, to avoid knocking vases off tables or hitting one another. You had the sense all the time of sidling between pieces of furniture, stooping in doorways, taking care not to bark shins or knuckles. Anyone claustrophobic would scream and run into the garden – but that was pretty cramped, too, a lawn like a handkerchief, an orchard not much bigger than a bedspread, the road almost under the windows.

Nicola was the sufferer. Alice could have lived in a biscuit-tin, but youth ought to be served. When she was small, she should have been able to dash from room to room; when she was a teenager, she should have been able to give huge parties; now she had to keep her wheelchair to a snail's pace, threading her way across rooms and through doors.

It was hardly fair.

Alice could have lived in a biscuit-tin, but that would have been a terrible shame. She had always been very pretty; now, at forty-five, she was beautiful. She was slim and graceful, a beautiful mover. She had a broad brow, and cheekbones which gave a hint of Slav somewhere in her ancestry. Her hair was ash-blonde, her eyes a bright pale blue. Her face was full of strength and humour. She was somebody who, at a party, most strangers wanted to meet, but who frightened some people by an appearance of impatience.

'Hello, darling.'

'Hello, Mum.'

'Have you had tea?'

'Hours ago. I needed it.'

'Did David come?'

'Yes, he was here.'

'And?'

'I don't know.'

'He asked? Properly? Asked right out?'

'Yes.'

Alice had foreseen this. Everybody had foreseen it. Everybody knew that David would ask, though nobody knew how Nicola would answer.

Although she had foreseen it, Alice was utterly dismayed. She was frightened for Nicola and for David, because history was repeating itself.

Controlling her face and voice, she said, 'What have you decided?'

'I can't decide. I'm not sure I can do this to him.'

'He thinks you can,' said Alice, with an effort at calmness.

'When I'm your age I shall be fat and my breath will smell, because I shall never have taken any exercise at all. Unless he gets a girl he'll never have a sex life. He'll never have his own children. He or somebody will have to get me in and out of the bath, on and off the loo. I'm getting used to that, but what about him, in five years, in twenty-five years?'

'I understand,' said Alice in a neutral voice. She wanted to say: You're right! Hold back! Be careful! Announce nothing! Don't get engaged to David! Don't even see David! She was terrified of not saying these things, but she was terrified of saying them, in case she pushed Nicola in the wrong direction. That also had happened before.

'All my life,' said Nicola, 'I should be using a kind of emotional blackmail: "Be my slave, because I'm crippled, because everybody pities me." If he ever put a foot wrong, he'd feel ten times more guilty than if I were normal. It's all too difficult, too sick. It's asking too much of anybody. I'd be getting a lifetime nurse, and he'd be getting a life of celibacy and sacrifice.'

'There are worse things.'

It was only later, when she was alone, that Nico understood the odd note in her mother's voice. 'There are worse things.' Alice had condemned herself to a life of celibacy and sacrifice.

Jack Parkinson left the office. He would rather have stayed, and talked to David about fencing contractors and the syndication of the trout-fishing and Nicola Maude, but he wanted David to be in charge of the estate and of his own life, and the only way not to interfere was to remove himself physically, to go home and have a drink and potter about in the garden.

As he went up the three steps to the side door of Normandy Farm, in the Jacobean part between the cramped original building and the Victorian addition, he wondered if Nico would ever live there. The problems would be formidable. The whole house, built on a slope and at different times, was on different levels. All the passages were punctuated by steps; almost every room had a step up or down into it. There were two staircases, neither of which, Jack thought, lent itself to one of those chair-lifts.

'Hello, Jacky,' called Monica, his wife, from the kitchen. 'I've been wondering.'

'What?' said Jack, almost sure he knew the answer.

'I've been wondering if Nico could manage in this house, supposing the problem arose, and I don't think she could.'

It was always happening, this telepathic sharing of thoughts. It was the result, no doubt, of thirty years of happy marriage. It was something Alice Maude would never experience, which was terribly unfair.

David forced his eyes from the window to the papers on his desk. He kept them there until the telephone rang. As he spoke to the feed merchant his eyes wandered to the photograph. When he hung up they stayed there.

It was like a photograph taken in 1914 or 1939, the last sunshine, the last and unrepeatable laughter.

Hugh Jarvis was his friend. They had been together at Magdalen, David reading agriculture and Hugh modern languages. Unlike many university friendships, theirs had survived, being the result of choice rather than chance. It was definitely the attraction of opposites. That was, no doubt, the origin of it: mutual curiosity verging on incredulity. David the bumpkin was startled by the smooth cosmopolitan; Hugh, the man of streets and salons, was intrigued by the kind of countryman he had only read about, in the novels of Surtees. David stayed with Hugh and his mother (divorced) one spring vacation in Tuscany. Three years later, when Hugh was a journalist and David a probationary landowner, Hugh came to stay at Normandy Farm. He walked by the river, looked at the Cathedral, rode a horse for the first time in his life, and met Felicity Peacock.

Little dark Flickie was the adopted daughter of the Dean of Milchester. Clever, ambitious and funny, with a pointed nose and a pointed chin and enormous eyes, she was the miniature knockout of Wessex. She was the friend and the foil of Nicola Maude. When Felicity and Nicola came into a room together, whom did you look at first? Nico first, because she was taller, because she was fair; so Flickie contrived, on the whole, to make her entries alone.

That March, Nico was away, abroad, studying. She was going to be an art historian. Strange as it seemed, she already had a job lined up in that rarefied world: if all went well, and with further specialist qualifications, she would be a kind of librarian and archivist attached to the Milchester Museum and Art Gallery. To this end she went to Rome and Venice. That was where she was, that March. That was why she missed Hugh's visit. She did not know what she had missed. Nor did Hugh.

David took Hugh to a recital of Renaissance music at the Chapter House. Different as they were, this was one of the tastes they shared. They went afterwards to a party at the Deanery. David introduced Hugh to Felicity.

Hugh had a trick, most attractive to most people, of devoting his entire attention to anybody he was talking to. He never, ever, looked over anybody's shoulder to see who had come into the room. He devoted his entire attention to Felicity, leaning from his great height to hear what she was saying in the hubbub of the party, oblivious to his empty glass and of anybody else.

Flickie, by contrast, was one of those restless and impatient conversationalists, for whom the grass was always greener at the other end of the room. It was difficult to hold her attention at all, and impossible to hold it completely.

Not for Hugh. David saw that they really clicked. Nobody could be surprised. It was amusing to see them together, as he was more than a foot taller than she. They were both dark and lively and voluble, exotic in the English West Country, visitors from a Mediterranean place of wine-jars and olive-groves.

Hugh extended his holiday, his visit, charmingly apologetic to Monica Parkinson, having no need to explain. He repeated his visit, weekend after weekend, all that spring. Felicity went more than once to London, sleeping (so she said) on the sofas of friends. One long weekend she spent in Tuscany. She came back saying that Hugh's mother had been very kind to her.

David had been missing Nico terribly, but he was relieved that Hugh was meanwhile neutralized. A lot of girls at Oxford had been crazy for Hugh, and probably dozens in Italy and scores in London. Nico might be falling for Romans and Venetians, but at least she had not had the chance to fall for Hugh. And now Hugh was Flickie's property. It was a great relief.

Hugh and Nicola coincided in Milchester in June. It might have happened before, but it happened on 10 June. Felicity introduced Hugh to Nico, her new friend to her old friend. It was another cultural function in the shadow of the Cathedral, the opening of an exhibition of Victorian photographs.

Hugh gave Nico his full attention. He did not have to lean down so far as when he was talking to Felicity. They had heard about one another, from Flickie, from David. They stood in a window of the gallery, in the evening sun. The sun set fire to the silvery-tawny mane of Nico's hair, and slid over the sleek darkness of Hugh's head. Neither of them looked at any Victorian photographs. Felicity and David were both pleased that they got on so well together – they said so to one another, right there at the exhibition.

The picnic on the river-bank was six weeks later. The photograph was taken by a man called Roddy Plumb. He had enlargements made, and gave them to all four. It was a kind thought. David knew that Nico still had her copy. It was one of very few photographs of Hugh she did have. David did not know about Felicity's copy, or about Hugh's.

Two weeks after the day of the photograph, David thought: if Hugh and Nico had to meet, it's lucky they met when they did. If Hugh had married Felicity and then met Nico ... David imagined that Flickie felt the same. Anybody with any sense would. He did not ask her about it, then or later.

David finished the VAT returns, from the figures put together by the secretary who came in once a week. He walked back to the house, thankful to stretch his legs after sitting for so long; he had a bath and changed, in what was now his self-contained flat. (Working at home meant living at home, but they all agreed he had to have his own space.)

David was committed to a party which, in local terms, was strange and even louche. It would not have been so elsewhere, but the society of Milchester and its countryside was unusual. It was archaic and intolerant. It was like an outpost of Empire, rather than a place with winebars and discos. The strictness was not the doing of the Bishop or his clergy. On the contrary, they were mostly so modern that it was possible to wonder if they were Christians at all. A lot of guitars were played in the churches, and the old pews abandoned in favour of cosy huddles of chairs. But the older and stiffer laity – colonels' widows, retired bank managers – breathed the air of an earlier discipline. They did not wear top hats on Sunday, but they came near it. David and Felicity once agreed that they were all acting parts in Trollope, self-consciously dignified. They were censorious, narrow-minded and purse-proud. In that stiff world, the evening's party was certainly dubious. It was being given by a couple to celebrate their marriage, and for the neighbourhood to meet the new wife. They had actually been married in San Francisco. Both had been divorced. The man and his first wife had lived locally. The divorce had been a shock, the ensuing unpleasantness felt over a wide area. People took sides.

The party was in the so-called ballroom of the White Hart Hotel, a flimsy addition to the old building, used by local firms for sales conferences. At least one of the waiters would be drunk.

David's parents had been asked, but would not go, because they had taken sides with the wife at the time of the divorce. She might hear that they had gone. It would seem like a betrayal. Her feelings would be hurt.

David had to go, because he had promised to.

Alice Maude would be there, because she would think that a stranger from a far place might be feeling forlorn, and ought to be welcomed. Nicola would not be there, because big noisy parties bored and exhausted her.

The Bishop might be there, exuding modernity and tolerance.

The Dean and his wife had probably made an excuse, the sin of telling a social lie being less than that of condoning adultery and bigamy. But their daughter Felicity would be there, because she had never been known to miss a party.

In the event the party was better than David expected. The people who disapproved were enjoying doing so, and they were enjoying the champagne at the same time. The new wife was a soft-spoken woman, not young, with a deep California suntan and a lot of gold chains. It was reckoned in her favour that she was nervous. Word got about also, behind hands at the party, that her first husband had been a brute.

There were not too many people at the party. There was room to move. There was no overpowering noise. Nico could have steered herself about the room. She might have enjoyed it. She ought to get out and about more. It was a pity she had not come.

David saw Alice Maude in the middle of a group. Alice was always in the middle of a group, but for no obvious reason. She was not a celebrated wit, a mimic or raconteur. She was usually rather serious. You had to watch what you were saying in front of her; you had to watch your language. She did not draw every eye, nor break unnumbered hearts. But she was always in the middle of a group, the person everybody wanted to talk to.

She had been an attractive girl, a sweet-looking girl; there was a wedding photograph in a silver frame at the cottage: Alice the bride of the Reverend Barnabas Maude. David remembered him well, a man of calmness, of smiles, of quiet, considered answers: a man who seemed slow to the impatient but strong to the weak. He was very good to the young child David. David imagined he had been singled out for favour, but then realized that Barney Maude was very good to everybody. It was obvious, even to a ten-year-old, that Barney and Alice adored one another.

As he had expected, David saw Flickie Peacock at the party. She did draw a lot of eyes, and she had already broken her share of hearts. She was very smart, in lime-green, with a new short hair-do. She had changed since the river-bank photograph. That was two years ago, but she had changed more than two years' worth, more than the difference between twenty-one and twenty-three. She had acquired a surface of enamel, hard and bright. She was more beautiful but more formidable, if any girl so small could be formidable. Like Alice, she was the centre of a group, but it was a different kind of group from Alice's, and she was a different kind of centre.

Flickie was laughing and gesticulating in the middle of her group of young men, telling a ridiculous story, recounting a catastrophe of which she was the victim, making herself out to be a ninny, perfectly aware that none of her listeners would believe a word of it ... She was alive, bouncing, almost dancing as she talked and laughed.

Nico would never again bounce, never dance.

Nico should have been the centre of that group, this party, every party, alive, vibrant, quick as a swallow, as a flame.

It was not fair.

Alice was aware of Felicity Peacock telling a long, funny story to a group of admiring boys. It was a thing Alice sometimes wished she could do – could ever have done. Her sister Vi could tell a story about eight different people, talking in eight different voices, an elaborate comic set piece – but it was something Alice was obliged to leave to other people. It was probably lucky, Alice thought, that the world was not over-filled with raconteurs. Life would be like that proverbial Central European navy, all admirals and no sailors, if everybody was a storyteller and nobody was a listener.

'Picture the scene,' said Felicity in her high, clear, penetrating voice. 'F. Peacock standing on the station platform, holding an exploded suitcase, knee-deep in sponge-bags—'

There was a burst of laughter from her audience. It was indeed a comic picture – little jewel-like Felicity in the middle of a surging commuter crowd, holding a suitcase which had burst open and ejected a pile of intimate belongings all over the platform. Felicity painted it in – bank clerks picking their way between petticoats, families tripping over hairbrushes ...

Alice moved away, sickened by the hatred she felt, unable to stand the sight and sound of this unspeakable girl.

Even if she had not known what she knew, she would have found it difficult to bear Felicity's liveliness and confidence, her fizzing and springing physicality. The contrast was too savage. The irony was painful. It was heart-rending. It was not fair.

Nicola would never have said so.

Nicola did not know how unfair it was.

Nicola thought that she had been crippled by accident; that Hugh had been killed by accident.

Alice was the only person who knew the truth, and there was nothing in the world she could do about it.

CHAPTER TWO

'ACCIDENT.'
A joyrider, a teenager, a hit-and-run kid, maybe drunk, some kind of itinerant layabout, the car taken from outside the Village Hall, abandoned after it had skidded into the ditch, no fingerprints from gloved hands in the cold, no footprints in the frozen ground, no motive, no witness, no suspect.

Hugh was a beginner as a rider, though nobody would have guessed it. The Parkinsons put him up on one of their old horses when he first came to stay with them; then his equestrian education had been taken over by Felicity Peacock, as well as everything else about him; then Nicola was the one he went riding with, on horses belonging to Hilary and Vi. They had always mounted her, all her life; their groom had taught her, and had taken her hunting, and shown her off to the county. She rode beautifully. Many people said it was a pity she was never interested in competition, in show-jumping or cross-country or racing, but Alice understood that, for Nicola, riding was so elegant and so exciting that it was only vulgarized by turning into a battle. Hugh did not take that view. As soon as he was first in the saddle, he set himself to be good, to be the best. He said he committed himself to the pursuit of excellence. It was an attitude that had to be admired. He had private lessons in London that they only heard about afterwards; he read the manuals of horsemanship, and sat in front of instructional videos from Portugal and Germany. He took great pains to make it seem effortless, to be admired for talents he did not have, instead of guts he did have. He became an effective horseman, quite able to pop over painted jumps in a show-ring, or tackle a series of mixed obstacles across country. And when he did have his smash, it was somebody else's fault: he was hit by a murderously skidding car in semi-darkness.

'Accident.'

Hugh and Nicola riding back in the early dusk from a hack round the new cross-country course at Lower Bendon, laid out over the farm of friends, designed by one of the stars. Hugh was undoubtedly imagining entering a three-day event there; if he found the right horse the dream was perfectly attainable. Nicola as usual was riding a horse of Hilary and Vi's, Hugh one of the Parkinsons'. They were both safe, reliable, experienced animals, steady in traffic, not ones to spook or shy. Both riders were wearing luminous green crossbelts, glaringly visible in headlights, and Nico had a reflector on her right heel. It was dark at that corner, under those oak trees, but coming up behind them the driver could hardly have failed to see them.

'Accident.'

Any number of people might have known that Hugh and Nicola would be riding back that way at about that time. They were unlikely to go any other way. Since they had gone to ride round the course, leaving home after lunch, they could not have been much earlier. Since they wanted to get home before pitch dark, they could scarcely have been later. There was no reason that very many people knew all this, but there was literally no limit to the number of people who might have known.

'Accident.'

The only witness was Nicola: her evidence was a long time coming, and added nothing when it came – a skid, a scream, a crash. Hugh and his horse were both killed instantly, not by the car but because of the car – the horse breaking its neck as it fell, Hugh losing his crash-hat and falling on his head. Nico's horse dragged a broken foreleg into Bendon village, where it was caught. The vet put it down immediately. The search-party went out, and found the scene within twenty minutes. Nico was still unconscious, and remained so for fifteen hours. The car was damaged by skidding into the ditch rather than by hitting the horses. The mudguards were crumpled, the windscreen shattered. There was no way of knowing if the driver had been hurt. The driver was not found then or later.

'Accident.'

The car, by a sickening irony, belonged to Hilary Cavenham. It was a ten-year-old Volvo, built like a tank, normally used for towing a horse-box. Hilary had left it outside the village hall, while he went to a meeting of the trustees of the hall. The keys were in the dash. Hilary bitterly blamed himself for this negligence, but who would think of locking an old car in the car-park of the village hall? Nobody saw anybody take the car. Nobody would have been standing round in that car-park at teatime on a weekday in February. Any of fifty million people might have taken the car, for any imaginable reason or no reason.

Accident?

The Coroner's Inquest was adjourned, pending police enquiries, since it was evident that a crime might have been committed – manslaughter, dangerous driving, or something lower down the scale. Nothing could be done by the courts until a suspect had been identified and charges brought. Nothing more was ever done. There was nothing to do. There never was any suspect.

Alibis? Did anybody have an alibi? Did everybody have one? Nobody asked. The question never arose.

Everybody talked about the 'accident'. The police file was labelled 'accident'. 'Fatal accident' was the headline in the local paper. Nico referred afterwards, when she had to, to the 'accident'.

In the shock of the news, the reeling and shuddering moment when the bare facts were conveyed, Alice accepted the word that everybody was using – accepted that it was luck, hazard, chance, an antic fall of cosmic dice. She would have preferred that illusion to have persisted.

'Accident.'

It might have happened to anyone.

Necessity took Alice along that road seven weeks after the event. She would not have chosen to go by that place, of all the places in the world, but unless they moved to the other end of England, she could hardly deny herself the use of indispensable roads. None of it was the fault of the road. The trees were trees, the corner was a corner. They were neutral. None of them showed any signs of being the scene of such a thing, except that you could see where the bumper of the car had scraped the top of the verge and drilled into the side of the ditch.

Here the car had come, here where Alice's car was, pointing like hers towards the corner, travelling no doubt much faster, not in full daylight ... after a gentle bend the road straightened, giving a full view of the corner four hundred yards away. The horses had been there, going in the same direction, at the edge of the road, or on the verge where the road did a sudden forty-five degree turn to the right. The horses had not yet turned right: they were at the corner, the outside of the corner, about to turn right. The luminous sashes of the riders would have been in full view for four hundred yards, in the undipped headlights of the car.

This was all obvious to everybody. It had been obvious to the police and the Coroner and the local newspaper. It had been obvious to Alice, even before she found herself in the same place. The driver that evening must have been very drunk, or going very fast, or both.

Probably the driver climbed out of the car, unhurt because he was drunk, having only taken the car for a joyride because he was drunk. He staggered away, found himself somewhere to lie down in the warm, woke up hours later with no memory at all of the—

Of the accident. Accident?

Somebody must have been aware of somebody getting drunk that afternoon, disappearing for a while, reappearing probably bruised, shaken, shocked, probably incoherent, maybe with a dim notion of being horrified. Somebody was keeping quiet, a wife or mother, knowing maybe that it was out of character, telling herself that it would never happen again—

That an accident like that would never happen again...

Alice drove slowly towards the corner. She felt, as she drove, a sensation new to her, so strong that she was at first uncertain if it were mental or physical, so strange that she did not recognize it.

It was a charge, a stab, of the most vicious malevolence. It was bitter hatred and envy. It was outside sanity, morality. It was far outside seeing greener grass, or harmlessly coveting somebody's emeralds. It was sickening: it was murderous.

The car had been driven at the horses. The driver had wanted to hit Hugh or Nicola or both. He had wanted to kill or maim. There was no room for doubt. This was certain. Alice had not invented, could never have imagined, that surge of bile, of murderous jealousy. She would never forget it, nor disbelieve it.

None of it could be proved. None of it would be believed by anybody else.

Alice was not, never had been, the smallest bit psychic. She was not telepathic or clairvoyant. She was not even fanciful. She was commonsensical and ordinary, even to a fault. She had had no glimmer of experience of anything supernatural. But when it came it carried its own total and immediate conviction.

Alice stopped the car just beyond the corner. She needed a moment to recover. Her hands were shaking and the trees quivered.

She tried to rationalize, to explain to herself what she had experienced. Along the road had come this person hunting the two on horseback. A person so poisoned by hatred, so determined to commit an act of unspeakable ferocity, that a kind of trail had been left, a plume of hatred in the air overhanging the verge of the road, like the trail of exhaust left by the diesel of a tractor ... She, perhaps, had inhaled and absorbed this vestige as she drove on the track of the murderer, she rather than another because she was so close to the victim ...

Something like that. That was near enough.

It was not necessary to understand how she had come by her knowledge. What mattered was that she knew.

★

It was no longer possible for Alice to believe in the 'accident'; but neither did it become possible for her to tell anybody the truth about it. Her thoughts were terrible and they were private. To an extent she could share the burden of looking after Nicola – with Vi and Hilary, with the Parkinsons – but she could not share this new secret burden.

Hatred. Whose hatred? The answer was supremely obvious. As soon as the question was asked, the answer gave itself.

She did it. Yes, *she* did it. She had caught the man and then lost him. She was jealous.

Now that she had destroyed one life and ruined another, she could relax and congratulate herself, live and laugh and tell funny stories. For her the world wagged happily on, sweetened by her revenge. It was not fair, but what was Alice to do?

Probably nothing.

Alice would play detective, if she could. Perhaps she would play prosecuting counsel. But she would not play God. Though judgment was not likely to come in this world, it was very certain to come in the next.

Alice could do nothing, but she would keep an eye out. She was not blind or stupid. And she might not always be powerless.

Nico saw at the time that something had happened to her mother. She saw it with a wobble, because she saw everything with a wobble, lying in the bed in the private room in Milchester Hospital (paid for by Hilary and Vi).

She asked, but her mother would not tell her. The habit of a lifetime held – Alice's habit, of Nico's lifetime. Nico sighed, as often before, lying there in a bed from which she might never get up. For fifteen years, since her father's death, Nico had lived inside a plastic bubble of her mother's making. At least, her mother thought she had. Once started, Nico indulged herself in great warm baths of memory, because memory was the only indulgence possible. It was pretty small beer. There was precious little glamour, until the last bit. Even her sins were sinless.

Her earliest memories were like anybody's – unreliable, almost meaningless. Probably the images were all hearsay and photographic albums, nothing authentically seen and recorded – the faces, gardens, church towers, birthday parties.

Sense began with her father's appointment as Vicar of Grimworth (with Lower Grimworth and Grimworth St Andrew). There was a flint-and-brick Vicarage near the church, with a smell of damp, with an upright piano in the hall and a room for prayer meetings and the Bible Study Group. Daddy wore a collar unlike the collars of other fathers. He was more cheerful than others. He never sulked or swore or got drunk. Nico's friends said he must be strange to live with, but Nico did not find it so, since she was used to it.

Being an only child was no hardship, because she had so many friends. She seemed to live in a dozen houses, with a score of aunts and uncles and a gross of cousins.

At the age of six she was often – too often – told that she was pretty; she soon – too soon – knew that it was true.

Foremost among the aunts and uncles were the real ones: Aunt Vi, Uncle Hilary – the Cavenhams. March Court was the principal home from home, although – perhaps because – there were no other children there. Of all houses, March Court had the softest cushions and the biggest pictures; in the winter, great fires winked on the steel fenders, and in the summer everyone shrieked and splashed in the pool.

In her hospital bed, in the blazing early summer of 1990, Nico smelled the smell of March Court, brought to her by memory and the visits of Aunt Vi: the smell of freesias, and vodka, and something Nico recognized but could not define.

Aunt Vi was in the middle of these memories. Uncle Hilary must have been there, but he was on the edge.

And then she remembered that November morning, the year of her sixth birthday, well inside the floodlit area of clear memory. The mist lay impenetrable on the water-meadows, trees standing knee-deep in the milkiness like wading birds, the sky plumy with apricot in the east; a robin piped, trying to remember summer, and then came the thumping of the Vicarage's ancient central-heating pump; and then the policeman came in by the back door, his helmet under his arm—

Nico remembered her mother's involuntary wail of loss and misery.

Aunt Vi was there, almost at once, herself exhausted.

Hands were held, tea brewed, telephone calls made. Nico was drawn onto laps for comfort. People came and went. Voices were kept low.

There was a funeral, voices chanting among echoing stone arches, dim light through stained glass, the coffin on trestles. The day was all blurred with tears in Nico's memory, either because she cried at the time, or because she cried at the memory afterwards.

They moved from the Vicarage into Turner's Cottage. Everything was compressed into smaller spaces, put closer together, piled higher.

Each year, as Nico grew, the cottage seemed smaller.

It seemed very small when it was full of their friends.

They had just as many friends as when they lived in the Vicarage; now when they came they had to be squeezed in among the chairs.

Many of the same people went to Aunt Vi's house, where they had plenty of room. Nico's mother and Aunt Vi were sisters. It seemed extraordinary to Nico, when she was young, that they lived in such different houses. It was only gradually that she came to understand this oddity.

Many people said it was not fair. Nico once overheard Monica Parkinson saying it was grossly unfair. Nico's mother never said so.

The sisters married such different men because they were so different from one another. In every dimension, every direction, Aunt Vi was bigger than Nico's mother. She was taller, ampler, louder, more brightly coloured; she moved faster when she walked about, but she was more relaxed when she sat down. Her hair was either much longer than Alice's, or much shorter, and so were her skirts and her parties and her telephone conversations. She was more generous because she had more to be generous with.

Everybody said it was a pity Vi had never had children, but she almost had Nico for a child.

If March Court was Nico's number one extra house, the Deanery was her number two. Felicity Peacock was her best friend, all those years. The Deanery was a big dark house in the Close, full of oak panelling and gloomy pictures. Felicity had two older brothers who were not really her brothers, because she was adopted. When Nico understood what this meant, she understood why Felicity looked foreign. She *was* foreign, perhaps Italian or Spanish. Nico envied Felicity her exotic quality, her dark strangeness. Although Felicity's adoptive father was a parson, as Nico's had been, she knew all kinds of interesting things. This was because she had older brothers who had friends. Nico was accordingly not as ignorant as people supposed, as her own mother supposed. When they were teenagers, Felicity took Nico to parties that their families knew nothing about.

Nico tried not to lie to her mother about such things, but she did not tell her the whole truth about everything. Felicity said nobody told their mothers the whole truth about anything – their mothers had not told *their* mothers everything, or they would never have got married.

When Sir Robert Armstrong said in an Australian courtroom that he had been 'economical with the truth', Nico knew exactly what he meant.

Flickie was bouncy and restless and energetic, and variously talented, and into all kinds of activities. She was the *ingénue* in the productions of the Milchester Amateur Dramatic Society (known to its members as the 'Mads'); she organized the jazz concert for the Milchester Arts Festival when she was only nineteen; her photograph popped up in the local paper more often than the Bishop's.

The person who never appreciated Flickie was Aunt Vi. She said Flickie was a tart. Flickie said (not to Nico, but it was reported) that Vi was a tart. Nico knew they were both wrong, but she understood how they thought as they did.

Felicity and Nico were never in love with the same boy at the same time. This was fortunate; it was odd, however, as they shared nearly everything else.

Nico at school was good at art and at history, and it seemed logical to combine the two in her choice of career. She enrolled in a two-year diploma course at the

Milchester Poly. Felicity was meanwhile studying business administration, which was extraordinary only to people who did not know her well. They remained as close as ever, though they had grown up apparently so different.

Being a student did not much change Nico's life – she lived at home, and went in on a moped for lectures and tutorials. She went to parties and dances; she wore jeans and T-shirts and sloppy sweaters; many of the lads wanted to kiss her, and a few succeeded.

Local gossip linked Nico and David Parkinson, who had come down from Oxford and was working as his father's farm manager. The parents of both were known to be in favour. David was known to be passionately in favour, but he was not one of those who had kissed Nico.

Roddy Plumb was.

Most of Nico's new friends were students, but Roddy Plumb was a lecturer. He was an academic art historian, with a special knowledge of Germany and Scandinavia; he was also a working artist, occasionally selling his semi-abstract landscapes, and a brilliant photographer, never trying to sell at all. He was only twenty-seven, and probably on his way to more glamorous launching-pads than the Milchester Poly. He was a tall, narrow man with a beaky face and big, bony, effective hands. He looked as though he might have been a surgeon. The girls said he had burning eyes; the girls thought he was lovely. He lectured with passion. Nico sensed that he was lecturing directly to her, and she was right.

He shaved off his beard, because he thought she would prefer him without it.

He was exciting because of his excitement.

He kissed her after a fancy-dress party at the

Milchester College of Art. He was trembling more than she was. He became physical but too nervous to undo buttons. It was easy for Nico to make him stop; she did so half reluctantly.

The following day he met her for a drink in a pub in the Buttermarket. Among the farmers and travelling salesmen, he asked her to marry him. She was so surprised that she knocked over her glass of white wine. He meant it all right.

'I'm too young,' she said. 'This is too soon for me. You've come into my life too early.'

'Yes, I know, but I couldn't control that, could I?'

They managed to end the conversation with smiles, with promises of friendship.

It was Nico's first proposal, and she remembered it with excitement, amusement and gratitude.

Nico's course included the option of six months' study abroad, for students who could arrange it and could afford it. Nico yearned to see Italy. It would be a kindness to Roddy to go away. Vi waved her chequebook. Alice hid her dismay . . .

Nico's hair was a sensation in Rome. In the streets she needed a bodyguard, for which there was no shortage of recruits. She wrote letters to her mother, to her aunt, and to Felicity; she sent cards to David and a few dozen others.

Flickie reportedly came out to Italy while Nico was there. Somebody mentioned this in a letter. She stayed with friends. It was the normal thing to do, if you had friends in Italy and the price of a ticket. Nico thought they might meet, but apparently there was no time, it was impossible.

Nico had so many admirers in Italy that, for a time, she had no one single boyfriend. Life was a party, lived in large, noisy groups. Nico knew that people had thought that going away would be liberating for her, that distance would sever the apron-strings. Her mother had thought so. In the event, for a time, it was rather the opposite. At home, she could be up to many more things than the grown-ups realized: there were opportunities for privacy, time for twosomes. In Italy, they all went in gangs from bar to bar.

Then Jefferson McCabe appeared on the edge of their group, a craggy American of thirty. Jeff had pale blue denims and a thatch of straw-coloured hair; he had notebooks, camera, tape-recorder, the energy of a demon. He was doing research for a book about ... he never really said. He was assembling so much material that his subject had got lost. He could not see the wood for the twigs, for the pine-needles. He was an attractive personality, generous, enthusiastic, interested in everything.

He became immediately and obsessively interested in Nico.

She became his honorary research assistant, and thus learned about many unexpected things.

In that group there were some other English girls, and American and German and French girls, and Italians from every part of the country, and some of these girls made a play for Jefferson McCabe.

'I don't believe I can do myself the honour to accompany you at this time,' he would say to the girls, 'since right now I am obligated to meet with a terrible fraud from Copenhagen who claims to have something to tell me about Mantegna.'

He used mock pomposity, and genuine old-fashioned

good manners, to get away from the girls, after which he met Nico somewhere out of sight and took her to new places.

He was rich. He was kind. And he made Nico laugh. He wanted to re-educate Nico. He wanted to take her to Des Moines to meet his family, and then bring her back to Italy to live.

Nico kissed him, and more, but she felt like patting him on the head and tucking him up in bed. Jeff was a great dear, but it would be a few years before he grew up. As Nico knew that she herself was far from grown up, they were a pair of babes in the wood.

It was lucky, though intensely sad, that her time in Italy was coming to an end.

At this point, somebody mentioned Hugh Jarvis in a letter, as being somebody Nico would be interested to meet. Somebody else mentioned him, as a figure of glamour who had blazed over the neighbourhood like a comet. Though preoccupied, Nico was mildly curious. Few comets came to Milchester, and those not the guests of the Parkinsons.

Nico came home lugging sheaves of drawings, reams of notes, boxes of reproductions of paintings and details of paintings. She had to work hard not to bore everybody about Italy.

There was not much local news, no deaths or scandals among their friends.

Had nothing of interest happened? What was the name of the stranger they had mentioned in their letters?

'Hugh Jarvis?' said her mother. 'Oh, David's friend. Yes, I just met him. He gives the impression of being rich.'

'In a nice way? Like Uncle Hilary?'

'Oh yes. Not at all like that dreadful ... not like some

rich men. Mr Jarvis has what I should call quiet certainty in every situation. You need lots of money for that. And he has a sort of high polish. Beautiful clothes, expensive hair-oil.'

Nico burst out laughing. 'Mum, you can't possibly know how much his hair-oil costs.'

Alice laughed too. 'I'm just giving you my impressions, after a fleeting encounter.'

Nico was more than ever curious to meet Hugh Jarvis, and expected some time to do so: but not so soon, and not at the opening of the exhibition of early photographs of the locality (horses and carts, tinker families, haymakers, the Cathedral bellringers).

As a thumbnail sketch, her mother's description was pretty good. You could not doubt that his hair-oil was expensive. He was wearing a pale-grey suit and a pink shirt and a silk tie with a foulard pattern. He was very well dressed, but not in the least overdressed. He looked sleek, like a seal or an otter, but not at all slimy, not smarmy, not like some of the Italian young men who had tried to pick her up in Rome. Hugh looked like a diplomat. He looked old-fashioned, Edwardian. He looked older than David Parkinson, although they had been Oxford contemporaries; he looked more experienced and worldly-wise.

Nico had allowed herself to be quite pleased with her own appearance, before she left home. She had lost weight in Italy, all the remaining ounces of puppy-fat. She was very slim but shapely. She thought her figure was about right. Her hair was long, longer than it had been for years, because it had been so much admired in Italy. Her face and arms were lightly tanned. She wore a little blue cotton suit, white shoes, and a crazy necklace of chunks of coloured Perspex, from Milan.

She and Hugh both said that they had heard so much about one another. As an opening it was marvellously banal. Nico wondered what Hugh had heard about her. She wondered what there was to hear. All she had done so far was to prepare for what she did from now on. The only thing that she could remember that she had heard about him, at that moment, was that he used expensive hair-oil, and that, though obviously correct, was no more than a theory.

She saw that he was staring at her necklace, as though mesmerized.

'It comes from Italy,' she said.

'So do you, I understand.'

'I've come back,' she said absurdly.

'Carrying your loot. You and the necklace suit one another.'

'What?'

'You both have an air of sophistication without being too serious.'

'Oh. That is exactly how I would like to seem. But I didn't think I managed it.'

'You don't manage it.'

'Oh.'

'I mean, you achieve it without effort. I mean, it is how you appear to be, not how you appear to have made an effort to be. I mean, you do not appear to have made a conscious choice in the matter, but simply to show yourself in your true colours. That is what I mean.'

Nico realized, to her great surprise, that he was nervous. He seemed younger and more vulnerable. She was astonished at the idea that she could frighten anybody, and especially a world-weary cosmopolite like Hugh.

She told him, because he asked, where she had stayed

in Italy, what she had seen. He did not want to talk about his own extensive and glamorous travels, but only about her small student journeys. He wanted to hear exactly what her reaction had been to everything. She found it difficult to remember exactly what her reaction had been to anything, when he smiled with such warmth, when he listened so intently to all that she said. For him, the rest of the gallery, the other people, the exhibition might not have existed. It was flattering.

Everything about him was clean, well pressed, polished. But he was not in the least effeminate or dandyish. He gave no impression of vanity. The impression he gave was that he took trouble about his appearance out of pure good manners.

Nico would have been equally engrossed, but she was in her own place, surrounded by neighbours and lifelong friends – she had to have regard to appearances and to people's feelings. There were friends of her mother that she had not seen since she came home. Duty compelled her to break out of the charmed bubble of their private conversation. It was awfully difficult.

'Whatever were you talking about, all that time?' asked Felicity Peacock.

'Italy.'

'Then I'm glad I wasn't listening.'

This was a joke, but not altogether. Flickie seemed out of sorts. Probably she needed a break. Her parents were pretty overpowering. Her brothers were both working in London, but when they were at home they were overpowering, too. Flickie was too small and brittle to be surrounded by such powerful and moral people.

She had been, all along, so fascinating and capricious, so hard to please, that although she had been so very much admired she had never, as far as Nico knew, had a steady boyfriend. She was by no means too young for such a thing, not nowadays, and it would surely be a comfort.

People talked about independence, but how independent did any girl truly want to be? You didn't have to own or be owned, but you did want your hand held.

Hugh was not yet holding Nico's hand, but Nico knew he wanted to, and she wanted him to. She did not try to see further than that.

It was funny that although Italy had been adventurous – wine, smiles, admiration, proposals – Nico's heart had not really been touched. But the moment she got back to dreary old England, here she was on the brink of something exciting.

Hugh telephoned from London on Sunday evening, the moment he got back. Nico was out. There was no message. Nico's mother, telling her, looked as though she wanted to say something more: but she picked up the Sunday paper, and read an account of a Glyndebourne production she would never see.

Other people in that week, as it seemed to Nico, were nearly but not quite saying something – something to do with Italy, her friends there, her romances, her return, her longer hair or her shorter skirts?

Even her oldest and closest friends, Flickie Peacock and David Parkinson, stepped back from whatever brink they were on, and talked about something different.

Nico thought much later (when she was lying paralysed in bed, when she could do nothing except think) that she might have realized people were nearly telling her something vital; she might have realized that it was about Hugh and Flickie. But at the time she was busy and preoccupied and excited, and she had no time or energy to spare for unspoken speeches.

Hilary and Vi came back from India – one of their holidays in the Maharajahs' palaces – and life for miles around was lit up by the golden glow of their hospitality.

They were often away, but they were terribly missed when they were. All round Milchester, life went into a kind of grey hibernation, springing to life the moment they got back, when Vi picked up the telephone and Hilary waved the shaker.

They always brought back new records, new clothes, new enthusiasms, crates of presents.

Vi came back golden. Her skin was golden; so was her hair (which had been a kind of purple when they set off). She wore gold bangles, gave gold presents, and laughed her gurgling, infectious, golden laugh.

Hilary was brick-red. He was some years older than his wife, and probably, when they were abroad, went to fewer nightclubs. He grinned in the background, looking after everybody who was not actually talking to Vi. He was a king who acted as consort. Everybody said he was generous, but not everybody said he was amusing. Nico thought he had the best and greatest sort of kindness, because he let it seem that it was Vi who was doing the giving.

Nico went over for tea, driving her mother's little car. She knew she was one of the first people to cross the threshold of March Court since the Cavenhams' return – but Vi already knew the gossip.

'Oh yes, yes, yes,' she said. 'I met him with Monica Parkinson, just before we left. I do understand, darling.'

'You're jumping the gun, Aunt Vi,' said Nico, laughing in spite of herself. 'There's nothing to understand. I've only met him once, and that was in a crowd.'

'I haven't mentioned a name, have I?'

'No, but—'

'But you know exactly who I'm talking about. Ha! Got you there! I'll tell you what I thought. I thought that his being a friend of David Parkinson does them both credit.'

'They were at Magdalen together.'

'Pooh. I knew men who were at Magdalen with the Prince of Wales. That didn't make them friends. I refer to Edward VIII, not the one who does the watercolours.'

Nico knew what she meant. Hugh must be simpler, and David more complex, than either seemed. Hugh had been nervous when they met. Hugh had given her his total attention for a lovely long time.

'On balance,' said Vi, 'taking everything into account, I generally feel I should hate to be young again. All that love and hassle and going to the loo to weep during dances. It's so exhausting having one's heart broken, and it happened to me constantly. But when I meet a young man like Hugh Jarvis, which, I may say, I practically never do ...'

Nico said again that her aunt was jumping the gun.

Nico went straight from her aunt to her mother – from Vi, sitting on the great canopied Edwardian swing-seat on the terrace, precious miniature plants in the cracks between the flagstones under her beautifully shod feet, looking out over the barbered lawn which sloped to the river, with the horses grazing on the water-meadow beyond – straight from that picture of pampered elegance to her mother in the kitchen of the cottage scrubbing potatoes for their supper ...

Nico's mother never said it wasn't fair, but she couldn't stop Nico from thinking so.

CHAPTER THREE

Hugh was sent abroad, by the serious political weekly for which he worked. It was not a summer to be travelling, leaving week after flamboyant week of the most glorious English weather in living memory.

Hugh's farewells to Nico were hurried, scamped, inadequate. Their meeting was not exactly furtive, because they had nothing to be ashamed of, but it was not under anybody's eye. They might have taken some advantage of that, but there was no time, and the mood was wrong. Nico was supposed to be at a lecture and Hugh on the road to London.

Nico did not know who else Hugh said goodbye to, or where or in what way or for how long. It was not yet any of her business; she had no rights in him at all.

Nico tried to concentrate on the set books of her course. Many of them were obtainable in paperback; she read them by the Cavenhams' pool, wearing a Roman bikini and trying to make sense of Vacari and Michael Levey. It was difficult when the sun caressed her shoulders and the thought of Hugh caressed her mind.

It was a waste of the hot weather not to share it. It was a waste of herself and her bikini to be seen, most of the time, only by the swifts wheeling and screaming over the water-meadows.

★

'I haven't said anything,' said Alice to her sister, 'but on the whole I'm relieved. It must be difficult enough, trying to concentrate in this weather. And that young man will have time to sort his ideas out.'

Nico, fifty yards away, put down her book. She bounced on the springboard and dived into the pool.

'If I was him,' said Vi, 'I wouldn't need any time.'

Later Vi said to Alice, having coffee in Alice's small garden, 'How well does Felicity Peacock know Hugh Jarvis?'

'I've no idea,' said Alice, surprised by the question, surprised that Vi should be interested. 'I suppose they must have met. Yes, certainly they've met, the Peacocks and the Parkinsons being such friends, Hugh being David's friend ... I wouldn't know where or when but they must have met.'

'I had the impression they met more than once, and a bit more than just met, if you know what I mean. Didn't she go to Italy to meet his mother?'

'Did Felicity go to Italy? And for that reason?'

'Darling, do you never listen to anything?'

'Well, I thought I did,' said Alice. 'But news about Felicity's travels seems to have passed me by. Actually I don't hear nearly as much gossip as you do, because ...'

Because, as they both knew, Vi had two garrulous women coming in daily to clean the Court, while Alice did her own Hoovering and dusting; because Alice – without pretension, without affectation – was simply above the tinkling provincial tittle-tattle of a place like Milchester.

'You're just too grand for the likes of us,' said Vi affectionately.

★

David Parkinson was better informed. He had watched, with rather more than benevolent neutrality, the developing relationship between Hugh and Felicity.

He did not know how 'relationship' should be interpreted. He did not know what had happened when Felicity went to London. His mind shied away from prurient speculation. He had no idea how either of them envisaged the future.

David did not discuss either Hugh or Felicity with Nico, because he hardly saw Nico. He hardly saw anybody. He was very busy, all that June and early July, working long hours made longer by his father's interventions and non-interventions in the affairs of the estate. He knew that Nico was working hard, or supposed to be; she was doing a paper on the influence of middle-class prosperity on fifteenth-century Italian painting. There were thus two good reasons why they were out of touch during those blazing weeks.

David did not see Felicity. She, too, was studying. Everybody was battling against torpor and lotus-eating.

The Parkinsons received a card from Hugh, from Athens, addressed to the family, saying that he was coming home shortly. David thought that his mother mentioned the card to a number of people. Soon after the card arrived, Hugh telephoned from London. He asked if he might come to Normandy. There was nobody in particular that he said he wanted to see.

David said he would take an afternoon off; he would organize a party of welcome for Hugh. Some of the people he asked were away, but most accepted. It would not be a large party. The picnic on the river-bank was Felicity's idea.

Nobody knew if Felicity had heard from Hugh: but, if

anybody mentioned him, she wore an expression which suggested that she had.

Alice, at the time, wondered what was in Nico's mind, knowing that she would shortly be seeing Hugh. Was it important to her? How important? Was Hugh good news for her? Was there something in him – or did Alice entirely imagine it? – a little suspect, a little false? And what was this about Felicity Peacock?

Nico, much later, lying in her hospital bed, wondered what had been in her own mind, knowing that she would shortly be seeing Hugh.

Certainly nothing that had been in her mind before he came prepared her for what happened when he finally arrived.

A horseshoe bend of the river, a clump of willows and alders, sunshine and shade and the cheerful company of running water.

It was a day when nobody was fishing, and there were no bullocks in the water-meadows.

David sank half a dozen bottles of Muscadet in the edge of the river, in bright water murmuring over bright gravel, cold even under that sun, the water seeping through hundreds of feet of chalk and welling up from the depths gin-clear and chilly. People paid huge sums of money to try to catch trout in that water. It was anarchic and improper to be having noisy parties, lighting fires, drawing corks beside that holy stream. Jack Parkinson would have had a fit if anybody else had done such a thing.

Felicity appointed herself manager of the picnic. She put Roddy Plumb in charge of the fire; she set Hugh and some of the others to collecting wood for it. She herself unpacked the hampers and cold-boxes, and spread their contents over the cropped grass, in the dappled shade of the willows.

It was a magical day. There were no flies or wasps or stinging-nettles. Under the far bank a little trout was snatching at bugs which fell into the water from a clump of forget-me-nots. A water-rat nuzzled the bank, and upstream a moorhen ridiculously wagged her white tail as she puddled across the current towards her nest in an overhanging thorn-bush.

These things were later engraved on Nico's mind.

There were more trees two hundred yards downstream, a mixed copse with some heavy undergrowth. Nico strolled that way, to get wood for Roddy's fire. She found without surprise that Hugh was there. He was looking tired but very well. He had picked up half a dozen sticks. He turned at Nico's approach. He dropped the sticks. He stood looking at her, his hands spread as though he was about to catch a ball.

He said, 'I'm so excited to see you that I can't think of anything to say.' They were far enough away from the others not to be overheard, but near enough to be in full view of everybody. 'All I can do is say something,' said Hugh, 'and that's exactly what I can't do.'

'You've dropped your sticks,' said Nico. 'I'm glad to see you, too.'

'You look glad,' he said, with a note of wonder in his voice. 'You look happy.' His face had been serious. He suddenly smiled, widely and warmly. He said, 'You're not capable of telling a lie, even by the expression on your face. So it must be true. You are happy.'

'Yes.'

'To be seeing me.'

'Yes.'

'My God. I feel as if I'd just been given a million pounds. No, that's ridiculous.'

'Oh,' said Nico.

'The happiness in your face is worth far more than a million pounds. An untold number of millions of pounds. No numbers of millions of pounds could come anywhere near the value of ...'

His voice petered out, like a car running dry. He made a small, helpless gesture with his open hands, to one of which was clinging a piece of bark from a stick he had dropped.

They stood smiling at one another, all that needed saying having been said, no action being possible on account of the others in the party.

River-bank birds were active at the edge of the clump of trees, reassured by the silence and immobility of the monsters in their territory – chaffinch, wren, grey wagtail, creatures with chicks in the nest, with heavy responsibilities, too busy to stand and stare at one another with silly grins, which was what the humans were doing.

'Wood!' shouted Roddy Plumb. 'Fuel for the flames, for the love of God!'

Switches were thrown in their heads; they came back to life, and rejoined the normal world. Nico thought nobody had noticed anything. There had not been anything to notice.

They picked up armfuls of sticks, willow and silver birch, and walked back along the bank to the others. Nobody looked at them meaningfully, or smiled knowingly. Roddy was fussy about breaking up the sticks into lengths, and placing them carefully on his fire.

There was no need whatever for the fire, all the food being cold, much even iced, but Felicity had insisted. The excuse was coffee, but the reason was romantic or picturesque. The campfire made it more of a party, more of a welcome. Everyone saw the point of this, including Hugh, in whose honour the fire was crackling. But everybody shrank away from the heat of the fierce little flames, almost invisible in that brilliant sun, except Roddy Plumb, who was proprietorial of the fire once it had been given into his charge.

Flickie said it was time for a drink. David hoisted two bottles of Muscadet out of the river; he twirled the corkscrew that lived under the strap in the lid of the Parkinsons' picnic hamper. It was an antique, inefficient corkscrew, but using it was part of the ritual, part of the party. They drank out of proper tulip glasses, to the surprise of some of the guests. Wine glasses on a picnic, said a girl called Miranda Jolly, were impractical, heavy to carry, expensive, easy to break, dangerous, pretentious and silly.

'Drinking wine out of plastic,' said Felicity, 'is like...' She sought for an activity equally crass.

'Kissing a man who doesn't wax his moustache,' suggested Hugh.

Flickie looked at him in astonishment.

'Kipling,' he explained. 'One girl to another. Said to be like eating an egg without salt. Curious piece, product of the author's youth, dramatic in form, called *The Story of the Gadsbys*. Not to be confused with *The Great Gatsby*, from which it could hardly, in fact, be more different. Why are we talking about the history of English fiction?'

'We aren't,' said Nico. 'You are.'

Hugh laughed, with Nico and some others, but

Felicity did not appear sure if there was anything to laugh at.

Several people had cameras, and took photographs. It was expected that Roddy Plumb's would be the best, once he could spare attention from his fire.

The heat, the wine, the relaxed and festive atmosphere, made some of the people look their best and some their worst. There were men who looked awkward and oafish sitting on the ground; there were girls who looked scrubby and sluttish when their hair was mussed and their noses shone. Self-aware, they cowered from the camera. Nico did not think she needed to do this. Felicity Peacock knew very well that she did not need to. Hugh seemed indifferent. He looked as he looked. If people wanted to include him in their photographs, that was all right with him; at the approach of a lens, he did not smooth his hair or rearrange the position of his legs, or smile self-consciously or pretend not to know that it was happening. Nico thought again that he was without vanity – that he was beautiful out of politeness.

Nico suddenly said to him, aside, 'How much do you pay for the stuff you put on your hair?'

He blinked at her. She had surprised him as much as he had surprised Felicity a moment ago.

'Oh God,' she said. 'How weird that must have sounded!'

'I didn't put any on this morning,' he said. 'I forgot to bring any. I left it in London. I don't know what it costs. I get it from Trumpers. It's quite expensive, but it lasts a long time. Our subjects of conversation get odder and odder.'

'Somebody said, um, you looked like somebody who put expensive stuff on their hair.'

'Is that good or bad?'

'I think it was meant kindly.'

'I tell myself it was. I don't think I should like to be taken for a man who puts cheap stuff on his hair. I still find this a bizarre topic.'

'Not as bizarre as your crack about kissing a man with a waxed moustache.'

'That simply arose. Its irrelevance was more apparent than real. Shall I grow a moustache, in order to wax it? In a spirit of scientific enquiry? How otherwise shall we ever know if Kipling was right?'

'No,' said Nico.

It was possible that Felicity caught some of this; but impossible that she should know what they were talking about.

What *were* they talking about? It was a nonsense conversation, almost entirely without rational meaning. But it was full of irrational communication, of eyes and smiles and tones of voice.

Flickie could not possibly have absorbed any of that.

Nor the others. There were seven others, including Roddy and David Parkinson and Miranda Jolly, ten in all, five of each (not easy to arrange, in midsummer), none as old as twenty-eight: Peregrine the grandest, in an old-fashioned snobbish sense, his father being an unimportant local earl, Miranda the least grand, her father being the owner of a Milchester garage, none of them admitting the faintest interest in such distinctions; of the ten Hugh the most widely travelled, David Parkinson the richest, Nico the most beautiful (a view with which Felicity would have pretended to agree), Roddy the best known, or least unknown; but none hopelessly homebound, none impoverished, none illiterate or stupid or ugly: a party certainly containing people of future distinction – nobody could doubt that, even as they splashed one another with river-water, and shrieked and behaved with abandoned childishness.

Somebody might have wondered if it was really the sort of party that Hugh liked, he who looked as though he was most at home with ambassadors. But it seemed to be exactly what he liked. He laughed and sported. Probably he did not splash anybody, but certainly he was splashed.

Louise Trenchard went to sleep under a willow, in spite of the laughter round her. Perhaps it was the combination of sunshine and Muscadet, perhaps late nights in London, where she worked for an interior decorator and was often photographed at parties. For a while the others tiptoed and whispered, farcically dramatizing a need not to waken Louise; this was amusing for a few minutes, but too great a bar to conversation. Nico and Miranda rinsed the plates in the river. David said that any scraps, including smoked salmon, would be welcomed by the trout. They boiled water for more coffee, and polished off the wine. It might have been nice to swim, but that would have been stretching too far the forbearance of the trout and of David's father.

They straggled back at long last, across a meadow to the track where the cars were parked. They carried rugs and cushions and hampers and a basket of empty bottles. It seemed natural for Nico to be walking with Hugh. She did not notice who otherwise walked with whom. People might not have been walking in couples. There was no reason to do so. It was not that sort of party. It was a lunchtime picnic, not a dance. There was nothing romantic about it.

It was the most romantic occasion of Nico's life.

This was extraordinary.

She had known this river-bank, some of these people,

almost all her life. It was a healthy, sinless, aseptic midsummer afternoon, spent in a cheerful crowd, in a press of people and a babble of voices. She compared this humdrum reality with the recent memory of an April evening in Venice, the first warm evening of the year, a full moon over the Piazetta and Jeff McCabe murmuring words of adoration ... That was ordinary, compared to this.

The ten of them had come in four cars. Miranda Jolly was taking Felicity back to the Deanery, and with them was to go Roddy Plumb, who also lived in the town. David Parkinson filled his Range Rover with people and the paraphernalia of the picnic. Perry Tallant went off on his own, because he had an appointment with a man who wanted to buy his vintage MG. Hugh took Nico.

Of course. Who else should take her? Who else should he take?

Nobody made any comment. What was there to say? Nico needed a lift and Hugh had room. It was not much out of his way. There was a general flurry of farewells, thanks, laughter, cars starting, wheels turning. Felicity's face could be seen looking out of the rear window of Miranda's car as it disappeared round a clump of thorns at a bend in the track.

The cars might have gone in any order. As it happened, Miranda went first, then David, then Peregrine. The noise of their engines altered as they reached the road and accelerated away on the tarmac.

Hugh's car was a new VW hired for the weekend. Living in Central London, often abroad, he found this the best and cheapest arrangement. The car was consequently unusually clean. There were no bits and pieces in the dashboard and pockets – dark glasses, boxes of tissues, plastic cups: it was as tidy and impersonal as a Swiss train.

It was an intimate little box, a bubble insulated from the world, a private place.

Hugh shut the driver's door. He sat with his hands on the wheel, looking straight ahead.

He said, 'Didn't somebody say it's your birthday soon?'

'The week after next.'

'Which?'

'Twentieth.'

'My God. You're only nineteen. I suppose I knew that if I'd thought.'

'It's not so terribly young,' said Nico, sensing anti-climax. 'Do I seem so terribly childish?'

'Do you think you're grown up?'

'Yes. Yes, I do.'

She did. She felt grown up. She felt ready for anything. She felt beautiful.

'I'm on the horns of a moral dilemma,' said Hugh.

Nico felt shameless. She thought that dignity and decorum were less important than other things. She said, 'I'm grown up and tough and experienced, and it would be a terrible shame to waste a day like this, and I do hate your having such a tidy car . . .'

She realized that her sophisticated, adult speech had lost its sense of direction. She was not grown up or tough or experienced, none of those things, not at all.

But still it would be a terrible shame to waste such a day.

Hugh turned to face her, and smiled.

It was not clear who first reached out towards the other.

Never had there been a kiss so long, so abandoned

and shameless, so passionately friendly, so frightening and reassuring. Nico heard herself whimpering with joy, and making little high mewing sounds, like a distant bird. She felt his hand on her cheek and breast and thigh. She was frightened and excited. She was almost twenty years old.

The steering wheel was in the way.

'Drive somewhere,' said Nico into Hugh's neck, speaking with difficulty, her voice an unfamiliar squeak.

'Where?'

'Anywhere. I'll tell you.'

'I don't know if I can. I don't think I can.'

His hands shook holding the key, on the wheel, changing gear. His perfect hair was mussed. He was lovely.

'Where?' he said.

Where? Why? For what? Was she drunk? Her father had been a man of God. She and her mother were strictly moral, Christian, puritan, setting a good example, giving witness to the world by their lives . . .

'Next left,' said Nico.

Meadowsweet and brambles and rosebay willow-herb, the rustling of birds in the hedgerows, a pelmet of small clouds fringing the western horizon over the slow downs, the heat of the sun on cotton shirts, on bare shoulders and breasts and legs, the crackle of dry grass and the click of friendly insects, hands and lips, fingers exploring, caressing, broken words of love, wide smiles, eyes intent and distant, eyes tight shut and wide open, flesh on flesh, skin adoring the stroking palm, moist skin slipping leg on leg, breast on breast, the dance of tongues, the kisses on eyes and ribs, the hard and the soft, fingers twined in silky hair, intolerable sensation, agony, intensity of joy—

Surrender, victory, tears, the never-ending embrace, the love everlasting—

Nothing like it ever before: revelation, miracle—

'Marry me,' said Hugh.

'I expect so,' said Nico.

They telephoned from a pub. Nico's mother sounded wary.

Nico thought she should drink whisky, to celebrate being grown up, but Hugh argued her out of it. They had bread and cheese and lager. In the saloon bar of the pub they contrived to keep their hands to themselves.

Later and later, and after the setting of an infant moon, it was still warm, a caressing windless night, the sky purple rather than black, the trembling as helpless and the cry of heavenly amazement . . .

'I suppose I'd better,' said Nico.

'What, darling?'

'Marry you. This sort of thing is habit-forming.'

She felt his smile under her lips, their faces resting together in the darkness.

'Can we announce it on your birthday?'

'Oh. My aunt's giving a party. Oh.'

'Is that the one called Lady something?'

'Cavenham.'

'Like a very smart barmaid?'

'Like a *poule de luxe.* Yes. She's sweet. She's paid for my whole life, up till now.'

'It's a pity you haven't got a father, for me to have an interview with.'

'You can have one with my Mum.'

'Yes. I'd certainly better do that.'

'Not tonight.'

'Perhaps not tonight.'

She felt their mingled smiles, the cheek of each massaging the cheek of the other.

Alice knew.
She said nothing; Nico said nothing. But Alice knew.
Nico was late back. She came up the path to the house, the lights of his car already disappearing, the sound of its engine fading among the wild roses and the dusty oak trees.
'I'm sorry. We were talking. I lost track of the time.'
'Talking.'
'I can't do any more of it tonight.'
What should Alice say? The child was not a child. A student, among those wild young students. Those months in Italy, sunshine and unaccustomed wine. A knowing, beady-eyed, adventurous bosom-friend like Felicity Peacock, certainly a ticket to all kinds of experiences. Alice had always been aware of that, and not seriously dismayed. Nico was not a child; no good would come of treating her like one. No lectures or cross-examinations, no questions at all. She could not be made to stand in a corner, or sent to bed without supper.

They were not Catholics. There was no confessional. Was that good or bad?
Was it a sin?
How dared this smooth Hugh Jarvis insert himself into their lives, slide himself into a neighbour's household, seduce little Nicola? How *dared* he? Alice felt a great rage – with him, with the Parkinsons who had produced him, and with the Peacock girl who had devised the picnic.

She told herself she did not want Nicola's confidence. Not everything should be told, brought out into the open, as though they were shameless Buchmannites, 'coming clean' in an orgy of self-indulgent confession. It was unseemly and essentially selfish to force confidences on people. Some things should remain private. Bathroom doors had locks; the locks should be used. Bedroom doors should be closed. A part of Alice found repugnant the thought of hearing in detail about that evening: a part of her was intensely, painfully anxious to know the worst or best, not out of prurience but out of love and concern, unalterable maternal instinct—

Alice tried hard not to deceive herself. She must accept that her daughter was grown up, her own woman, in charge of herself, custodian of her own virtue, guided and guarded by her own conscience. The Parkinsons and Felicity Peacock had done nothing wrong. Neither their motives nor their actions could be criticized in any way. It was childish and unreasonable to blame them for anything that had happened.

Blame who, then? For what? Hugh Jarvis, for cynically exploiting his worldliness to dazzle an innocent child . . .?

Alice struggled to be fair, in the small hours of the morning. She found that, try as she might, she could not like or trust Hugh Jarvis. She did not think her hostility was the jealousy of a possessive mother. God knew that nowadays it was normal enough. Chastity was bizarre. Perhaps it was not so very terrible, but it was premature, far too soon, a relationship certainly doomed, probably dangerous – it was irresponsible and it would end in heartbreak. And if Nicola was starry-eyed with love, it would not help to say any of that.

'To *marry* him?'

'Don't look so astonished, Mum. I'm not much younger than you were. You can see we had things to talk about.'

'But you hardly know one another!'

'That's why I didn't say yes. Well, not actually and finally.'

'Nicola, are you in love with this man?'

'Well, I'm new to all this, you know. To this feeling. I haven't got anything to compare it with. That's another reason I didn't quite absolutely say yes.'

'I think nothing should be said, then. Not for the moment, not in public. There is nothing yet to say, in fact.'

'Hugh wants to announce it at my birthday party.'

'Oh no. Oh good heavens, at that party, no. You will still only have known one another for a bare *moment*. He's gone back to London? Yes, of course. You will only have met a very few times. You can't be so impetuous, so crazy, as to make such a huge decision so ... You can't commit yourself to sixty years after sixty minutes, be so sure about one man when there are so many million you haven't met, decide before you're twenty what you're going to want at thirty and forty and fifty ...'

'Mum, you protest too much. I agree there's no hurry. I want to finish my course, for one thing. But I don't see why it should be a secret that we like one another.'

'That, I suppose, is already known.'

'Yes, if anybody's interested.'

Nine months later, in her hospital bed, Nico remembered that her mother had known. She supposed it had been written on her forehead in letters of fire: Hugh has made love to me by sunlight and by starlight, and I want him to do it by firelight and lamplight and moonlight and no light and in the dawn, again and again until I burst from joy.

She supposed it had been so immediately obvious, and she was embarrassed by the memory. It was a nuisance to be so transparent; it was undignified.

Hugh's name was mentioned by other people she saw in the next few days – by Miranda Jolly, David Parkinson, Aunt Vi – and she wondered later how obvious it had been to them. She felt that she must have blushed and trembled, and that stars shone out of her eyes, as in old sentimental ballads. She felt all the most mawkish emotions of the Victorian music hall, and imagined that it showed.

Her mother did not mention Hugh. That was odd, but Nico thought she understood.

Felicity did not mention Hugh. Probably she was just not interested. Flickie always had her own fish to fry, of absorbing interest to her. Her current preoccupation might not last long – the grass was greener behind every locked gate – but it was a relief for the moment. Flickie always found out anything she wanted to know.

Perhaps Aunt Vi looked at Nico a little oddly. From what Nico had almost subliminally gathered, Aunt Vi had no business to look oddly at anybody, pillar of respectability as Her Ladyship might now be. Did being married to a millionaire put you in a position of moral superiority, whatever you got up to in your youth? Certainly it shouldn't, and certainly it did, and it wasn't fair.

Nico put the telephone down. She looked at her mother defensively.

'I didn't say anything,' said Alice.

'You complain that we don't know each other well enough,' said Nico. 'So we're trying to put that right. So now you're complaining about that.'

'I am precisely not doing so.'

'Well, you look as if you wanted to.'

Alice did want to, and Nico knew it, and neither of them knew why.

Of course everybody saw Nico leaving the picnic with Hugh. People had noticed them at the picnic, too, and picking up sticks under the trees oblivious of anybody else; and both Felicity Peacock and Miranda Jolly had rung up during the evening to be told that Nico was not back.

And people saw Nico during the following days, the many days before Hugh could get away again from London.

If she had been experienced and tough, it might all have been less important to her – she might, at least, have been able to act as though nothing earth-shaking had happened. But she had little experience and no toughness. Her apprenticeship, under the tutelage of Felicity Peacock, had been dim, meek and provincial, and Italy had been untouching of any emotional depths. Sleeping Beauty had gone to that picnic.

The Close at Milchester was a great place for the invention of theory and the spreading of news. Theory became news as the ripples widened, from the wives of the Cathedral clergy out into the parishes, from the shops in the Buttermarket out to the houses of retired colonels, from the waiting rooms of doctors out to the herbaceous borders, the tea parties, the bridge-tables and the art clubs.

This tiny sensation was more discussed than it deserved because Nicola Maude was so beautiful; because she was the fatherless only child of a clergyman; because she and her mother were popular and pious and held up as an example all over the diocese; and because Hugh Jarvis was a glamorous outsider, a metropolitan exotic with a mother in Tuscany, a journalist writing signed articles in a magazine everybody had heard of; and because there had previously been gossip about Hugh and a quite different girl, about whom quite different things were said.

By Milchester standards it was hot stuff.

So that although nothing had been announced – no questions answered, no questions, publicly, even asked – the party for Nico's twentieth birthday was abuzz with speculation.

The Cavenhams had laid on a disco and a steel band and a barbecue, and there were Japanese lanterns in the trees near the pool, and Nico was wearing sky-blue. It was extremely generous of Aunt Vi. Though only a twentieth, it was like a twenty-first, as though it was expected to be an occasion of great significance, a milestone, a time of announcements, toasts and speeches. (Nico's actual twenty-first, no doubt also to be given by the Cavenhams, would be something to tell your grandchildren about. Everybody at this party wanted to be at that party. Whatever would they come up with?)

Nico blew out the candles on her cake, and showed off her new bracelet; and the dancers were reflected in the water of the pool; and Felicity Peacock, in peacock-green, was thought by some to upstage even the heroine of the evening.

Hugh Jarvis came late, driving straight from London, having no time even to change.

There was no doubt that he brought something with him, a larger world of operas and treaties and takeover bids, French literary prizes and international film festivals and distant revolutions. The locals were abashed by the power and glory which Hugh represented, by the secrets they did not know and the celebrities they had not met.

'Everybody's frightened of you,' Nico said to him.

'I'm frightened of everybody,' said Hugh. 'These are the people I want to make a good impression on. Your old friends, your family and neighbours. I don't know how to go about it.'

She laughed.

'These are the people,' he said seriously, 'I want to be accepted by.'

'You are.'

'Not altogether.'

Not altogether.

The Very Reverend Leonard Peacock, Dean of Milchester, felt as he found and spoke as he felt. He said Jarvis was an interesting fellow who worked very hard for his living. The Dean knew what was going on in the world, and in his Cathedral, but not in his house or in quiet bars or in London flats. His wife was better informed. She was not fully in Felicity's confidence, but she had eyes in her head. She was cool to Hugh Jarvis.

Flickie herself was neither cool nor warm. It was an evening when she wore her most shining carapace; she was a fascinating, heartless mechanical toy. She was restless, almost hectic; she darted like a dragonfly.

'She acts as though it were her party,' said Vi Cavenham, a little sourly.

But most people were amused by Flickie's antics, and some people were sorry for her.

Alice Maude was cool to Hugh Jarvis.

Nico saw and suffered, and said something about it to Felicity Peacock.

'Darling, it's inevitable,' said Flickie. 'You're an only child. Your Ma isn't obsessive or over-possessive or anything, she's not Diana Rigg in *Mother Love* on the telly, but she's still seeing her ewe-lamb transferring allegiance.'

'Am I doing that?'

'Of course you bloody are. At least, you look as though you were, when you look at him.'

'I wish I wasn't quite so transparent.'

'It's one of the things we all love about you.'

It was not always easy to tell when Flickie was joking.

Later, much later, lying helpless in bed, Nico remembered this conversation held under the Japanese lanterns, to the humming and bonging of the steel band by the pool. She wondered how she could have been so stupid, so insensitive. But she had not been there in the early summer. She had not seen it happening. Nobody had told her. And Flickie had guts and generosity. And nothing had really been decided between them, matters had not come to a head, as far as Nico knew ...

Later, much later, Nico wondered what she would have done, what she would have felt, if she had known what they eventually told her, about Hugh and Flick. Anything different? How different? How far could she have helped herself?

Alice knew later that Nicola and Hugh were rushing blindly towards the 'accident' on the bend in the road. They might have avoided it. In July and August it was not inevitable. Until they were formally engaged to be married, perhaps, it was not inevitable.

Their safety lay in parting, and in staying apart for ever.

But nobody knew this until after the 'accident', and only Alice knew it then.

CHAPTER FOUR

RODDY PLUMB'S BIRTHDAY PRESENT TO Nico was a framed enlargement of one of his photographs of the picnic. It was a very happy picture.

Roddy had given the same enlargement to Flickie and Hugh and David. This did not reduce the value of the present to Nico, but simply increased the level of Roddy's generosity. Enlargements were expensive. Also, she had the frame, a pretty antique in the Chinese manner, intended for a drawing or watercolour.

'Happy memories,' said Nico, looking at the photograph, and at Roddy over the photograph.

'I hope so,' said Roddy.

'Oh yes, whatever happens.'

Already there were these memories, her favourite memories.

'Life is all a question of timing,' said Roddy. 'People say it is a question of semantics or mechanics or whatnot, but it is a question of timing. Now if I had clumsily charged at you not when I did, but immediately after you got back from Italy, after you had sufficiently grown up, before you had met the viper Jarvis—'

'Darling Roddy, I would have adored you, but I do anyway, and I always did, and I always will.'

'That is nice, but it is not what I mean at all.'

The picture joined Nico's other presents, on a table in

the hall at March Court. Luckily it was a big table. She had been given records, tapes, books, a Majolica vase, a big Dutch plate, two framed Victorian woodcuts and a set of unframed eighteenth-century prints, a stuffed goldfinch under a glass dome, a Moroccan doll, a gold bracelet (from her Aunt Vi).

It was a good haul, for a twentieth birthday. It was a good party.

'Fantastic, Aunt Vi,' said Nico, drifting by on her way to the table where the drinks were.

'Enjoy yourself, darling. But wait till next year. Then you'll have to buckle your seat belts.'

'You can't do better than this, Lady Cavenham. There isn't any party better than this.'

'You wait, Roddy. Everybody's in for a surprise. This is – pah!' Vi flapped her hands in disdain. 'A scrubby little high tea. But a twenty-first ought to be . . .'

'What?'

'Not so much a party, more a . . . happening. An event. An explosion. A sensation. You just wait.'

Roddy asked Nico, aside, 'What is she planning?'

'I tremble to think,' said Nico. 'So does Uncle Hilary, I bet.'

Hugh had a ring in his pocket, a diamond between sapphires. Nico would not let him give it to her, even secretly.

Monica Parkinson said, 'It's difficult for Alice Maude.'

'Why?' asked Felicity Peacock.

'She's out of it.'

'She doesn't have to be. She can come into it whenever she likes. All she has to do is relax. She should. If she's sulking and skulking she should stop, if only for Nico's sake.'

'That's easy to say, Flickie. It *is* awkward for Alice. She's a poor relation at her own daughter's party.'

'I'm a poor relation at the Deanery,' said Felicity. 'And I'm not even a relation.'

'Yes, but you're a bold hussy.'

'I bet Vi Cavenham was one of those. Not that I want to sound ungrateful. It seems to have worked for her. P'raps it'll work for me.'

'Oh, it's worked for Vi,' said Monica. 'If you like this kind of life. And I never heard of anybody who didn't.'

'Would Alice?'

'Of course she would.'

'Yes, of course she would. It's not fair, really, is it?'

'I think that every time I see them together. And I usually think it when I see them separately.'

That conversation was the longest that Felicity had, all that night. It was the longest time that she stood still. There was no man there for whom she would have stood still for so long. There had been in the spring, but not now.

Alice would have enjoyed the party more if Tommy Johns had been there. But Vi would never have thought to ask him. Vi hardly knew him. She didn't know about him. Nobody knew about Tommy. Nicola knew there was such a person – a respectable, self-effacing middle-aged man, product of a famous school and an ancient university, chartered surveyor and senior partner of a firm of estate agents in Milchester: Nico knew that much. Everybody knew that much. Nico knew no more than that, and nor did anybody else.

Everybody else had secrets. Why shouldn't Alice have a secret?

Alice was only forty-three. She had been married at

twenty-one, widowed at twenty-nine, and strictly virtuous ever since. She asked herself: in God's name, why?

A baby daughter, becoming a child and a teenager and a student and practically an adult, totally absorbing her emotional energy.

The spirit of Barney leaning over her shoulder, his unforgotten face on the pillow, his continual presence, a third party in every twosome.

Opportunity. Ridiculous as it sometimes seemed to herself, to Tommy, it would have been most awkward to arrange. He lived in Milchester, just off the Close. There was practically no chance of a female arriving alone, staying two hours, silent and uninterrupted, leaving alone, unseen, the implications unnoticed; and her face was well known there; and people had been asking for fourteen years when she would find another man. And then, even when Nicola was away, there was precious small chance of Alice entertaining a solitary male visitor for two hours without the neighbours noticing. Hotels? Motels? Anonymity? False names? The whole furtive rigmarole? Imagination recoiled, as at improvisations, car-rugs under hedgerows . . .

Conscience came into it. Alice was not sure where she stood, since the question had not really been faced. Would God mind what a middle-aged widow did with a friend?

But if the friend was married? And the friend's wife spent nine months of the year in a mental home?

Candles guttered in pools of tallow, petals dropped from the great bowls of virginal Iceberg roses and the swags of clematis and honeysuckle, the steel band had packed away its oil-drums and gone off in a Dormobile to a

Midland city. A grey-faced woman was collecting empty glasses from the window-sills, and a man from the caterer's sat in the hall, fast asleep, with a broom between his legs.

Nico in her Roman bikini dived into the pool. She was twenty. She had been given everything you could think of, except an engagement ring.

It was no surprise, no surprise at all, to receive a letter from Jefferson McCabe two days after her birthday. The letter enclosed a present. The only surprise was that the package arrived late.

The letter began, '*Nico carissima,*' and proceeded, in Baroque terms, to wish her a happy day, a happy year, a happy life. It ended, '*In devotion at least to the grave, and probably beyond, Jefferson (Marius the Epicurean) McCabe.*'

The gift was a bronze-gold copy of a Renaissance medal, the obverse showing the laughing head of a faun, made into a pendant with a heavy gold chain. When Nico put it on she felt like a slave-girl.

'I'm spoilt,' said Nico.

'Yes and no,' said Alice, half aloud, thinking of the party she would have liked, herself, to have given her daughter.

Hugh had taken his holiday entitlement for the year before Nico had even met him. He had been prodigal.

'Skiing,' he explained. 'And I do like Italy in the spring. The sun's arrived but the crowds haven't. We might have met. I don't understand how they let you out of the country. You'd better not go back again by yourself. There are weekends I shall have to work.'

'There are weekends I shall have to work, too,' said Nico, 'when the term starts.'

'Then we'd better try to arrange that they're the same weekends. I don't want you mooning about down here with nothing to do.'

'I have a great deal to do. That is the most arrogant remark I ever heard in my life.'

'Well, do you want me mooning about in London with nothing to do?'

'You'd be safer here, I expect.'

'No. Not safer. Who wants to be safe?'

Nine months afterwards, Nico said from her pillows, with embarrassment, 'I can understand why you didn't tell me.'

'Tell you what?' said Felicity Peacock, pretending not to know what Nico was talking about.

'But I can't understand why Hugo didn't tell me.'

'Tell you what?' said Felicity again. 'There wasn't anything to tell.'

'He needn't have said anything about somebody I'd never heard of,' said Nico. 'A girl in London or Paris or Timbuctoo. I wouldn't have cared about them. I expect there were dozens. David Parky says he murdered them all at Oxford. I didn't want to hear about any of that, except that it made me all the prouder. But you ...'

'Stop talking about it,' said Felicity. 'You're exhausting yourself.'

A week after the party, Alice went to March Court to collect a present that had arrived there for Nicola. It had been sent by somebody who had received an invitation, who did not know that March Court was not the Maudes' home. It was a perfectly understandable mistake. It was not a hardship for Alice to drive a couple of miles to have tea with her sister in that garden.

They sat in a sort of bower of rampant Nevada roses, which grew over an archway of iron hoops copied from those at Kenwood. In front of them the lawn sloped to the river, three miles downstream of the copse-clad bend of the picnic. The towers of Milchester were invisible from this spot, the traffic inaudible. No humans, no human habitation, were to be seen or sensed. The only sound was the tinkle of Vi's teaspoon, as she stirred a non-fattening sweetener into her Lapsang Suchong.

Hilary was there, eating cucumber sandwiches, wearing a Panama hat with an Eton Ramblers ribbon. He was as amiable as ever, a figure infinitely reassuring but tending to merge into the background. It was said that he had increased the fortune he had inherited, but nobody knew how – he was too gentle, too tolerant, too tender of everybody's feelings, ever to have been a tycoon. It was amazing he had hung onto anything, married to Vi, who stinted neither herself nor anybody she liked.

Alice found that she was disgusted with herself.

Hilary stood to leave them, to go indoors to write letters (perhaps to watch a children's programme on the television). He bent to give Alice the invariable peck on the cheek. He took and held Vi's hand for a moment. It was a gesture of tenderness touching to see after so many humdrum years of marriage, a gesture which filled Alice with a sick and contemptible surge of envy.

Barney had been killed fourteen years before. Tommy Johns was not allowed to make such gestures, by the world or by his own conscience.

There would have been no room in Alice's garden for that arch with those roses over it – such a feature would have dwarfed its neat little surroundings, looked gross and pretentious and out of scale.

There was nowhere Alice could sit in her garden out of earshot of passing cars.

She had no silver teapot.

If she wanted cucumber sandwiches, she had to make them herself.

China tea tasted of jealousy.

Most of that blazing August, Hugh was, by his own account, miserably imprisoned in London. Nico did moon about, preparing lackadaisically for the imminent term, toasting her shoulders by the Cavenhams' pool for the benefit of the swifts and martins, feeling an itch and urge which she identified, with astonished awe, as simple lust.

Alice struggled against irritation. Nicola's preoccupation was self-indulgent and undignified. She could have helped more in the house, especially having been away for six months. The heat should have been conducive to tranquillity – but not that summer. Not for Alice.

With September, schooldays returned, and so did Hugh.

It was at this point that he showed himself, so surprisingly, as a fearless and effective horseman, impressing Nico, who had ridden all her life, impressing the Cavenhams' groom, old Jim Clayton, who started by mounting the London smoothie, mischievously, on a fresh and queer-tempered mare called Sadie Hawkins (because it was very seldom her day). Sadie bucked Hugh off in the end, but it took her a long time, and she only did it by bucking after an awkward jump, screwing in the air, over a tiger-trap. Next day, Sunday, Jim bought Hugh a drink in the Blue Boar in the village, a thing he was not given to doing, by way of apology.

David Parkinson told Nico that Hugh had never in his life crossed a horse until the spring of that same year. Nico flatly refused to believe him. It remained difficult to believe, even after she knew, from Felicity and others, that it was true.

It made him quite a man. Even Nico's mother admitted that it said something for his guts and his fitness.

Nico asked Hugh to stay at Turner's Cottage, where there was a perfectly good spare bedroom tucked into the attic. Alice was not keen, but she was obliged to second the invitation. She did not want a show-down; and with herself in the house there was nothing improper in the idea – not even the Milchester Cathedral clergy could have criticized. But Hugh declined.

'I will not be responsible for giving your mother extra trouble.'

'You won't,' said Nico. 'You can make your own bed and help with the washing-up. You can *save* us trouble, by bringing in the firewood and getting the dead leaves out of the gutters.'

'I'll do those things anyway. It's actually because I should go mad, being under the same roof as you and not being able to get at you.'

'Get at me. Goodness, how poetic.'

'Get at you and tear you to pieces and eat you up.'

'Well. My Mum is a light sleeper.'

'I wouldn't be a sleeper at all. *Youth that spent the light in crying, in the dark should cry no more.*'

'You don't spend the light in crying.'

'Yes, I do. I keep it hidden, like the Spartan boy with the fox. I want to make love to you now.'

'Don't say things like that. We can't. I shall burst if I think about it.'

But now and then, with infinite trouble, they could. Nico thought that it improved her understanding of the arts. There was no doubt that love made her even more beautiful.

'I don't know when or how,' said Alice to Tommy Johns. 'I don't even know how I know. I just know it's going on.'

Tommy nodded. He looked tired. He always looked tired, because he always was tired. He worked too hard and worried too much.

He was a thin, sandy man of fifty-two, his forehead sunburned in the summer, his physique younger than his years but his face older. Tragedy dwelt in his eyes, invisible sometimes, when he hooked a trout on a Mayfly, when he met Alice for a drink, but constantly rekindled when he visited his wife in the hospital, or coped with looking after her at home.

'You say you know,' he said to Alice. 'But you're using the word "know" in a slightly special sense. Have you asked her?'

'Oh no. A row would be terribly counter-productive. As it is I can't influence her much, but if we had a fight I wouldn't be able to influence her at all. She is grown up.'

'Barely.'

'Well, she thinks she is. All the more so, now, which is one of the sickening things about it. Of course you're right. She's too young for such strong emotion. She thinks she's being adult, and actually she's being childish. She only comes to life when he appears. Heaven knows what it's doing to her academically.'

'That may not matter as much as it did.'

'Because she need no longer worry about independence? Because she won't want a career? If I were a feminist I'd hit you for that remark.'

'It's something to be young,' said Tommy. 'It's something to have the power to grab the moment as it passes. Herrick had it right.'

'*Gather ye rosebuds while ye may*,' quoted Alice.

'Some may, some mayn't. Andrew Marvell had it right, too. I wouldn't blame Hugh Jarvis for thinking so. I don't blame myself for thinking so.'

'I'm not coy,' said Alice. 'And unfortunately I'm not your mistress.'

Tommy laughed ruefully. Discussion of English lyric poetry was not what they wanted, but it seemed to be the best they could do.

Tommy could not help Alice in this situation, in the problem she thought she had with Nicola, except by reminding her that he existed and that he loved her.

Alice could not help Tommy, either.

At the end of October, three months after that twentieth birthday party, Nico had one of the weekends without Hugh which she loudly hated and which her mother quietly welcomed. It was a change to get some reading done, some solid work, without the interruption of lectures, the distraction of student functions, the Milchester parties. That was the theory. In practice it was a time for mooning about and missing Hugh and not answering questions.

Alice fought down her irritation. She bit back remarks which would have been a relief to herself, but which would not have helped Nicola or the relationship between mother and daughter.

What would Barney have done? For once, Alice had no idea.

They went to Matins in the Cathedral, mother and daughter in their Sunday best. Nicola glowed like a lamp under the black arches, against the carvings of the roodscreen, below the quiet blaze of the transept windows, tawny-silver hair badged by the medieval colours. Nicola's voice was raised in the singing, louder and sweeter than her mother's. She had more to be joyful about. She would see Hugh within a week.

Nicola was too well bred, too well trained, to look round in the Cathedral during the service, to see who was there that she knew, to see who was looking at her. But a sensation between her shoulder-blades assured her that many people were looking at her. More than ever she was a girl people looked at. This was partly the result of Italy, but mostly the result of Hugh.

After the service they went to a demure little sherry party in the Close. It was a very parsonical party – a bluff archdeacon, a colonial bishop like a colonial rodent, whose diocese was a thousand miles across, a retired missionary and his leathery wife, a stained-glass expert, an organ repairer, the retired head of a theological college who had known Barney Maude as a student. This was Doctor Gregory Gardiner, who gobbled and gargled and bobbed up and down like a turkey-cock, who was ridiculous and full of kindness and friendship.

'Oh my goodness,' he said to Nicola, 'I knew your father quite as well as most. I was supposed to be responsible for training him for the priesthood, but it was perfectly unnecessary! He was awfully well organized, and I never was at all! Without the ceaseless ministrations of my dear late wife, I could never have survived! Never have reached my study with the right books, in the right clothes, at the right time! Barnabas Maude. What memories the name brings back! I suppose I am speaking of the early sixties? Those would be his days as an ordinand? Dear, dear me. We kept in touch, after his ordination. He gratified me intensely by asking me for my advice on a number of occasions. Quite purposeless, I assure you! But pleasing to a silly old man. One such occasion was his betrothal. Yes, to your mother! How could I advise? I had not then the pleasure of the young lady's acquaintance. But I shortly made it! An errand, so to say – an expedition of a quasi-professional character and utterly devoid of interest or relevance – took us in our motor-car close by the scene of Barnabas's labours and the residence of his intended bride! It was a most happy coincidence, in which I was tempted to see the hand of Providence. Thus, as matters turned out, Cynthia and I found ourselves taking tea with the family of Dr Harold Bolton, in their small but gracious home in the city of Portsmouth.'

'My grandfather,' said Nico.

'No longer with us, I think? I believe I recall writing to your mother a letter of condolence on the occasion of his death. No, no, your grandmother, to be sure, your grandmother.'

'They both died. A long time ago. I hardly knew them.'

'That is your loss, and was theirs.'

Nicola took a moment to sort this out. When she had done so she was pleased.

'My memory,' continued Dr Gardiner, 'is intermittent in operation, but at its optimum moments of a most gratifying clarity. Scenes present themselves to my eye as though photographed, to my ear as though recorded! Thus I remember those two most attractive young ladies, the Misses Viola and Alice Bolton, even to the colour of their earrings!'

'What colour were their earrings?' asked Nico, bursting out laughing.

'Do not press me to the issue. I remember being startled that they were sisters.'

'People still are. I still am.'

'It would be so, of course. It might now be supposed that they were so very different because of the differences in their lives. Viola, I believe, is a wife of a man of substance? Of hereditary title? I recollect being told so, probably by Barnabas. Difference in fortune, with all that it entails, might be held the cause of the difference in personality, but I assure you that it was already most evident when I met them, a quarter-century ago. That was, you understand, before either of them was married.'

'How were they different?'

'How are they different now? In all ways, I hazard. Just so were they then. It was to be explained not at all by environment, since Miss Alice had spent all her life, Miss Viola most of hers, in the self-same household, attending the same schools, church and all such. No. Heredity is seen to be at work here. The fathers. I am sure you know far more about this than I. I would be interested in your account, in what you will have heard throughout your life, as I suppose. I did not meet Viola's natural father, of course – did not know of his existence, until Barnabas told me of him. Barnabas told me the bare fact only – that the young ladies were half-sisters, that Viola's father was gone out of her life. Perhaps abroad? Perhaps dead? You shall tell me. The man was, at any rate, presumably of a complexion of character notably different from Harold Bolton, most devoted and respected of general practitioners, as the world knew. Come now. You must know. Elucidate. What of Viola's father? Whence and whither? I should tell you that my curiosity is almost wholly frivolous.'

'Are you sure you've got this right?' asked Nicola, aware that she sounded impertinent, but not knowing how else to ask.

Dr Gardiner was quite sure. He was long-winded and absurd; he bobbed up and down when he spoke, as though preaching a sermon in a pulpit too big for him; but he was not senile or stupid. He was inquisitive but not mischievous. He might be wrong but he was certain he was right. He was amazed that what he said was news to Nico.

'I wonder,' he said, 'if I have been lamentably indiscreet. But cats should not be kept in bags.'

'You'd better ask my mother about it. Or come and ask Aunt Vi.'

'The latter I shall most assuredly not do. No indeed. Mister Valiant-for-Truth is a fine fellow, but tact remains a necessary condition of civilized life. As to your mother – well! I *might* have asked her. Yes, time was, I might, indeed. A bare half-hour ago! But now I will not! No! Because if she were minded to talk about it, she would have talked to you about it.'

'Oh. That is true,' said Nico. 'But why did my father tell you that Aunt Vi's father—'

But before she could complete the question, her mother was plucking at her sleeve and saying they must go. It was true that their glasses had been unfilled for a long time, and the room had almost emptied.

Alice had completely forgotten Dr Gardiner. At her parents' house in Portsmouth, when she was engaged to

Barney? He came for tea? That little aged parson with a red nose? No doubt he looked different then; no doubt she was preoccupied; and she was at that time meeting an awful lot of parsons.

Whatever had he and Nicola been talking about, all that time?

Vi's father? Why in heaven's name did a strange old parson tell Nicola about Vi's father?

'He didn't know he was telling me,' said Nico. 'He assumed I knew. You can't blame him. Anyone would assume it.'

'Why did he even mention it? Whyever did it come up?'

'He said it was pure curiosity,' said Nico. 'But I think he was just thankful to find something to talk about. *Is* it a secret?'

'I don't know if it is. Yes, I suppose it is.'

'Why is it?'

'I don't know. Whatever happened, it was before I was born, and I never heard anybody talk about it. I grew up not knowing anything about it. It never occurred to me my father wasn't Vi's father too. It wouldn't, would it? To a child?'

'But your names? She wasn't a Bolton.'

'Yes, she was. That's to say, she'd taken my father's surname. Or rather, she'd been given it. He'd adopted her, made her his daughter. It quite often happens, you know. The idea is to give the child a firmer emotional base.'

'I understand that. Are you telling me Granny was divorced?'

'Good gracious, no. She was a widow. Vi's father was killed in the war, in 1944, I think.'

'Crossing the Rhine, or something?'

'I expect so.'

'But that's something to be proud of,' said Nico. 'Why would you change your name if your father had been killed in battle?'

'I don't know. I grew up thinking Vi was my full sister. I saw her being treated exactly as I was, my father's daughter ...'

'When did you know?'

'I can't tell you, exactly. It sort of grew on me, that Vi and I weren't quite ... There wasn't a thunderclap, a moment of revelation. We were so different we had to be different, and it turned out we were different.'

'That's what my old parson said ... I wonder what Aunt Vi's father was like.'

'I've wondered that. I did ask her. She doesn't really know. She doesn't remember. She was too small. He was away fighting.'

'But Granny? Did you ask her?'

'No. By the time I would have dared she was dead.'

'Was she so frightening?'

'It wasn't that. But I thought there must be a reason why nobody ever mentioned him.'

'Aunt Vi must have asked her.'

'Yes, I think so. Yes, of course she must. Her own father. But I never knew what Mummy told Vi.'

'Haven't you asked her?'

'Not really. I don't think Mummy told her much. I don't know why. I don't think what she knows is very interesting. It's none of my business. To tell you the truth, I've never given it much thought. Vi and I weren't close as children. Five years is a big gap when you're small. To all intents and purposes, Vi's father was my father, and by the time I knew he wasn't ...'

'But it means,' said Nico, pondering, 'she has a whole

other family. Maybe cousins all over the place, maybe fascinating, her flesh and blood—'

'Perhaps not,' said Alice. 'Perhaps my mother's cousins and the Bolton cousins were enough. They were more than enough for me, when I was small. I wouldn't have wanted any more relatives. And then, you know, it's possible Mum headed Vi off her real father's family.'

'On grounds of snobbery?'

'Possibly. She was a snob. They all were, that generation. But there might be all kinds of grounds. It was a wartime marriage, probably done in a hurry. A lot of those were calamitous, awful mistakes, people from different backgrounds wildly mismatched, okay in wartime when everybody's jolly and democratic, not so funny in peacetime, when you find how differently you live ... That sounds awful, but it's realistic. I think it could easily explain why Vi's never had contact with her father's lot. Mummy was thankful to be rid of them.'

'What was he called?'

'I don't know,' said Alice. 'I never did know. Now that you mention it, I wonder myself. I don't think I'll ask Vi.'

'I shall,' said Nico.

'Bolton,' said Vi.

Nico blinked.

'Carnegie-Bolton, to be exact. Captain Denis Carnegie-Bolton, MC, The Lennox Highlanders. My mother had the medal and the citation. She showed them to me, of course. I tried to find them after she died, but they'd disappeared.'

'What a pity.'

'It wasn't a pity. It was a crime. They were stolen and destroyed. I wonder if you're old enough to be told this?

If you're tough enough? I want to tell somebody, but I don't want your Mum upset. You're a big girl. Are you big enough to know the truth and not talk about it?'

'I think it depends what you tell me.'

'You'll understand when I do. Your grandfather stole those things. My stepfather. He stole them and destroyed them, as well as everything else that might remind my mother of my father.'

'Why?'

'He was jealous.'

'My God.'

'He met my parents. He and my father were distant cousins. My father was the Scottish branch, a much grander branch.'

'Oh I see. The name. Not a coincidence.'

'No, not at all. They met because they were cousins, in the middle of the war. Rather a contrast between them. My father was a dashing captain in a kilt, from a castle in the Highlands. Harold was a medical student from a middle-class family in Chelmsford. I imagine he fell for my mother there and then.'

'She for him?'

'Oh no. Oh no. My Pa was the love of her life. He was dashing, glamorous, aristocratic. She was married to him. She was intensely proud of him. She adored him. She would hardly have noticed Harold was there, in his ready-made grey flannel wartime civvy suit ... And there's this about it, darling, a touch of unfairness. My father was killed. He is eternally a gallant, decorated, virile, beautiful young army officer of twenty-five. How about that for an unfair advantage? *They shall not grow old as we that are left grow old—*'

'*Age shall not wither them, nor the years condemn,*' murmured Nico.

'And,' said Vi, 'as I realized more and more, at the going down of the sun and in the morning, my poor old Mum remembered my father. However, she had me. We both had to be supported. She took on Harold, and she spent twenty years making the best of a bad job. Don't get me wrong. Harold was a worthy, dependable, conscientious doctor, never one to get drunk or go bankrupt. But his life was poisoned by jealousy of somebody dead. Can you imagine anything more mean-minded than pinching and destroying that medal? You can see why I don't want your Mum's nose rubbed in any of this.'

'But why didn't Granny keep in touch with your father's family? Highland castles and all that? Wouldn't that have been nice?'

'Poor Nico. That would have been fun for you. But it had all gone. All disappeared between the wars. My Pa inherited bugger-all. The castle was sold, the people were dead or disappeared, nothing left but a few antique great-aunts gibbering in nursing-homes in Aberdeen ... Probably there were some others, but Harold was so obsessively set against the contact, and she never had the energy to defy him. Don't forget he was paying all the bills for me as well as your Mum.'

'Carnegie-Bolton,' said Nico. 'You could look them up.'

'I have. There aren't any. They're extinct. All except for me. I'm the last. Maybe there are some in Australia or Canada. I looked for them, but I never found any. It's a shame. If my father had lived, he might have had sons.'

'And so that's how we explain,' said Nico, 'the difference between you and my Mum?'

'I daresay it's a factor.'

★

It was not a secret. It was public knowledge which nobody happened to know. Vi's father had been killed in the war; her mother had remarried and had become Alice's mother. No secret, no problem, no interest.

So much and no more.

On this basis, Nico could mention the matter to Felicity Peacock. Why did she? Why would Felicity care one way or the other? No reason, except that for some reason conversation was sticky. Odd, unnerving, after a lifetime of easy intimacy. Nico found herself making conversation, while drinking a mug of instant coffee in the Deanery kitchen.

Making conversation with Flickie? Weird. But so it was.

'Hugh's coming down on Friday night,' said Nico, supposing that Flickie would share her excitement.

'That's nice,' said Flickie.

Nico was stopped short. Laboriously she started again.

'He's staying with the Parks again. He won't stay with us.'

'Nice for the Parks.'

Nico had expected Flickie to ask why Hugh would not stay at Turner's Cottage. She would explain his reason, as little boastfully as she could. That would be a pretty good conversation. But Felicity was obviously too preoccupied with her own emotional life to be interested in anybody else's. Fair enough, perhaps. Not very friendly.

Nico dredged about for another subject. It was too large and gloomy a kitchen for companionable silences. (The Turner's Cottage kitchen was too small and bright for them.)

'My Mum and my Aunt Vi are half-sisters,' said Nico. 'Did you know that?'

'I didn't, but nothing could surprise me less, as they clearly belong to different species.'

'It surprised me at first, because I'd never heard of it. It doesn't now I'm used to the idea.'

'Vi had a different father?'

'Killed in the war.'

'Do you know about him?'

'Dimly.'

'Christ, how I envy you.'

'Having a dead great-uncle?'

'Having any relations at all.'

'Oh.'

Nico wondered if she had been tactless, unfeeling, in mentioning the subject of families. She thought not. Felicity had never minded discussing people's families before. She liked a good gossip.

'As you know, I'm some kind of orphaned Wop or Wog,' said Flickie. 'Or Dago or Spic or Yid. If I've got any living relatives they're brown or black, and they speak no known language.'

'Don't be ridiculous,' said Nico uneasily.

'But you all know all that, and make allowances.'

'Rubbish.'

Nico wondered how many allowances the Dean and his wife had had to make, and the Parkinsons and her own mother and everybody else.

'Nobody has to make allowances for you,' lied Nico.

To somebody far away – to a schoolfriend now prematurely and miserably married – Felicity said: 'How am I supposed to feel? She's tall, fair and beautiful. I'm beautiful too, but it's not enough, not in that company.

She's got relations all over the British Isles, all tall, fair, beautiful and Anglo-Saxon, all knowing all their bloodlines, knowing exactly who they are and where they came from. So obviously she got him. How could she help it? You can't blame her. I can't blame her for winning. It was inevitable. I just think it's a bit unfair.'

CHAPTER FIVE

Hugh came almost stealthily, on Friday evening. He had booked a room at the Green Dragon, a pub that had found itself on the main Milchester bypass road, and had consequently sprouted a filling-station and a sort of tentative motel among its outbuildings. Hugh said he had presumed too far on the Parkinsons' hospitality. He could not go to the Deanery, though asked by the Dean. He could not go to Turner's Cottage, though asked by the Maudes. He might have gone to March Court, certainly asked by the Cavenhams, but they were away shooting partridges in a waste of Midland turnips.

The Green Dragon was under new, indifferent management. The patrons were a mixed lot, with big grey company cars. Nobody gave a damn who came and went.

Alice sat watching Nico leave, after Hugh telephoned. She sat in a silence which spoke more clearly and bitterly than words. Nico tried to walk normally, and to leave the house with no particular expression on her face.

She parked among Peugeots, and crept to the front of the pub at the edge of pools of sodium light. She did not feel brazen.

She might have imagined herself repelled by the sleaziness of all this – by laminated plastic and pastel lights, the mini-bars in the 'chalets', the dash past the reception desk while the girl was looking for somebody's key, the muffled giggle through the paper-thin party wall. She might have supposed herself to feel corrupted by deceit, degraded to the level of furtive gropings in car-parks, at one with the overweight girls from the offices on the new industrial estate, the orange-rinsed girls from the supermarket checkouts and their gentlemen friends from Head Office. But she felt a great tolerance for these her sisters, wriggling naked between motel sheets even as she was; she felt a childish glee at the easy manoeuvres of getting in and out unseen; she felt a self-forgetting passion which made all of this unimportant, an intensity of physical sensation to which nothing in the world could be compared.

The bedclothes were found to be strewn over the room. It looked as though a bomb had struck. Nico thought a bomb had struck. She lay back on the pillows in a daze of wondering happiness, feeling wet, used, defiled, fulfilled, wise, beautiful. His magical hand stroked her thighs and breasts. She looked down at her body, amazed. Lazily she shifted her legs and pelvis under his hands, as though to prove to herself that she could still command them.

She had grown up a lot since July.

Nico felt drunk when she got home, although she had not had any drink at all. She blundered about the kitchen, laying breakfast as a kind of penance.

Her mother had gone to bed. On the drive home, Nico had prepared a story about a meeting with a colleague of Hugh's, an art critic, who might possibly be able to offer ... Something on those lines. She felt guilty about preparing a lie.

That was the only part of the evening she did feel guilty about.

She was astonished at herself.

On Saturday evening there was a party in Milchester of a strange and special complexion: a meeting of the ancient fellowship of the *Cantatores Milcastienses*. The original intention had no doubt been sacred, but there were copies of secular madrigals composed for the society in Tudor times, and of dreadfully ribald lyrics being contributed by the Duke of Buckingham in the reign of Charles II. The eighteenth century saw a long period of abeyance, when nobody connected with the Cathedral could be bothered with anything; the nineteenth an excessively high-minded revival; the earlier twentieth a phase of folksiness, the 1950s a happy combination of Renaissance music and claret-cup.

The singers met half a dozen times a year, in the homes of members. The Precentor and Succentor of the Cathedral were often present, but most of the members were amateurs. They had to read music pretty well, as most of their pieces were unaccompanied part-songs. Nicola had been the youngest member, when elected at the age of seventeen, but now she was only the third youngest. Milchester was full of precocious musical talent.

At noon on Saturday Nico had tried to cry off, pleading every reason except what everybody knew to be the true reasons.

'I beg you to come, dear girl,' cried the Master of the Holy Cross Hospital. 'We are short of treble voices. Neither Cynthia nor Marigold, nor that other one nor the fat lady, and in any case without you we lack attack at the top of the harmonies, and your young man, whom

I remember to have met at the Deanery, will be welcome at the Lodgings, especially if he will take a part.'

'I don't think he sings.'

'Then he shall be at once audience and wine-steward. He has a steady hand with a ladle? That is all we require of him.'

Thus Hugh heard Nico sing – properly, seriously sing, with others, music of beauty and merit. He was the audience. He sat with an expression of happy amazement. He was judged a good audience, and then a good hand with the ladle.

They sang in the big, bare gallery of the Master's Lodgings, uncarpeted, with an enormous open fire in the middle of the inner wall. The walls were linenfold panelling, badged with the black portraits of previous Masters. Oak settles were the only furniture. The singers stood in a semicircle at one end of the gallery, in overlapping pools of light from three standard lamps. Hugh sat at the far end, almost in darkness. The claret-cup was in a punchbowl on a hob by the fire. The firelight winked on the punchbowl, and a dancing flame caught a jewel on the breast of a frowning portrait opposite.

The music washed along the gallery like a blessing.

Nicola's tawny-silver hair gave back the firelight and the lamplight. Her voice in the embroidery of sound was now like a boxwood flute, now like a silver flageolet. She neither looked nor sounded real.

Felicity Peacock was a member of the group. She sang. Her voice was clear and pure, a hard, accurate voice like a platinum wire.

They sang a complicated twelve-part anthem by an anonymous Italian of the time and school of Palestrina.

The voices of Nicola and Felicity twined contrapuntally, living strands of light over the riper tones of the altos and the dark voices of the men.

Felicity was hardly visible from a distance, from where Hugh sat, being small among the singers, being dark in the darkness.

The Master was a big man, with a fringe of white hair round a dome of skull. He wore a gigantic cassock, though the two other parsons present wore suits with their dog-collars. In the singing, the Master disciplined his tremendous bass to a kind of crooning foundation for the polyphony; when they broke for the wine-cup he was thunderously jovial; and then he drew a friend aside – a singing stranger, a performing guest – to satisfy his curiosity about the company. He was tactful. His voice was low. He was far from the group, the fireside. He had perhaps forgotten Hugh on his oak settle in near-darkness.

He did not see, probably, that little dark Felicity was nearby. It would not greatly have worried him. He was speaking confidentially but not unkindly. Nothing he said was so very secret. It was unknown to strangers, but common knowledge locally. At least, the Master might have supposed that it was.

'That girl,' he murmured to his friend, 'the raving beauty with the angelic voice, her father was a very nice fellow, incumbent of a parish in the diocese, who fell out of a train when he was spifflicated, poor chap. The widow's life has been a bit of a struggle, but the girl's won't be. She's the only living relative of a very rich aunt.'

'Does the aunt see it,' asked the stranger softly, 'the way you see it?'

'Oh yes. I know the family. They've always loved this

child. There's never been the least doubt. I daresay they'll make old bones, mark you, but when they finally pass the threshold into the neighbour room, Nicola Maude will be a rich lady.'

Perceptibly, questionably, there was another listener, possibly not in fact listening, not interested, a figure hardly to be discerned in the gloom, dark-suited against the dark panelling, his face turned away. He was the one young man among the singers, younger than Hugh, a teacher at the preparatory school which the Cathedral choirboys attended. He taught English and History. He sang tenor, his voice reedy but accurate. He was called Gerald Orchard. It was thought that he had found his niche, but he did not think so.

Nobody would worry about Gerald Orchard overhearing anything.

The Secretary of the *Cantatores*, Doctor Frank Gray, called his singers to order. They regrouped themselves in their semicircle, and shuffled through their scores to find the next madrigal. Hugh was again isolated in the dark distance of the gallery. Nico shone once again in the light of the fire and that of the lamps overhead, and with the inner light which everybody could see.

Of course, to anybody who stopped to think about it, it was obvious that Nicola Maude was the heiress of Hilary and Viola Cavenham. Hilary's was the will that mattered, because he owned everything. He would leave this and that to old friends, colleagues, brother-officers if any survived – silver cigarette-boxes, minor pictures, firescreens or pieces of porcelain; he would give his widow a life interest in everything else he possessed; and Nicola would be his residuary legatee. There would be an awful lot of inheritance tax to pay, so she might have to sell the house. She might want to sell the house anyway. It depended on whom she married and where they lived.

It had become obvious whom she would marry. Everybody was simply waiting for the announcement. He was apparently rich himself. People said he was. He acted rich, in a nice way. What a waste!

Nobody had actually asked Hilary Cavenham about his will. Nobody had asked his wife or her sister or her niece. Nobody would. It was not the sort of conversation anybody had.

Local interest in the matter was not academic; it was not simply impertinent curiosity. The future of March Court was important. It was a beautiful house in a beautiful setting, to which terrible things could happen if it fell into the wrong hands. Hotel, conference centre, multi-national corporate headquarters, the stables converted into residential blocks, a car-park where the lawn was, heavy traffic, noise, outsiders, strip-lighting – it had all happened in other places. It was the sort of prospect which gave the Milchester Close a collective nightmare, as had the new hypermarket and the office blocks and the industrial estate near the station.

Some people wanted to make sure all this was averted, in perpetuity; they wanted Hilary to give March Court, with a sufficient endowment, to the National Trust. The stables would be turned into a tea-room, but it would be a gracious tea-room. There would be a gift-shop, but done in good taste. Local ladies would be engaged as guides and waitresses. This idea was not popular among Nicola's friends.

It was all a long way off. Hilary was barely sixty; Vi forty-eight. They were both overweight, but not gross.

They had given up smoking. They swam in their pool. Hilary played a little golf; Vi sometimes walked a small dog.

Nico might be fifty and a grandmother, before she inherited.

On the other hand, accidents happened, especially these days, on the roads . . .

The wife of the Master of the Hospital of the Holy Cross, a well-meaning but insensitive lady, told Nico she ought to make a will. Nico, incredulous, told her mother. Alice told Tommy Johns, hardly believing that he would believe it. But Tommy took it seriously. Nico's fortune was potentially large. Of course she ought to make a will.

'That's rubbish,' said Nico, upset enough to be rude. 'He asked me to marry him months ago. I told you. You were horrified. We'd only just met. It was before he knew anything about me, weeks and weeks before he came to the Holy Cross, before that silly old . . . before the Master was broadcasting about . . . before he could have known about Uncle Hilary's will. How could he possibly have been influenced? I think you ought to take that back. If it was anybody else, I'd think you ought to apologize.'

'Oh, don't be so touchy and defensive, darling,' said her mother. 'Hugh knew about you before he met you. You knew that. He'd stayed several times with the Parkinsons. Do you call Monica Parkinson reticent?'

'How would she know about the will? How could anybody?'

'How could anybody not guess? How could Hilary or Vi not say anything to anybody in all those years? I didn't say Hugh proposed to you *because* he knew about it. I simply said that he knew about it when he proposed to you.'

'The implication is that it was cause and effect. And I think it's a cheap and rotten thing to say.'

'Oh heavens. It's nice to stand up for your friends. But it gets boring when it leads you into being silly and naïve.'

Nico left the room abruptly, white-faced.

Alice was slightly aghast. Of course the implication of what she had said was exactly as Nico said it was. She was close to accusing Hugh of fortune-hunting. She was not sure if this was quite what she had meant. It was not far from what she meant. She was no nearer fundamentally trusting Hugh. Her gut reaction, as the newspapers nowadays put it (vividly if rather crudely), was still to see him as a double-tongued, plausible London smoothie, equivocal, unreliable, phoney. She was not blindly trusting her instinct, but she was not ignoring it, either.

She was shocked and unhappy about the whole situation.

Nico left the house in a rage. She was still in a rage when she met Hugh, when he began to kiss her and take off her clothes. An edge was added to her rage by a nagging sense of guilt at the lies she had been telling. Rage and guilt intensified passion, giving it a degree of exquisite explosive fury which broke all records.

Nico lay slippery and glistening, and certain, and impatient.

'Yes,' she said. 'When you like. Where and how you like.'

'What?'

'I will.'
'What, darling?'
'Marry you, you clod.'

The local bombshell was a damp squib. Nobody was in the least surprised. The announcement was not only expected, it was overdue. It was as though people were tired of waiting to be told an inevitable event was going to happen; as though urgent bulletins were issued warning of the probable rising of tomorrow's sun.

Nico felt a sense of anti-climax all around her, in the village and in the town, in the shops and the lodgings of the lecturers, in the dark houses of the Close and the bright choirstalls of the Cathedral chancel. The world smiled and said, 'I told you so.'

But they were not blasé at March Court. There they opened the champagne.

'Have you made any plans?' said Vi. 'Are we to pencil in dates?'

'Not really. His mother's in Italy and his father's in South Africa. Quite a lot of to-ing and fro-ing has got to go on. We can't even put it in *The Times* yet. And Mum's being po-faced about it, on account of me being her ewe-lamb.'

'No other reason?'

'What other reason could there be? Also, I want to finish my course and get my diploma.'

'That sounds as though we've all got to wait until July.'

'Yes. Eight months. It's hell.'

'It'll just about clash with your birthday. What day of the week is your birthday?'

'Saturday.'

'Well now,' said Vi. 'That does give me an idea. Will

you get married in the Cathedral?'

'I don't know. Mum will have to talk to the Dean, but at the moment she's trying to pretend that none of it will happen. I'd like to get married in the village, but our church only holds seventy. We've got plenty of time. All too much time.'

'What about the reception? You won't want it in a pub. I shouldn't think you'd want the Corn Exchange or the school hall. You haven't got room in the cottage, and your lawn hasn't got room for a marquee. So, obviously, if you agree, the reception is here. We'll combine it with your birthday. My God, what a hooley. The very thought gives me a hangover.'

'You've done too much for me.'

'We've hardly started. Wait till we roll up our sleeves.'

'We'd love it,' said Hilary. 'Don't deny us the fun.'

The spontaneous generosity of this remark almost made Nico burst into tears.

'To London?' said Alice.

'Yes, of course,' said Nico. 'That's where we shall be. Naturally. His job's there. Did you think he was going to commute from here?'

So, in the weeks before Christmas, Nico stole days from her studies to go flat-hunting in Wandsworth, Battersea, Paddington and Fulham.

'What did you expect?' said Vi to Alice.

What *had* she expected? Hugh to get a job on the *Milchester Herald*, to settle in a cottage in one of the villages? Her chick to remain for ever in the shadow of the nest?

Nicola must spread her wings. If London, then London; very possibly abroad. But that man – what was it about that man?

★

Nico found that a surprising number of people looked exactly as you would have expected them to look. Curly Cobbett, who owned the best butcher's shop in Milchester, was big, red-faced, affable, deep-voiced, with little blue eyes fringed by sandy lashes – he was exactly as a successful provincial butcher would have been portrayed in an Ealing film of the fifties. The Master of the Hospital of the Holy Cross; Roddy Plumb, gaunt, clumsy, passionate, artist and lecturer in art history; Gerald Orchard, the rabbity young schoolmaster – these people were so perfectly typecast that they were caricatures of themselves.

Hugh's mother also.

Hugh told Nico not to be frightened of his mother, but in such a way that she was frightened. She expected a thin, intensely elegant lady in marvellous Milanese clothes, who would be foreign and aristocratic and remote, a gourmet and connoisseur, the intimate of celebrities, as familiar with New York as with Paris and Rome...

Like Nico herself, Hugh was an only child. His mother, proud and adoring, would demand something very special in the way of a bride – something far beyond the half-educated milkmaid Nico was made to feel.

'Don't be frightened,' Hugh said.

Nico quaked as they sat in a restaurant in South Kensington, waiting for Mrs Jarvis.

And then in the doorway, handing a Fortnum's bag to a bowing waiter, stood the personification of cosmopolitan elegance, a slim woman of fifty, dressed with a perfection Nico was herself just sophisticated enough to appreciate. Her features were strong, slightly beaky, with high cheekbones and a high-bridged nose. Her eyes were a hard pale grey in a face which retained a little tan from the previous summer, or had recently acquired it in Australia or the Caribbean; her hair was dark, with a few dramatic streaks of silver. Clothes, shoes, bag, gloves, jewellery were all beyond the imagination of Milchester.

Nico was horribly conscious of ill-cut hair and inexpensive clothes. She stood up nervously. She felt like an awkward teenager. She nearly knocked over her chair.

She found herself presented, shaking hands.

'Nicola,' said Mrs Jarvis, keeping hold of Nico's hand for a moment. 'What a lovely girl you are.'

'How do you do?' said Nico stupidly.

'My name is Maria. Everybody calls me Miggy, although for forty-five years I have tried to stop them. You know the problem?'

'Well,' said Nico. 'Nobody has ever called me Miggy.'

The cool face crinkled into a quick, cool smile.

'Why,' said Miggy to Hugh, 'are we not already drinking champagne?'

'Because it gives you indigestion,' said Hugh.

'Not today it won't.' To Nico, Miggy said, 'I am a figure of farce. I am the doting mother for whose son no girl would be good enough. My friends have been saying for years that my daughter-in-law, if any, will have a terrible time. But now that I have met you, I doubt if *we're* good enough. I can't imagine how Hugh had the courage to approach you. Where's that wine? I'm beginning to gabble, on account of nerves.'

'Nico has that effect on me,' said Hugh.

Once released, Hugh's mother's goodwill was abundant, overflowing. She made Nico laugh. She herself laughed, so that Nico was made to feel wonderfully witty. It was a happy lunch.

Nico agreed to spend a week in Tuscany in the spring.

Miggy was much delighted, much amused, at the thought of the spectacular July combination of wedding and twenty-first birthday.

'I am beginning to plan my hat now this minute,' said Miggy. 'But I shall go on changing my mind until long after the last moment. I shall require the world's best hat. Hugh's told me about your aunt. She sounds a good aunt to have. Will she lend you a tiara?' Turning to Hugh, she said, 'Have you written to your father?'

'Yes, of course.'

'He'll come if he can. It'll be midwinter for him, an extra reason to spend all that money. No, that's rude, he won't need an extra reason. I shall be glad to see him. And interested to meet his eighth wife.'

'Fifth,' said Hugh.

'More, surely? I expect we've all lost count, including him.'

Hugh and his mother spoke lightly about all those marriages. Perhaps they were right to joke about them. But Nico felt a chill, a sense of revulsion. In some ways she was still a child of the Vicarage. She was a romantic and she was in love. She thought the vows of the marriage service meant what they said.

That afternoon they looked at a marvellous flat in Notting Hill Gate, with views east and west over rooftops.

'In this room,' Nico said, 'I can see terracotta walls and peacock-blue curtains.'

'In this room,' said Hugh, 'I can see myself in my slippers with a cup of Ovaltine, while you in your tiny apron are singing in the kitchen—'

★

The flat was nobody else's business, but it only had to be mentioned, in one or two Milchester drawing rooms, to be described and discussed up and down the town and in two dozen villages. It was as though nobody in the area had quite enough to do; as though nothing of importance was happening in the world that Christmas except Nicola Maude and her fiancé finding somewhere to live.

At the Deanery the subject was discussed and dismissed.

The Dean's attitude was aloofly benevolent. He said it would be sad for Alice Maude, her daughter moving so far away, but that a wife must go where her husband went, as in the armed services and the missionary field.

Douglas Peacock, the younger son, home for Christmas, said that he knew the particular street, having friends who lived there. Some of the flats were lateral conversions, across two houses, making spacious two- and three-bedroom apartments with very big living rooms. Those flats had long leases costing at least a quarter of a million. Hugh's father might be helping. Wasn't he in South Africa? They all seemed to be rich, though the future was probably chaos. Hilary Cavenham might help, perhaps with an interest-free loan, perhaps buying the lease himself as an investment. Hugh was pretty well paid, one supposed – he seemed to be quite a star on that paper of his; he could get a large mortgage, though on such a sum the interest would be crippling.

Mrs Peacock said that, no doubt, they knew their own business best. She began talking rapidly and with unconvincing vehemence about a new series on the television. She did not want Felicity's feelings to be lacerated any further.

Felicity seemed never to have heard of Hugh, Nicola or London. She smiled brightly, uncomprehendingly, like someone showing good manners in a foreign country.

Gerald Orchard was Drusilla the Witch in the school's end-of-term Christmas pantomime. All the staff of the school and many of the older boys took part. It was an annual event. Governors and parents sat on hard little chairs in the assembly hall, and the music master thumped on the upright piano. The pretty assistant matron got the loudest applause. The following day, all the trunks were carried down from the dormitories, and by evening the place was deserted.

The older masters looked forward to exactly the same thing, for all the remaining active years of their lives, just as they looked back to the same thing. They were men who knew their destiny. They were resigned to their obscure places in the world.

Not so Gerald Orchard.

He went back to his mother's cottage five miles from Milchester. He made out some dozens of school reports. It was a detestable job. His colleagues were resigned to doing it at the end of every term, for the rest of their lives. They took it seriously, tempering honesty with tact for the boys' fathers, encouraging ambition but salting it with realism . . .

Gerald Orchard put away the school reports, and got his bicycle out of the shed in the garden, and went plunging angrily across the misty countryside.

There had been some sharp early frosts, and some nights of high wind, scouring away all traces of summer; but now the air was warm, damp, still, the distance a dim yellow-grey, the foreground spangled with scarlet berries and with drops of water strung along the cobwebs. There were gulls on the ploughland and speckled fieldfares on the pastures, and a few little birds, deluded by the weather, clicked and rattled in the hedgerows.

Gerald Orchard sweated as he bicycled. He gave himself the illusion of purpose. His legs were pumping so hard that he must be getting somewhere.

Through the mist loomed March Court, towards which some instinct had propelled him. The house looked larger, grander, because half-visible through the pearly veiling; its sentinel trees looked immemorial, its park limitless. There was a hint of gold in one upstairs window, as though somebody there was reading a very expensive book.

And he, Gerald Orchard, had missed the bus.

The golden apple had been plucked from the tree under his nose.

Somebody should have told him, a year before. Evidently they had all known, had always known. Somebody could have told him! His mother could have told him!

Could the damage be repaired? Was there any hope?

His mother always said there was nobody as attractive as himself.

Probably as a start he should have asked Nicola Maude to the school pantomime. The *Cantatores* showed only one side of his rich and complex talents. Now it was too late for that, too, and by the time next year's came round she would have been married for months . . .

His bicycle lay on the sodden verge at his feet, one wheel slowly revolving. He stared and stared through the mist at everything he had always wanted.

★

For Christmas, Hugh joined his mother at the home of cousins in Sussex. The arrangement had been made months before, when the current situation was not at all foreseen. He could not now ditch them, his bed being already aired, flowers already in a vase on the dressing-table in his room.

He had left with Alice three presents for Nicola and one for herself.

The cousins went in for party games after dinner, for charades and dumb crambo and 'Can you hear me, Moriarty?' Hugh was thought to fit in wonderfully. All the cousins were pleased with him.

Nico was given an insight entirely new to her. She thought she understood, for the first time, how her mother must have felt the first Christmas after her father was killed.

Among the Christmas post was a letter addressed to Miss Nicola Maude from South Africa. It was written from Stellenbosch, and signed by Anthony Jarvis. The writing was a little wayward. Here and there a word was illegible, and the pen had twice gone through the paper.

My dear Nicola,
My son Hugh tells me that I am to have most delightful and accomplished daughter in law and altho this news makes me feel v old I am simply delighted and quite [word illegible] *to meet you, wch I wd come and do at once only I cannot get away from here at this moment, wch you are please not to construe as the smallest reluctance, on the contrary, I am agog, but just now things here are fraught with politics and worries of all kinds but I am* [word illegible] *to drop everything here to*

put on my ancient morning coat and topper and dance at your wedding wch I understand is to be in July. It is many years since I saw a midsummer in the UK or any other time of year and I am wondering what I shall make of it all pretty rum by some accounts but what isnt, but I understand from Hugh that whatever is wrong about the old country you are one of the things that right about it and he tells me that [phrase illegible] *every day.*

I am really looking fwd to meeting you Nicola dear and you are not to be put to any trouble on my account when I come in the summer. Hugh will let me know the date as soon as its fixed and then I will make all arrangements to put everything here on Hold and packa bag wch I lood fwd to immensely. My v great and most sincere hope is that yr marriage will be truly happy and enduring and more successful than mine was.

Yr v affectionate future f in law,
Anthony Jarvis

Nico read it through twice, and then realized with a shock that it was the first letter she had ever received that had been written by somebody who was drunk. This was more evident in the handwriting than the words. Of course it was possible that the writer was ill or disabled rather than drunk: but if his father had been wounded in the war, or injured in a car-smash, or had a stroke, Hugh surely would have said so? If he knew? How could he not know? They were not things to be ashamed of, embarrassed about.

Hugh had not told her anything at all about his father, except where he lived. They needed to know a bit more, before the wedding. Would Hugh tell them, without being asked? Would she have to ask him? It was an awkward question: 'Is your father drunk or senile or what?'

'Perhaps this explains why the marriage broke up,' said Alice, when Nico showed her the letter.

'I'm not saying anything about the sins of the fathers,' said Alice to Tommy Johns, 'and I'm not saying that what's born in the blood is bred in the bone, but just the same it makes one uneasy.'

'You're allowing it to confirm an existing prejudice,' said Tommy. 'I knew a man you would have sworn was drunk all the time. All he had was a hole in the head, which he got on the Normandy beaches on D-Day plus three. And there's a woman whose door I pass when I go and see Julia. Drink got to her all right, but knowing what I know I don't blame her.'

'Nicola says the mother's frightening but friendly.'

'I imagine that's how nearly all mothers-in-law seem. I imagine that's how you seem to Hugh.'

'I don't know that I seem very friendly. Nicola says I don't.'

'You can't put on a friendliness you don't feel.'

'I ought to be able to.'

'Not you. That's one of the things about you. If when you see me you look glad to see me, I know it's because you're glad to see me, not because you're good at making that kind of face.'

'I'm not sure we're going to be glad to see Hugh's father.'

That was putting it mildly. Alice did put her doubts mildly to Tommy. He had enough to worry about; she was prepared to add to his burden a little, but only a little.

Hugh's father was probably a drunk, and certainly had been married at least five times. There seemed doubt about the exact number of his wives. That was as bad as it could possibly be. It was equally bad if you believed in heredity or environment or any combination of the two. Hugh might not now be influenced by his father, but he had been in the most formative years of infancy and childhood. And what had he inherited?

It seemed there had been some kind of relationship between Hugh and Felicity Peacock. Alice had not known anything about that, but Vi had heard about it. Vi always heard about that sort of thing. Then, as soon as Nicola appeared, he dumped one girl and went off with the other. His father's son. Exactly what you'd expect of a man whose father had had five wives. What of the future? How could you suppose he would suddenly become a pillar of loyal rectitude?

People couldn't escape their genes. Alice herself couldn't; Vi couldn't. They were as different as, presumably, their fathers had been. Alice's very earliest memories were about that difference: not about their nursery, their mother, the grimness of life just after the war – rationing, shabbiness, bomb-sites, the people waiting in her father's surgery, her toys and dolls; all of those large matters were overshadowed in Alice's earliest memories by that big bulk in the foreground, that extraordinary fact of life, the difference between Vi and herself.

It was not quite true, what Alice had told Nicola – she and Vi were not really treated alike, not because her parents were unfair, but because Vi was always in trouble. Alice never was. Vi was rebellious and secretive. She was punished for being sly and deceitful. Alice was not a saint, not really such an awful little prig, but she was a naturally well-behaved little girl, obedient, tidy, truthful. Looking back nearly forty years at her five-year-old self, Alice was a little dismayed at how conformist she was, how anxious to please; but it was the way she was constituted, the personality she had inherited from a father whose principal motive was his sense of duty.

Predictably, the difference between the girls became more dramatic than ever when Vi entered puberty. Those were the fifties, when the bomb damage had been cleared up, and poor old Portsmouth was being redeveloped into the ugliest city in England. They lived on the edge, in a middle-class enclave with gardens round the houses. The life of the nation had become comfortable, but their life was still drab. It was worthy and glamourless. It was not what Vi liked. Even in her very early teens she was noticeably different, a stranger in that street. Alice began to be afraid of her, afraid for her. She had a precocious bosom, and she did exercises to make it bigger. She was quite clever at school, but she was already more interested in boys. There was a frightful row involving a boy, when Vi was caught upstairs in a friend's house with her knickers round her knees. Alice was too young at the time to understand what might have been going on, what was so terrible.

It might have been better for Vi if her stepfather had been anything except an overworked, underpaid, humourless, provincial National Health Service doctor. As they grew older, Alice understood more and more: she understood that Vi had a completely different set of values from the rest of them. The things she thought were important the grown-ups despised and deplored; the things they valued she found boring and irrelevant. She wanted glamour and glitter and mink, she wanted to drink champagne in nightclubs and play roulette in Monte Carlo and have her photograph in *Tatler*. Possibly once upon a time, when she was a teenager in the thirties, their mother might have wanted these things, but she had outgrown all that with one silly marriage and one sensible one, with years as a doctor's wife and mother and home-maker. She might have understood Vi's yearnings. Alice's father would never have understood. To him Vi's values were frivolous and contemptible. Alice could see that when she herself became a teenager, at just the time when mini-skirts and The Beatles were changing the world for ever. Vi by then was almost grown up, a big sexy girl doing a secretarial course. Somebody said she had the shortest skirt in Portsmouth. Alice envied her liberty and her latchkey and her lipstick, and the handsome, sophisticated men who came to take her out to dinner. She envied the way Vi talked, and her popularity and the friends she had.

About this time Alice realized something else: precisely the things that made Vi different were the things that made her popular and successful. Being in trouble, being rebellious, was the other side of the same coin. Rebels were admired and they had more fun and they were bright-coloured and adventurous. It seemed that Vi's was a better way to be than Alice's, although you had to be nearly grown-up to realize this. Vi was a better sort of person to be than Alice, but Alice could do nothing whatever about that, and it was unfair.

That was how it struck Alice when she was thirteen, and how it still struck her thirty years later.

CHAPTER SIX

NICO WENT OUT WITH THE CAROL SINGERS, as Alice had so often done at the same age, as Vi had never done. They finished by tradition at the Deanery, and drank mulled wine in the hall.

On the telephone on Christmas Eve, Nico told Hugh about his father's letter.

'I'm surprised he didn't send you a Christmas present,' said Hugh. 'I'm sure he will. When he comes in the summer he'll bring something amazing. He's very generous. Of course, all that alimony makes rather a hole in his income. You'd think some of his wives might have died, but none of them have.'

Hugh waffled on cheerfully, not saying anything about his father being ill or disabled or in any way embarrassing. Nico would have to have it out with him some time, to make the right preparations, to send out the right warnings. But these were not questions to be asked on the telephone, or on Christmas Eve.

'A quarter of a million,' said Felicity Peacock on the telephone, at the same time, to her distant and miserable friend. 'I suppose it's coming from rich Auntie. Sort of anticipating the legacy. Nobody in this family ever heard of so much money. Nobody in Hugh's family, either.

They live on remittances from a trust. Of course I'm not saying it's her *fault* she's got a rich aunt, as well as everything else. I'm not *blaming* her for being dealt all the aces.'

Felicity laughed. She was being flip and light-hearted about it all.

Her friend heard the bitterness and hatred in her voice. She thought it was sad to hear such a tone on Christmas Eve.

They went to March Court after church, mother and daughter in their best clothes. They had drinks and a glorious lunch, and the Queen on television, and the ritual opening of their presents under the enormous tree.

Nico's presents from Hugh were: a framed reproduction of a Jacopo Bellini drawing in the Academia, which she had told him she liked; a necklace, also Italian, which she guessed his mother had found; and a cased set of German tapes of sixteenth-century polyphonic music. With each present there were two cards, one with conventionally hearty Christmas greetings, to be shown to other people, and one with a passionately loving message to be shown to nobody.

Nico had hardly before seen his handwriting. It was like himself – correct, even conventional, yet strongly individual. Nico was oddly excited to see the scratches of the pen on the cards, to touch the lines and loops that he had made.

Nico tucked away the private cards. She found herself blushing, although nobody was looking at her, and nobody would ever know what those cards said.

There were fine presents to the Maudes from the Cavenhams. Of course there were. Nico squealed when she tore the wrapping off a new coat. Alice gave a kind of squeal, too, but it was forced.

The opening of presents was a moment every year which dramatized – all needlessly – the difference of fortune between the sisters. Alice could produce presents which were carefully chosen and in impeccable taste, but nothing that cost more than a few pounds. Whereas Vi...

Of course it was a problem for Vi. Alice saw that. Every instinct was pushing Vi into being superbly lavish with gifts for her sister and niece – but she would draw back from too blatantly providing things that they wanted and could not afford. What constituted the truest kindness, in this situation? It *was* a problem for Vi.

Alice could have done with a bit of that trouble.

Alice would have liked a bit of Vi's trouble at Christmas 1964, as well.

Alice was eighteen, Vi twenty-four, and they were citizens of different worlds.

Alice was a pretty girl, slim, sandy; she was a good little mouse, living at home and working as a secretary at the hospital. She was taken to local dances by very young doctors, and by pimply sub-lieutenants in the Navy. Some of the doctors expected her to be easy meat. They were used to the shocking way the nurses carried on. Alice had been brought up to think they would respect her for saying 'No'. But things had changed. They were not respectful but cross and impatient. They thought she was priggish and ungrateful. She was sometimes tempted, but she was frightened. She was frightened of hellfire and her father and getting pregnant and men. The lurid conversations of the other girls at the hospital filled her not with courage but with revulsion.

She wanted romance, but that was not what they were talking about.

Of course Alice knew the facts of life – an eighteen-year-old in the middle sixties, a doctor's daughter; she knew what the otherwise useless parts of her body were for, and she understood the nature and function of the male equivalents. She faced the eventual invasion of the former by the latter, and the consequences thereof. But knowledge did not obliterate fear and distaste, as it should have done. She was deeply embarrassed at the thought of it all – the thought of being seen, being touched; she was shocked; she was frightened of being hurt. She was, as she later realised, young for her age; she was exceptionally unawakened and virginal. The girls at the hospital thought she was retarded.

She helped a good deal at home. She was needed.

Her father had become difficult, fussy and tricky-tempered. He was disappointed. He had chosen his way of life, which was humane and honourable, but he was disillusioned. He had to deal with suffocating bureaucracy on one hand, and whining, scrimshanking patients on the other. He had been a talented amateur painter, but he had lost the will to get his materials out, to sit down and do a picture; he had been a keen gardener, but he had lost patience with the repetitiveness of weeding and mowing and clipping. Much of the time he was exhausted, bored and in a rage.

Alice's mother, meanwhile, was in a fair way to being broken by the demands of her life. They were small demands, considered one by one, but there overwhelming numbers of them – housekeeping, cleaning, shopping, cooking, gardening, being secretary and part-time receptionist and telephonist and accountant and assistant ... Each year within Alice's memory her mother had grown smaller and greyer. She developed a stooped back and arthritic fingers. She wore an expression of indomitable pluck. She talked about soldiering on. Alice relieved her of what burdens she could, but it was not nearly enough. They needed help with the cleaning and cooking and the garden, and a proper secretary; but these were not available or affordable – or at least Alice's father said they were not.

Vi might have helped, but Vi was far away. Vi had run away to London, to a job in an advertising agency and a big shared flat near Paddington. She had emigrated. She was leading a new life in a new country. Alice understood that it had been neither possible nor even desirable to stop her. She would have been no use at home. She would have driven them mad. She would have broken the china, and stayed out all night, and smoked cigarettes in her bedroom, and hogged the telephone. Life would have been not easier but more difficult, Alice's father more tetchy and her mother more defeated.

Vi reappeared in Portsmouth for a weekend every couple of months. She always came for Christmas. She apologized for not coming more often – the journey was expensive and her weekends were full. There was a tremendous explosion of activity in London in those days – you could read about it in the newspapers – new nightclubs opening, new pop groups giving concerts, new marches and demos. Vi was involved in all of that. She said her advertising job required her to keep her ear to the ground of popular culture.

Alice felt like a country mouse when Vi talked about her life in London.

Vi was dark then. She changed many times later in her life, but in 1964 she had dark hair and a high colour and a voluptuous figure. At home in her stepfather's house she dressed modestly, but it was obvious to Alice that in London she cut a fabulous dash, not being one to hide her assets, not being shy or frightened of anything.

Vi didn't really confide in Alice, didn't much boast to her, but she let a few things drop. For instance, she said she was on the Pill. She just happened to mention that to Alice, in relation to some other pills, some ordinary aspirins in the medicine cupboard in the bathroom. Vi said the Pill was the most liberating thing that had happened since they abolished chastity belts.

Vi was up to all the same things as the girls at the hospital, but the effect on Alice was quite different. The nurses and radiologists and physiotherapists filled her with contemptuous distaste. Vi filled her with envy.

How glorious to be sexy and liberated and free! Vi's surrenders were conquests.

Alice was not sure, from the little that Vi said, whether Vi had one boyfriend at a time, or several. If the former, it might be love of the one person, rather than love of the act. But if the latter, it must be that there was something marvellous about the act itself. Literature and films sometimes suggested that there was. It was difficult to imagine in relation to the people she knew. It was easy to imagine in relation to Vi. She would give herself, with high glee, to loving and to being loved. She was made for it.

That Christmas Vi was in a muddle which caused her to make far too many expensive telephone conversations. If it had not been Christmas, there would have been a row. As it was, Alice saw that her father was sitting on his hands.

Vi said the muddle was about her social life, but actually, as Alice could tell, it was about her love life.

How many New Year's Eve parties was she going to? With how many men? Where would she wake up the following morning? Who with? Which of all those men was she in love with? Or were there still others?

Vi looked abstracted, preoccupied. Well she might.

She made the bathroom smell delicious.

In church on Christmas morning, people were nudging one another.

Alice ached for a bit of Vi's trouble. She would have been content with just a little bit; she had none at all. She was not in the way of getting any. She was stuck.

Because Vi had left home, Alice could not do so.

Even Vi saw that. She said so. She admitted that it was not fair.

In March Vi came home for another weekend (the first since Christmas), saying she was engaged. His name was Derek. He was a marketing manager. Vi had met him on business in her advertising agency. His divorce was coming through. He was thirty-two, seven years older than Vi. He was very well dressed, and his company had given him a Jag. She would bring him down to meet them as soon as they all had a free weekend.

'All our weekends are free,' said her mother.

'Speak for yourself,' said her stepfather. 'None of mine are.'

Vi said they would like Derek, and they would see the point of him more and more the better they got to know him.

Derek came for a weekend in April. He had a Cockney accent, and hair cut in a fringe across his forehead like an old-fashioned schoolboy. It was true about the Jaguar. He wore shoes which were like bedroom slippers, made of soft white leather; the rest of his clothes appeared to be made of grey paper.

Derek wanted to take them all out to dinner on Saturday evening; then he wanted to take them all out to lunch on Sunday. Vi whispered that he could easily afford it, that probably it wouldn't be him paying anyway. But it was against the custom of the household. Derek was awkward, eating with them at home. It was as though he was constantly looking round for a waiter with a bottle of wine. They left immediately after lunch on Sunday, so as to avoid the worst of the traffic.

After they had gone, the rest of them did not say anything about Derek.

In May Vi and Derek went abroad, with another couple. They were driving to the Italian lakes. The others were married, as Vi was at pains to point out.

When they came back from Italy, Vi said they were not engaged any longer.

Vi said nothing to her mother and stepfather about it, beyond announcing the bare fact; to Alice she said only that it had been a experiment that had not worked.

'Then it was a good thing to do the experiment,' said Alice daringly.

'No it wasn't,' said Vi. 'It was bloody awful.'

Derek had been mean with money or made passes at the waitresses or something.

It was just as well, because in July Vi met the love of her life. His name was Vernon Keegan. He was American. He was in public relations. He had come to Europe to make his fortune, and probably he would soon begin to make it. He was a great contrast to Derek. He was a success in Portsmouth, being terribly polite and appreciative. He was obviously very fond of Vi. He was proud to be seen with her. He used their names all the time. He said, 'Why yes, Mother Bolton, I certainly do find the

British climate quite a change from the weather back home.'

Vernon and Vi went for a long walk in the country on Sunday afternoon. They came back not looking at one another or speaking.

Before she went to the station, to get a train back to London, Vi said to Alice that Vernon was an oversexed pervert. She did not say what form his perversion took, and Alice did not like to ask.

That autumn of her nineteenth birthday, Alice thought she might be in love.

He was not what anybody would have expected. He was a new sort of thing for Alice: he was more Vi's sort of thing. He was a reporter on a local newspaper, not long down from university, doing his provincial apprenticeship before they allowed him into Fleet Street.

He said to Alice, the first time he met her, 'There's a kind of myth about people like me, a kind of proverbial wisdom. That I spend my entire time reporting flower-shows, and that the only important thing is to get people's initials right. And you know the truth? Can you bear it? Are you strong enough? The truth is that I spend my entire time reporting flower-shows, and the *only* important thing is getting people's initials right.'

Alice thought this was brilliantly funny. She laughed as she seldom had occasion to laugh, loud and long. He grinned ruefully. He was small and slight, a little fair man with pale eyelashes. That first occasion was the pattern of their relationship, cheerful, great fun.

His name was Francis Purdey. His father was a solicitor. He had been to Bristol University. He drove an old Volkswagen. When he was on the job he wore a neat dark suit and black shoes. He was not a figure of glamour, though he was diligent and unmistakably decent. He was not like a reporter in an American film. When you got to know him, you realized that after all he was Alice's sort of person, not Vi's.

Francis had a future. Everybody said so; his editor said so. That October and November, Alice thought she and Francis had a future. She was happy and excited. His kisses were tentative and respectful, but they were sure enough kisses. Vi might not have called them kisses, but Alice did.

Because of all this, Alice did not at once pay as much attention as usual to Vi's new boyfriend. He was worth a bit of attention. He was called the Honourable Colin Quin. His father was a lord. He worked in a merchant bank in the City, and spent weekends in the grand country houses of his grand country friends. It was some time before he was displayed in Portsmouth. This was because Vi was afraid not of what her family thought of Colin, but of what Colin thought of her family.

She said he was not a snob and, in truth, when he did come at the beginning of December, it appeared that he was a very cheerful and tolerant fellow. He was tall and beautiful, with thick chestnut hair and a turned-up nose. He was serious with Dr Bolton about the NHS, the future of health insurance, and so forth. He was matey with Francis Purdey; he was hearty and brotherly with Alice. He did his very best to make them all relax, but he was glittering and awesome in spite of himself. He could not help being glamorous. Vi was the only one in their circle who remotely matched him.

When Colin was in the room, Francis simply disappeared.

Seeing this, Alice realized with a painful new clarity that when Vi was in the room, she – Alice – disappeared.

In spite of all his amiable efforts, Colin Quin was

unmistakably everything Alice's father most disliked. The doctor deplored inherited wealth, the old-boy network, the Old Etonian Mafia, inequality of opportunity, easy charm, matinée-idol good looks, and all the amazing things Colin had. Yet the doctor smiled on Colin. He really did.

He neither smiled nor frowned on Francis Purdey. He ignored his existence.

A fortnight before Christmas, another family Christmas, Francis had an interview with Alice's father, an old-fashioned request to be allowed to pay his addresses. After quite a short time he left the house, looking stricken.

Alice's father would not talk to her about it. Her mother said that he could not bear the prospect of Alice leaving home, that they needed her, that their lives and his medical practice and all his patients depended on her . . .

'The bloody old blackmailer,' said Vi, when she heard. 'It's not fair.'

That Christmas Vi came only for the day, only for lunch, leaving in the middle of the afternoon in a borrowed Hillman.

Francis Purdey got his London opening in January; he left with the blessing of the local paper. He did not telephone or write to Alice.

This was not cruel or treacherous. He had been hurt. Alice had not put up any kind of fight for his happiness or her own. He was not apt to impale himself on the same pitchfork. One contemptuous rejection was enough. The only thing for him to do was to go away and start again. Alice understood that.

The only thing for her to do was to stay at home and start again. Start when? Why? To what end? With what hope of escape?

It had to be a dimmish, square, unambitious little man, to be interested in Alice, when there were girls like Vi in the world. And such a man did not have the guts or the leverage to get her out of her father's house.

Colin Quin could have got her out. Colin Quin did not want her.

Was she only to be released by her father's death? The death of both her parents? It happened, quite often. The English countryside was full of forty-five-year-old spinsters, their lives hijacked by selfish parents. It happened.

'Colin Quin?' said Vi. 'Don't talk to me about Quin.'

They did talk to her about him, all of them. She would say only that she had booted him out of her life. Objectively it was possible that he had booted her, but you could not look at Vi and believe that.

Vi was more gorgeous than ever. She did not at all accord with the waiflike ideal of the middle sixties – the pin-thin, bosomless, pouting model-girls who were said to earn more money in an hour than a GP earned in a lifetime. As Alice heard the young doctors say, you couldn't imagine screwing one of those models. But, as she heard them say, a man couldn't look at Vi and not imagine screwing her. She was yummy. She was opulent. She was a Rubens, a Renoir. She might not be fashionable, but she was what they liked. She visibly enjoyed food and drink, and everybody knew what that implied. She had already looked experienced at eighteen – not used or sluttish, just knowing. Now in her middle twenties, she looked as though she could teach anybody a thing or two, and get a bang out of doing so.

Alice wondered what it felt like, to look like that.

Alice had another suitor in the spring, a young man so

gentle and mouselike that he was even frightened of her. He never got up the courage to make a proper pass at her. One or two of the young doctors continued to do so. There was nothing personal in it. They thought that, working at the hospital, she was at their disposal.

'You know, you're getting really pretty,' said Vi. 'How do you manage to stay that shape?'

Vi had another boyfriend and another, mentioned at home during her rare visits, not produced there. There was no need for anybody important in her life to meet her family, because her family was not important in her life.

What was important in Alice's life? Just getting through it. It had no merit except that it would not last for ever.

The swinging sixties. Every part of England was swinging, except that suburb of Portsmouth.

And then, in June, the world was transformed.

He came into the office where she worked. He brought a golden light. It was a grey, weeping Tuesday, a day of wet feet, sweating armpits, short tempers. He came into the big, dingy office like a sunlamp. He was not hearty in manner. He was not bronzed, or very big. He was not offensively cheerful, or desperately friendly. He looked busy but peaceful. He was wearing a dog-collar and a rumpled grey-brown suit; he carried a scuffed briefcase and a dripping, flapping umbrella. His hair was fair, but darkened by the wet, and his trousers below the knee clung wetly to his calves.

Providence was specifically generous to Alice for the very first time: it was she who took down the particulars of the patients he had come about.

It was only his third day in Portsmouth, he said. Practically nobody had met him yet. Nobody had snapped him up.

He looked as though he played tennis and cricket. Did he have a fiancée somewhere?

He was shy but businesslike. He cared about what he was doing. He cared about the needs and troubles of old, ignorant parishioners.

Alice at twenty was inexperienced and unawakened, and she fell in love at first sight. She felt happy and ill with love as she asked him the necessary questions and filled in the necessary forms.

The forms took twelve minutes. It took two of those minutes for Alice to fall in love. The forms were things of benevolent magic, because they held him in the chair facing Alice's desk until every last box was filled in.

At the end he rose and smiled and they shook hands.

The tea-trolley came rattling like a streetcar into the office. A couple of the girls were on holiday, so there was an extra cup. The young Reverend Something had a cup of tea in the office.

Tea and biscuits tasted of love.

He smiled and chatted about the terrible weather, the difficulty of parking a car in the centre of Portsmouth, the business of finding one's feet in a new place, laundries, plumbers, the kindness everybody was showing. Some of the others joined in the conversation, but it was Alice he was really talking to. Alice thought she was the reason he lingered in that dreadful office, when he had so many errands to run, such a list of things to do. She really did think so. She thought she could see that in his face when he looked at her.

Did parsons feel like that? Were they allowed to? Was it all right with the Bishop, with God?

He went away knowing her name, knowing that she spoke like a lady and had never been anywhere or done anything.

Two days later, when she left after work, he was waiting for her. Her heart jumped like a trout when she saw him. She felt herself blushing, and she felt the width of her smile.

She knew she was not hiding her feelings. She supposed she was being undignified and forward. Her behaviour did not seem to disgust him.

The weather had changed. It was such a June evening as to make the angels feel at home. They walked amongst the concrete fortresses of the town, pouring questions at one another.

The miracle was that he had fallen in love, too.

He was terribly busy as a curate in a huge working-class parish, but his Vicar met and so much liked Alice – so clearly saw how Barney felt, how necessary she was to him – that he was ordered to take time off. They spent it out of doors. He could hardly afford to buy her a cup of tea, but she did not want to be bought anything: she only wanted to be with him.

When they drove out into the country for a walk, he was not wearing his clerical collar. Alice might have supposed that that might have made a difference – that they might both be more relaxed, less self-conscious, less on their best behaviour. Funnily enough, it made no difference at all. Being a priest was part of him – he was unimaginable in any other role. He kissed her enthusiastically with his collar and without it, and she responded with happy enthusiasm.

Faced with such generosity and unselfishness, such active and tireless goodness, Alice was abashed. She felt unworthy. She was relieved to discover minor weaknesses – to find that he was, after all, human. He was vain enough to be aware of his appearance, to be clean and well turned out. He was a little bit greedy about sweet things, guiltily having a second lump of sugar in his coffee at the Boltons' house. He was a little untidy and absent-minded. He needed somebody to look after him.

But Alice was already needed.

'I don't know what we're going to do about this,' said Barney. 'We must wait until I've got a parish and you're twenty-one, but then what?'

It was lucky that Alice was so young, because they faced a terribly long engagement.

Vi came home. She met Barney, who came in for coffee after supper on Saturday evening.

Vi said, 'Wouldn't you know you'd find yourself landed with a bloody parson?'

But Vi let Alice see that she was actually impressed. Vi had been around enough to know an attractive man when she saw one, even if he happened also to be an exceptionally good one. Barney would not have done for Vi, nor she for him, but they could like one another.

Barney's faith in the power and goodness of God did not have the effect of relieving him of decision, of action. There were holy men of other religions who never did or decided anything. They felt no need to. They thought it would be presumptuous. They were obliged by their belief to be totally fatalistic. Barney thought this point of view was attractive, in a way, but also an evasion. It showed a basic cowardice and laziness. It was not what God wanted of His people. Barney was for getting up and doing what needed to be done, trusting to God and relying on His help.

But in this situation, the future had to be left in God's hands. There was nothing they could do. Decisive action would be impossibly cruel. There it was.

'It's like the situation in *Emma*,' said Barney.

'Not quite,' said Alice, who was pretty well read. 'Emma's father didn't really need her. My parents do really need me. And Mr Knightley could move in with them. I don't think you could do that.'

'I don't think I could,' said Barney, after a pause.

'How about murder?' said Vi. 'It's the only thing I can think of.'

Vi was not altogether joking. Her sympathy was real. She saw that Alice and Barney were now deeply and permanently in love.

Barney turned to God for help. He turned to an older man he liked and respected, the principal of his theological college.

Alice did not think any easy answer was available from either.

Alice and Barney did not, on any particular day, announce their engagement. There was never even a formal proposal and acceptance between them. It simply grew. The future revealed itself. They found that they had travelled to a country in which they were always together, in which they did not exist as individuals, but only as a couple.

Alice had a ring with a very tiny diamond.

Vi was engaged, too. She rang up to say so. She was just off abroad. She was not asking permission or anything of that sort – just telling them in case they were interested.

'I know it's not fair,' she said to Alice, when it was Alice's turn to talk to her on the telephone. 'But I've got to live my life, as you've got to live yours. I mean, it won't do you any good for me to live like a nun.'

'You live like a nun?' said Alice, laughing in spite of the profound unfunniness of it all.

The next thing they knew, Vi was married. She telephoned from America, the first time an international call had ever been received in the Bolton household. She said she was Mrs Charles Bradfield-Copley. She spelled it out. There was doubt at home for a moment as to whether this was the one she had been engaged to, or a different one. It was kind to assume it was the same one. They were a long way off. They were in the Rocky Mountains.

Nobody at home was terribly surprised or horrified or thrilled or even (this was the worst part) terribly interested. Rushing off and getting married in America was typical of Vi. She had cut the apron-strings so very many years before. Probably it was time she got married; it was hoped that she stayed married. That was what was said at home, after the telephone was put down.

Alice found it chilling, that this sensational news should have so small an impact.

Vi came home sooner than expected. She was alone. Her husband was still in America. They would be reunited any minute – of course Vi missed him dreadfully. He might ring up. She would not ring him in America because of the expense.

He did not ring up but, on the contrary, instituted proceedings for divorce or annulment, on grounds which were never explained to the family, in accordance with the laws of Nevada, which were not like English laws.

Somebody heard from somebody that the marriage

had lasted six hours, from the moment of the disappearance of the couple into the honeymoon suite of the hotel, until the moment of the bride's reappearance, calling for a taxi to take her to the airport.

That was all anybody knew about Vi's marriage.

Alice's marriage? What marriage? How long would Barney wait? There was new desperation in their kisses.

They kissed with passion, with a growing boldness, but they did not go beyond kissing. Sex was legal if legalized, sacred if sanctified. Barney was quite clear about that; Alice was obliged to be clear about it.

Alice thought she would not be frightened of Barney. She would not be shy with him. But the question did not look like arising.

Things were in this state for six months. Long afterwards it seemed a little while; at the time it seemed an eternity.

Two things happened at the same moment. They were both effects of the same cause, which was the intervention of the old vicar, Barney's chief. Barney was appointed to the parish of All Saints, Igton, a kind of light-industrial suburb of a drab country town in the Diocese of Milchester; and a woman appeared who needed a home for herself and intermittently a quiet, untroublesome retarded child, and who would in return keep house for an ailing doctor and his exhausted wife . . .

She was a decent, competent, humourless woman, scrupulously honest, presentable but unpretentious, aged less than forty, active and strong. She had been deserted by a husband who had disappeared and who gave her nothing. She did not want and would not have accepted charity. She and the Boltons might have been designed to meet one another's needs.

Practical benevolence now worked in every direction. Everybody benefited, including the unfortunate child, who would probably after a while realize that she had a stable home; including Alice.

Alice was released.

Alice married Barney in the parish church; they had a small, staid reception in a local hotel; they went off to Cornwall.

The days were good – clifftop walks, bracing air, big simple meals, the first few nights were notable for dogged efforts in the dark, dreadful inexperience on both sides, and a certain inhibiting politeness and consideration, all too deeply ingrained. Then by happy accident they caught themselves in a mood of morning passion, and in daylight all suddenly came miraculously right.

Alice was startled into a storm of tears by the joy and wonder of her first climax.

It was as though she had only just then learned the significance of love, the experience of being in love, of belonging to another person. What she had felt before was merely shadow-play on the wall; here was the living reality.

The remaining days and nights of their fortnight went by at dizzy speed: but they faced the future, and their new life and love and ministry, with such excitement that they were almost glad when they came back from their honeymoon; when they moved into the modern little Vicarage and began playing house and pretending to be grown up.

They met great kindness. They met a small amount of enthusiasm in a large sea of apathy. People saw that Barney was to be liked and trusted. It became known that Alice had worked in a big hospital, that she was a doctor's daughter; her advice was therefore sought by women who were frightened to go to the doctor.

They had been three months at Igton before Vi came to see them. Vi had said, again and again, that she was avid to come, but there had been hitches, difficulties, prior engagements ... Anyway, she was at last coming, and Alice contrived a festive lunch.

The lunch was all in the oven and the table laid, and Barney was back from giving Holy Communion to a bedridden lady in a hospice, and they could sit for a moment on the sofa.

Their fingers touched and instinctively clasped. The previous night they had, as it happened, made rapturous love, and the magic lingered in their smiles.

A sound made Alice look away from Barney's face, and she saw that Vi was standing in the doorway. She cried out, and jumped to her feet. Vi laughed, and apologized for bursting in. She kissed them both. Without embarrassment, without being patronizing, she produced a bottle of gin and one of Muscadet, which she said she had herself been given. They had a merry reunion, although Barney had to go out immediately after lunch.

Alice realized that she and Barney had been perfectly, childishly transparent when Vi caught sight of them. This was not so dreadful, but it was a little undignified. Alice would have preferred to be less obvious, less lip-smacking. As a Vicar's wife, even at the age of twenty-one, she was supposed to be restrained and respectable. Oh well. If anybody could sympathize it would be Vi.

Nicola joined them in July two years later. Life became almost too full. There was much goodwill in the parish;

much miniature knitwear arrived in the Vicarage.

Complications followed the birth. Alice was quite ill for a time, the first illness of her life. She recovered completely, but she could not have any more children. This was a large tragedy; but Alice and Barney vowed that there would be no only-child syndrome with Nicola.

Everybody said that Barney would be a marvellous father; and it was true.

Vi got married again. She brought her husband to Igton. He was just the husband for whom her nature and her whole life had intended her. He was a rich baronet, twelve years older than herself. Like her he was divorced: but his marriage and divorce, unlike hers, had been conducted under normal English rules. He had inherited a huge, uninhabitable house in the Midlands, occupied by a school. He and Vi had a flat in Wilton Place and a villa in the Algarve. They were talking about finding a place in the country. Alice and Barney promised to keep their ears open.

They liked Hilary. They agreed afterwards that they liked him. They could not remember clearly anything much that he had said; Alice had a little difficulty even calling his face to mind, so unobtrusive was his personality. He smiled a lot. He had a pink vodka before lunch, the first time that drink had ever been drunk in that house. He was evidently devoted to Vi, in his quiet way. Vi seemed really happy, calmer, less restless than she had been for years, as though she had at last found what she had always been looking for.

Nicola was just four when they moved to Grimworth, a country parish almost in the shadow of Milchester Cathedral.

Alice found it very different from the previous induction: not because the parishes were so different, though they were; not because Barney was any different, because he was not; but because she had grown up. She had learned confidence. Her strength showed.

The Vicarage was large and cold, but it was often full of children and of music and other noise, of laughter, of the banging of nails into wood when Barney found time to shore the place up.

Though they were always broke, Alice thought they were without doubt the happiest family in England.

March Court came on the market, after a couple of deaths and a heavy tax bill. Was it what Hilary and Vi were looking for? Too big, too awesomely grand even for them, surely?

Too close to Barney and Alice, surely?

Hilary said that property was underpriced; that land and bricks and mortar were at that moment the best possible investment. He had a lot of furniture in store which needed big rooms and plenty of them. They liked entertaining and they had never had room for it. Vi wanted to be near Alice and adorable Nicola. It all added up to a surprisingly quick decision, considering what was involved.

Alice was ashamed of her dismay.

If Alice had doubts about Vi and Hilary so short a distance away, nobody else in the neighbourhood did.

Had popularity been for sale, they would have bought it. Insofar as it was, they did. People liked drinking their drinks, and telling the less fortunate that they had done so. But there was genuine, widespread and rapid appreciation of the authentic kindness of the newcomers. All but the most censorious agreed that they were lavish without being vulgar. In that neighbourhood, in the shadow of that Cathedral, that was not an easy trick.

The Maudes were asked to March Court pretty well every time anybody was asked. They could not always go, what with the pressure of Barney's parochial work, the visits he made, the clubs and groups he ran; what with Alice having an active young child with a vast number of friends. When they could not go, Vi came to the Vicarage. The sisters became closer than they had ever been in childhood. This could be put down to the tapering effect of getting older – a five-year gap, enormous in the teens, pretty well disappeared in their twenties. There was more to it than that. Everybody changed. No doubt Alice had changed as a result of being married to Barney – no doubt she was readier for intimacy with someone so different. Vi had changed as a result of marriage to Hilary, becoming more relaxed and tolerant. Alice was changed by motherhood; Vi just as surely, if less obviously, by aunthood.

In one way Alice had not changed. She had always been very poor, and she still was.

Barney's father had been killed in 1941, commanding an infantry platoon in North Africa. Barney never saw him.

A small family trust had paid for Barney's education, which was therefore, ironically, more expensive than it could possibly have been if his father had survived. He went to a good school, with a well-known tie and many famous Old Boys.

As a theological student, as a penniless curate, he had lost touch with his schoolmates. He received notices of the annual dinner in London, and various other sporting and social reunions, but he had neither leisure nor money for such frivolities. He was in any case a man given to looking forward rather than back.

And then one September, two months after Nicola's sixth birthday, Barney met by chance in a Milchester street a man called Gregory Dawlish: a schoolmate, once an intimate friend, one of a small, close group in that house, in that school, at that time. The others had remained close, meeting often in London with or without their wives. But Barney had gone off on his own pilgrimage.

Barney could not have kept up with them. He could not have afforded his round of drinks.

The group included an insurance broker, an oil company executive, a diplomat, a barrister. They were all, of course, the same age, thirty-four and -five. They were all going to the Old Boys' dinner in a London hotel in November, where they had arranged to sit at the same table.

Gregory Dawlish was entirely delighted to meet Barney again. The others would be, too. Surely something could be arranged?

Surely Barney could come to the Old Boys' dinner?

By strange, familiar rural magic, everybody in the neighbourhood shortly knew that the Reverend Barnabas Maude was about to do something he never did – he was actually going to London. The date and the reason became known. He would see a lot of old friends, and have a lovely, nostalgic time. They would all see how well his life suited him, how extraordinarily fit he looked, how young and clear-eyed and happy.

★

Barney drove himself to Milchester station, leaving the car in the car-park. It was a typical November morning – mild, damp, misty.

Alice, watching the car disappear round the yew trees of the churchyard, wondered if Barney would be fogbound. It was all too possible in November. His train home might be hours late, or cancelled. He could not afford a hotel room, even if one could be had at short notice. Would somebody have a bed for him? Should he have taken a razor, a change of clothes?

In the middle of the afternoon there was a little sunshine, watery but reassuring. Alice took Nicola for a walk, with Holly, the stupid, affectionate Vicarage mongrel.

Alice telephoned Vi in the early evening. There were arrangements to make for the weekend. But they said Lady Cavenham was away all day, was not expected back until late. She had not said where she was going, only that they were not to wait up.

It was not at all surprising. For somebody who had such a lovely house, Vi was often away from it.

Probably Alice had known that Vi was going to be away – probably she had known the reason. She had forgotten. She had a lot of things to think about.

The dark came down, and a misty drizzle. It was not foggy enough, Alice thought, to disrupt the railways, but there might be tons of wet dead leaves on the line, which were alleged to make the wheels slither, so that the train roared along in the same place. Alice put Nicola to bed, and cooked herself a frugal supper. She went back to her book in front of the study fire. Barney had told her not to wait up for him. By ten-thirty her eyelids were drooping. It would be two hours before he was home, even if the trains were running on time.

For her it was strange, getting into bed alone. She had not done so since Nicola was born.

She wondered with sleepy amusement how Barney had managed in London. Had he remembered how to find his way about? Tubes and buses? All the traffic?

There was no need to worry about Barney. There never was the smallest need to worry about Barney. Alice went to sleep with her hand stretched out to where Barney would have been.

CHAPTER SEVEN

THAT DAWN WAS A TIME OF PURE DELIRIUM. The following hours and weeks were lived in delirium. Faces were hallucinations, and pieces of furniture, and the times of day and night. Everybody said things had happened which could not have happened, that changes were taking place which were simply impossible. The waves almost closed over Alice's head, but she fought and fought – she clung to Nicola, and Nicola to her – and she never quite drowned in despair.

Vi was great.

Not all at once, but pretty soon, they had to move out of the Vicarage. The house went with the job, and a new Vicar was to be inducted. Mother and daughter could be taken in at March Court. Yes, of course, for as long as need be. Live there? God knew there was plenty of room, suites of bedrooms furnished and heated and usually empty. In many parts of the world, it would have been simply automatic for widow and orphan to live with rich relatives – in India and China and all of Africa and in Southern Europe; in England, in days of old, any other arrangement would have been unthinkable. But that Alice Maude should go to March Court, in the early weeks of 1976? Of course the offer was made. Of course the sisters discussed it. (All through Milchester, all over its countryside, the idea was discussed.) But Alice was steadfastly against it.

It was bad enough being a poor relation two villages away. She could not have stood being a poor relation under the same roof.

Alice felt miserably ungrateful. Sometimes she felt pretty stupid with it. But she was very sure she was right. It was a question of facing the practical realities, the daily business of getting through life. Comparative penury in a cottage was better than the luxurious alternative. When Vi and Hilary gave a dinner party, would Alice always be there? Did they have to ask a spare man every single time, to make the numbers even? Or have uneven numbers every time, the awkwardness of an extra woman? Or did they send a tray upstairs, as though to a governess or an unpresentable pensioner? Or did Alice eat with the servants in the kitchen? And what would guests think, if they knew that was where the hostess's sister was?

The state of somebody like Alice, in that household, was the subject of scores of novels. A grey, despised, put-upon figure in the background, obsequious, desperate to please – the child kept hidden, kept quiet, forbidden the public rooms in case she annoyed somebody, in case they were sent packing . . .

No, no, no. The offer was terribly well meant, but it was impossible. The unfairness could be borne at a distance of five miles, but not five yards. Nicola had to be allowed to shout and sing and run about with her friends, things not ever to be risked in somebody else's house.

Vi tried and tried, in the kindest way, to blow away these objections. She even showed herself a little insensitive, in pressing the practical advantages, the joy it would give her and Hilary. In the end it was Hilary, perhaps, who got it through to Vi that Alice needed a home of her own.

How was she to come by one of those?

Barney and Alice had never been able to save a penny, however frugally they lived. Alice could get a job, but not one that would enable her to get a mortgage – not one that would enable her to pay more than a peppercorn rent. If Alice was to have a home of her own, somebody would have to buy it for her. So Hilary did.

They found and bought Turner's Cottage, replumbed and rewired it, and squeezed the Maudes' belongings into a third of the space they had previously occupied.

Hilary said it was an investment. That was not the least of his kindnesses.

Since Nicola was at school, Alice could get a job in the termtime. In the holidays she had to be at home. What job could that be? Teaching. Only schools kept the same dates as schools. But she had no teaching qualifications. Therefore she could teach only under certain restricted circumstances – only in a private school, only the youngest children.

And because it was that kind of teaching job, it paid at the very bottom of the scale.

It was exhausting, physically and emotionally; and it had to be combined with cleaning and cooking, with washing and ironing and darning and dressmaking, with guiding Nicola's homework and her music practice, with making tea for Nicola's friends – David Parkinson and Felicity Peacock and all the others.

And much of the time, months and years after Barney's death, Alice had the sense of sleepwalking.

★

Nicola became more and more a person, a companion. Nicola became beautiful and beloved. Nicola gave a purpose and direction to Alice's life which would otherwise have been senseless.

It was obvious to Alice that David Parkinson had a strange, sweet schoolboy adoration of Nicola. He did not know that he had it, and Nicola did not know.

But sharp little Felicity Peacock, the alien waif that the Dean and his lady had adopted – she knew. She wanted David. She wanted everything and everybody. She was a people-eater. Knowledge of her own strangeness, perhaps, had made her predatory. It could be explained, but not excused. Often and often over the years, Alice wanted to warn Nicola against Felicity, against all hard and greedy people like Felicity. Vi said the same. But it would have been stupid to say anything to Nicola.

Nicola grew beautiful and beloved, and at the age of twenty she said she was going to marry this Hugh Jarvis; and Hugh Jarvis had driven a wedge between mother and daughter, and Alice bit back more than she said, and said more than she should have.

It was not their happiest Christmas.

They went all four to the Boxing Day meet of the foxhounds, at the Lamb and Flag in Lower Bendon. Nico would have been riding her usual horse, a twelve-year-old bay mare of sixteen hands called Molly, bought by Hilary five years previously specifically for Nico to hunt. But Molly had a sore foot. There was no other horse in the Cavenhams' stable that Nico would have been happy to hunt. There was none in the Parkinsons'.

Hilary would have found her a hireling, but she did not want to ride a strange horse. She had ridden very little that autumn, being busy, being preoccupied, being in love. She felt soft and coddled, and out of the way of strenuous adventure. She did not want to go hunting by herself. She wanted to ride knee-to-knee with Hugh. They would go hunting together – that was certain, a wonderful certainty for the future. A day with the hounds without Hugh was not worth the tying of a stock.

Alice saw this, and grieved.

So they went in Hilary's car to the meet, parking among all the cars in a field behind the pub in the middle of Lower Bendon. This was where the Boxing Day meet had been held, time out of mind. Other packs had lawn meets or market-square meets on Boxing Day, but these hounds met at this pub, and all the Antis knew where to come.

It was a moderate battle, the Antis led by a waiter from a Milchester wine bar. The Cavenhams and Maudes arrived after it was nearly all over, a few arrests having been made, a few dead thunderflashes lying charred and unregarded in a ditch. There was a sense of people rolling down their sleeves and buttoning their cuffs, and the potboy from the Lamb and Flag was busy amongst the mounted field.

It was another warm, wet day, the trees misty at the far end of the village, smoke vertical above the chimneys in the windless air. A wonderful scenting day, everybody said, a good day not to be sabotaged.

From the pacified crowd emerged Hugh, to Nico's astonished delight. Separated for a moment from the others, she felt able to throw herself into his arms, which were spread wide for the purpose.

'Why aren't you hunting?' he said.

'Why aren't you?'

'No clothes. Too frightened. Next year. I've just this minute arrived from Sussex.'

'You came straight here? What a funny place to come.'

'I was sure you'd be here. You told me you always came. I thought you'd be riding. I looked forward to feeling all humble.'

Nico laughed at the idea of Hugh feeling humble.

'Next year we'll come along trit-trot together,' he said, 'all dressed up fancy like ladies and gentlemen. The photographers will be stamping on one another's faces to get pictures for the *Horse and Hound.*'

'Has somebody been stamping on your face, darling?' said Nico, withdrawing from his arms in order to inspect it.

'Your boyfriend was nearly sacrificed in the cause of whatnot,' said a man on horseback, who had been listening with a grin.

'Hello, George,' said Nico, suddenly wondering about the warmth of her greeting to Hugh in a public place. 'Do you know each other? Hugh Jarvis, George Olney-Scott.'

'I know the fellow by sight and reputation,' said George. 'I think we met fleetingly at that marvellous party in the summer.'

'I ought to pretend to remember,' said Hugh.

George was wearing scarlet, with the incongruous crash-hat of the new rules. His horse was a big liver-chestnut, trace clipped, dribbling round the curb-chain. He was a leather-brown man of fifty, rich, a hobby farmer and racehorse owner. His wife and family accused him of being in love with Nico Maude, and it was just about true.

Nico said, 'What's this about your three-day event, George?'

'Ah. Three days. That's peeping ahead a bit. We are putting on some horse-trials. We're building the course now. Colin's designing it. Colin Blaydon. D'you know him? He's here somewhere.'

Nico knew of him – an Olympic individual medallist, twice winner of Badminton a dozen years earlier, now retired from competition, but in his day one of the half-dozen best cross-country riders in the world. George Olney-Scott was aiming very high with his horse-trials. That would be fun, a local excitement.

'Come and see it,' said George. 'Come in about a month. Ride over and hack round. Try the jumps, if you like.'

'Yes and no,' said Nico.

'I'd love to do that,' said Hugh. 'This is all new to me.'

'Don't you go trying the jumps,' said Nico. 'It's bad enough your getting bashed with banners.'

'It was a fragile banner,' said Hugh. 'Not as hard as my head.'

'It ought to be mopped with disinfectant.'

'I'll mop it with whisky Mac.'

Alice joined them, with an appearance of gladness; a slight shadow fell across the party. The Cavenhams then also joined them, and the shadow lifted.

Nico and Hugh made a date with George Olney-Scott, to ride over to his farm and look at the cross-country course.

Hounds moved off. The crowd dribbled away. Hugh came back to lunch at March Court.

Hilary took Hugh away after lunch, for a talk in the library about this and that.

They discussed the substantial, unsecured, interest-free loan which Hilary was making to Hugh so that they could buy the lease of the flat in Notting Hill Gate.

It brought everything closer.

Vi talked with high glee about the combined twenty-first birthday party and wedding reception they would have at March Court in July.

It was still less than a year since Hugh had first put his foot in a stirrup. This was still hard to believe. He rode Jack Parkinson's Merry Andrew, a solid, cobby, sensible, lazy animal. He was wearing corduroy riding trousers over jodhpur boots, a mid-length Barbour and a hard hat. The comparative newness of his trousers was the only thing that suggested he had not been doing this all his life.

Over the Barbour he wore a jerkin with a lime-green sash which was supposed to be luminous.

Nico wore old drab breeches and rubber riding-boots, and a long black shiny coat brought back by Vi from China. She had a similar luminous sash, and a little flashlight clipped to her offside stirrup and facing backwards, as advertised and recommended for the safety of equestrians. Nico felt a bit silly taking all these elaborate precautions, which she had never done before; but Hugh insisted, and he had been to school, so to speak, more recently than she.

There was a hint of early-evening frost, unusual in that warm, wet February.

They had jogged round George Olney-Scott's new course, its building nearly complete. The fences were of Intermediate standard, with Novice options. In that sad twilight they looked pretty gigantic. George was very pleased to show it all off. He was full of plans for making

Bendon a national and then an international venue. The sport was all the time growing, he said, in popularity and in sponsorship finance. George was loudly jealous of Hugh, which was a standing joke between them.

They did not attempt any of the fences. Nico was not much tempted to do so, and easily persuaded Hugh not to do so.

'We'll get home by daylight if we start now.'

'Barely,' said George.

'It won't be completely dark.'

'Leave the horses here. We've got empty boxes, spare rugs, plenty of hay. Come and get them in the morning. I'll run you back. I'd much rather.'

'Oh no, George. Thanks a million, but no.'

'I've got to go to London early tomorrow,' said Hugh.

'Jacky Parks can come and get Merry Andrew,' said George.

'I've imposed on Jacky enough. I can't ask that of him. David hasn't got time. No, George, really.'

He could not persuade them. They set off, chattering cheerfully. Nico knew that Hugh was picturing his attack on those formidable obstacles, daydreaming a clear round. She trembled as she thought that it might happen. Other people had started at the same age and become champions.

It was cold and damp, not foggy but clammy, the frost not yet crisping the mud of the verges or the sodden drifts of last year's vegetation.

They were happy as they rode. Nico felt obscurely frightened, because she was too happy.

That was the last day that Nico stood or walked. For a long time she thought it was the last day that she would ever laugh.

★

Usually, as everybody knew, concussion wiped the tapes of memory before and after the event. Not so with Nico.

She remembered her happiness.

She remembered how safe she had felt. She had never in her life had reason to be frightened – nervous and excited, certainly, plenty of times, approaching a hairy jump in the hunting field, walking with careful unconcern to the lip of a high diving-board – but she had no experience of terror. As the world went, she had been extraordinarily lucky and protected. She had never heard the scream of a shell, the snarl of hostile aircraft, the thud of bombs, the stammer of automatic small-arms. She had never seen violent death. She had been involved only in the most minor accidents – a bent bumper, a dented wing.

She had seen blood only from scratches, heard screams only of excitement.

She had never had reason to be frightened, and now had less reason than ever, because she was with Hugh.

But to be so happy was to tempt Providence. And on that dismal afternoon it was getting dark sooner than they expected.

They talked when either had something to say. But they were now so used to one another that they could be content in companionable silence. There was no need to fill the space between them with words. There was no requirement of politeness. It was comforting and restful.

Nico was happy, but a little bit of her wished they had let George Olney-Scott take them home in his car.

Car.

A car coming. There had been others, but very few. It was a back road, not a short cut to anywhere. This seemed like a big car, coming up behind them, going slowly, invisible behind its headlights. There may have been something distinctive about the sound of its engine – Nico had the notion it was a car she knew. That was likely enough, if it was a local car. It was surely local, on that little road, at that hour. If so, the driver would expect blind corners, horses, tractors.

The horses came to a corner, a sharp right turn under a clump of overspreading oak trees. The darkness was darker under the trees. The verge was trappy there, boggy and crossed by half-visible drains. They were better on the edge of the road.

The trees and the verge and the bank and the tangled brambles on the bank suddenly sprang into visibility. A billion drops of moisture were kindled to diamonds. Hugh's back, beside Nico, gleamed wetly in the light, as did the damp quarters of his horse. The road straightened behind them, so that they were in full view in the undipped beams of the car's headlights. It was a good place to be, the safest place.

'Stop, and let him go by,' said Nico.

Those were the last words she spoke to Hugh.

'Yes,' said Hugh.

That was the last word he spoke on earth.

It was obvious that the car would slow right down. It was something that was bound to happen. The driver would go quietly past the horses, giving them plenty of room, on a road sheened with wet and with a touch of ice.

Nico had time for a jolt of astonishment, of anger, as the light suddenly strengthened and the engine roared at them.

There was a confused and terrible noise, impact, screaming, the tumble of horse and man in the appalling glare of the headlights, her own lurch sideways, one scream, darkness.

★

That was all she could tell them. It was all they ever knew.

From the beginning they had to ration visits, keep people out, or the patient would have been exhausted and the hospital's linoleum worn threadbare. Nico on her back in the warm white room was like a monument, a shrine attracting an innumerable pilgrimage. Face followed face followed face, an interminable sequence of moons occupying the space between Nico's horizon and the zenith, faces concerned or crying or bright with manufactured cheer, low sickroom voices, voices heartily encouraging – questions: What's the food like? Is there anything you need, anything we can get you? – news, gossip, engagements made or broken, scandals ecclesiastical and lay, small local scandals, storms in the teacups of the Cathedral Close, anything to amuse her, divert her, take her mind off her troubles—

Could her mind ever be off those troubles?

The season marched through a warm and clammy spring into a breathtaking May, white sunlight pouring onto the white sheets, the white enamel of the bed-rails, the blue-white pallor of Nico's face.

All the local people came to see Nico: the Bishop of Milchester, the Dean, the Master of the Hospital of the Holy Cross, the organist of the Cathedral and the Precentor and the Bishop's Chaplain, and the Vicar of their own parish, and the wives and families of all these worthies, and all the other neighbours, the grandest and the humblest, and students and tutors and lecturers from the college and the other schools of Milchester; and Jefferson McCabe, come running from Rome the minute somebody told him the news, almost the first to make Nico smile; and Hugh's mother Miggy Jarvis, also come from Italy, all her cool sophistication in shreds, all her fashionable detachment dissolved in her tears, speechless, holding Nico's hand and weeping over it; and a little pale rabbity man, not well known to Nico before, but now most indefatigable of her visitors, Gerald Orchard, full of offers to run errands, read to her, anything she liked – it was kind, but puzzling that he should suddenly be so devoted – she did not exactly want him locked out, but she did not much want him let in ...

June was cold after the glory of May: people came into Nico's sterilized white box of a world wearing tweed coats against the cold east wind, some risking jokes about envying her, cosy in her bed.

Nico had a TV in her room. She watched some of the races at Ascot. It poured with rain on Gold Cup Day. Nico thought she saw Vi and Hilary huddling under a single umbrella in the paddock.

She was now spending many hours a week with the physiotherapist, and they lowered her into a hot-water pool and tried to get her swimming, and there was massage and electrical treatment and a lot of X-rays.

Nico heard that Vi and Hilary and her mother had decided what to do and were doing it – making Turner's Cottage fit for a wheelchair, fit for somebody who would never get out of a wheelchair.

Several times the hospital nearly let her out, to the fine new specially adapted cottage, but there was something wrong and then something else wrong, and after all they kept her in all through June and into July, and the last week of July ... so that Nico had her twenty-first birthday, after all, in her little white room in the hospital.

★

To see Nico came people who could walk, run, jump, dance, play games, ride horses, dive and swim, make love to their lovers. All of them who were not too old or frightened could do all these things.

They looked at Nico and spoke to her, and contemplated her present and future; and all of them said, to themselves and one another, 'It's not fair.'

The one person who was never heard to say it was Nico.

By the time of Nicola's twenty-first birthday, Alice had known for four months the truth about the 'accident'.

She was no nearer saying anything about it or doing anything about it. What could she say or do?

She knew that the 'accident' was the fruit of hatred, of a bitter and bottomless malevolence. She had sensed, almost smelled, that disgusting emotion, had been astonished and sickened by it. It was strange to her. She had never felt hatred. Now she did. It was ironic, that – as a result of meeting hatred, for the very first time she felt it. It was a sin to hate. Barney was incapable of hatred. Alice confessed her hatred, in her prayers. She was not saintly enough not to hate the person who had done that thing. Hatred became her single indulgence, her one secret sin.

She hid her hatred even better than the murderess hid hers.

Nico was astonished at the goodwill which poured into her little white room, from what sometimes seemed the whole civilized world, so dense, so numerous, so warm were the good wishes that she heard and felt.

Nobody else was astonished, but Nico was.

People rallied to help her in any way they could.

They rallied to help one another, too.

David Parkinson, for example, comforted Felicity Peacock. She also comforted him. They were not obvious about it, but they were not secretive either. They had no need to be. They had known one another all their lives. Of course, when tragedy struck at the centre of their circle, they would hold one another's hands. They would do so in private, but they would not mind if they were seen doing it.

Felicity had lost her love not once but twice. She needed comfort.

David had lost his love not once but one and – how many times? One and three-quarter times? One and ninety-nine hundredths times? Something of the sort. He needed comfort.

They held one another's hands; they were young and normal, abundantly healthy, physically attractive, lonely, abandoned, left.

July flared into glory, after the cold and wet of June. For Nico's twenty-first, Nature put on her most resplendent greens and golds, and the whole world was on holiday.

Those long evenings would have been long indeed for David and Felicity, spent alone, spent mourning.

Each might, perhaps, fill with the other the black holes in the middles of their lives. At least there was the possibility of forgetting for a little.

Nico's arms and shoulders had been little injured, but they were pathetically weak after five months of doing nothing. She set herself to strengthen them, with all the exercises given her by the physiotherapists, and others of her own, so that by the middle of August she could spin round the corridors of the hospital in her wheelchair, at speeds which threatened the tea-ladies and sent the nurses scurrying out of the way.

The porters followed her with hunting cries, and there were patients who waved their crutches and cheered.

There was still a sort of bleak fun to be had.

Gerald Orchard wanted to push the wheelchair. He could not be made to understand that she did not want to be pushed. He wanted to be the person she wanted to be pushed by, but there was no such person.

People mentioned seeing David Parkinson and Felicity Peacock together.

Vi told Alice that one of her daily women had seen the two of them in the bar of the Eastgate Hotel in Milchester.

Why not? Well, why not?

Alice was fond of David, and esteemed his parents, although she could not forgive them for introducing Hugh Jarvis into their lives. Here was someone she viewed with qualified affection caught by the murderously jealous, the mad and evil.

Alerted, Alice looked; looking, she saw.

Felicity had an air of proprietorship.

Alice was sickened and appalled.

It would not do to warn David against Felicity. There was nothing that Alice could do to help David, except to hope that Felicity fell under a bus.

Alice did not think herself capable of praying for such a thing. But she knew God knew what she was hoping for, and she knew He knew she was right.

Meanwhile Felicity could run about the tennis court, and bounce on the springboard of a pool.

★

It was difficult to know how to treat Nicola's homecoming. Of course it was cause for loud and long celebration, that she was released from the necessity of constant attention, examination, medication, that she would be back among the loved and familiar things of her life, that she was rejoining the world. But could you celebrate a girl of twenty-one beginning her new life as the prisoner of a piece of furniture?

To Alice, there was another aspect of the problem, a horrible and secret dimension unguessed by anybody else.

If family only were to be there to say 'Welcome home' to Nicola, that was fine – that was Vi and Hilary and herself and no one else; and this could be justified on the grounds that the day would be exhausting enough for Nicola without the hassle of noise, greetings, politeness.

Any party even a little larger must include certain lifelong friends.

Like Felicity.

The thought of Felicity welcoming Nicola home made the bile rise in Alice's throat. The imagined scene was the sickest and cruellest conceivable. That confrontation, that irony, was unthinkable.

If it had to be a party, then, it had to be a big one, an ocean of people to dilute the poison, a chorus of voices to drown her out. For lots of reasons, the prospect of a big party was horrible, but it might be the least of evils.

Vi assumed there would be a gigantic party and that Hilary would pay for it. It would be a sort of additional, delayed twenty-first birthday. But it was September, and many people were still away. And there was just not enough room for what the Cavenhams had in mind. You couldn't welcome the girl home anywhere except *at* home, and home had small rooms, a small garden, a parking problem in the lane outside.

In the event, there were to be not quite thirty people, rather more women than men, rather more old than young. Some who had been particularly kind to Nicola were included, though not close friends – on this basis the chief physiotherapist of the Milchester Hospital was asked; and on this basis Gerald Orchard was asked.

All the Peacocks were invited, but Felicity was in Scotland.

Nico looked forward to the party with moderate enthusiasm. She was longing to go home, but felt she would like her home to herself for a bit. Goodwill was what it was all about, and she was grateful. In any case she was helpless. She would make the best of it.

She thought this was a thing she had better get in practice for. She would be making the best of things for the next fifty years.

The specialist came round soon after eleven. His only business with Nico, that final morning, was to give her his blessing. They did not exchange extended or emotional farewells, since he would be seeing her soon and often.

There had been many goodbyes with nurses, cleaners, porters, the Friends of Milchester Hospital who brought round Bovril in the middle of the morning, the lady with the trolley of paperbacks – a kind of mobile library, the cheerful young man with mutton-chop whiskers who sold newspapers in the wards. Nico had become the mascot and the pin-up of all these people, and they were torn between joy that she was able to leave and sorrow that she was leaving.

Nico dressed after the specialist had gone. She

dressed the top half of herself, and a nurse the lower half. She looked out of the window as she buttoned her shirt. The sky was full of low, wet clouds. Rain was forecast, and it looked imminent. It was sad: Nico would not celebrate going home by drinking champagne in the garden.

Alice came. A porter loaded cases onto a trolley.

It was raining by the time they were downstairs.

Nico wanted to get wet. She had not felt rain on her face since February. Not to experience rain was to be only half alive. This was heavy, cold, drenching rain, bouncing off concrete and tarmac and the roofs of cars, hissing across the driveway and car-park in front of the hospital, already gurgling yellowly in overfilled drains and gutters, rain to batter the autumn flowers in the borders of all the gardens in all the villages, to knock the petals off the late roses and wash the cobwebs out of the long grass. They would not let Nico get wet. They thought she would almost want to be back in bed, safe and warm and dry in the hospital room. They did not understand about the necessity of rain on the face. The car was brought round to the covered loading bay; Nico was lifted in, and the wheelchair folded and stowed.

The wipers at double speed hardly cleared the windscreen. The glass immediately misted with cold rain outside and warm breath inside. Alice peered ahead as she drove, going slower than she had in all the years since she learned to drive. It was not a time to be skidding into a ditch.

An agency nurse was waiting for them at Turner's Cottage. Everybody agreed that she was absolutely necessary, at least at first; she was a condition of Nico being allowed to come home. She was a big, black, comforting young woman with a Yorkshire accent. She said it was a shame it was raining for the welcome-home party.

Nico tried her wheelchair in the cottage. It was more difficult than in the hospital; it was more crowded, with sharper corners, narrower gaps betweens obstacles; she threatened more damage if she hit things. She tried reaching for things in the kitchen, and in her new downstairs bathroom. Outside the rain hissed and bounced and tried to drown the whole of Wessex.

The party should have been dominated by Nico, but it was dominated by the rain.

They expected the Cavenhams to be the first to arrive, with a groom or gardener following them across the gravel with a case of champagne. But Gerald Orchard was the first. He came early in case Nicola wanted her wheelchair pushed. He was totally encased in oilskins, because he had come on his bicycle. He shed them in the little porch of the cottage, knocking over flower-pots and showering the doormat. It was evident that his oilskins leaked or gaped, as his pale suit was dark with patches of damp, so that it resembled the plaster of a derelict building. Rain had reached his hair, going through or under his sou'-wester, plastering it to his little skull. He looked pink, unusually healthy, disarming although so very anxious to please. Alice gave him a cup of coffee, because if he started drinking immediately he would be drinking for two hours.

The Cavenhams arrived, and with them the makings of a great number of champagne cocktails.

'We thought about Buck's fizz,' said Hilary. 'But it's the wrong sort of weather.'

They were wet, but not in the way that Gerald Orchard had been wet. They had dashed a short distance from their car across the streaming garden, laughing and shouting as they came. They were splashed rather than soaked. It was a game; the party was already beginning. The rain dominated the conversation, even as Hilary began peeling the foil off the corks of the bottles, and Pedro was unpacking tulip glasses from cardboard boxes.

Jacky and Monica Parkinson arrived, with David. They struck an in-between note – not ingratiating, not boisterous, but quietly breezy. They were people who got on with things, and what they were getting on with was the party. They accepted cocktails from Pedro, and talked about the difficulty of driving in such rain, the criminal folly of young men who went too fast, the misery of mud, the certainty of blocked gutters at Normandy.

There was a moment of uneasiness. Young men driving dangerously under difficult conditions – it was a subject to be avoided in that house.

The rain crashed on the window-sills, and continually shivered the leaves of the plants outside the windows; the rain drummed and hissed and hid the distances, and it was difficult to concentrate on anything else.

Gerald Orchard offered to push Nicola this way or that, with such anxiety that she almost allowed herself to be propelled up and down the room, simply to oblige him. But there was hardly room for that. With seven of them, besides the wheelchair, the drawing room of the cottage was getting crowded.

Nicola looked frail and pale. She sounded cheerful. It was worse, seeing her in the wheelchair in her own home. It institutionalized the wheelchair, giving it permanence as part of the life of the house.

David brought up a little chair, and sat beside Nicola.

She smiled at him. He was telling her a story, and she was laughing. Alice saw the laughter, but she could not hear it. Vi and Jacky Parkinson and the others were talking loudly about the rain, and there was the pervasive hiss and thrum of the rain itself, and Nicola's laugh was not a ringing, abandoned laugh. It might be a long time before she gave one of those. She might never again give a wail of loud, helpless laughter.

The Dean's wife arrived, Mary Peacock, invited but only half expected. The Dean's apologies were conveyed. Felicity had come instead, unexpectedly home from Scotland.

Greeting Felicity, Alice put on the mask she had been using since March. Alice doubted if she were successful, pretending to be glad to see Felicity. But her play-acting was needless. Felicity was looking past her. Felicity was looking at Nicola, at David sitting beside Nicola, at their unmistakable intimacy, the long-standing and loving friendship which they showed.

There was something frozen about Felicity's face: not an expression of any kind but an absence of expression so total that it was startling. It was a dead face.

Alice thought, with sudden giddy horror: my God, it's happening again.

Nicola had taken Hugh from Felicity.
    Felicity had found David instead.
    Nicola was taking David from Felicity.
    Now what?

CHAPTER EIGHT

NICO WENT BACK TO COLLEGE, recommencing her final year.

She had done some reading and re-reading in the hospital, and it seemed to her that her brain still worked. She had no difficulty remembering old things or acquiring new. There were practical difficulties, about going to lectures and tutorials, about getting to Somerset House and the National Gallery and the Tate, but nothing that could not be licked by will and goodwill. Other people managed, and Nico reckoned she had as much determination as any, and more friends than most.

She received a tremendous welcome when she re-appeared in Milchester. At her first lecture there was a standing ovation, in which the lecturer joined. It was not that she had done anything wonderful: it was just a very big 'Hello'.

It was impossible not to burst into tears at the intensity of this goodwill.

There were steps up and down, here and there in the college buildings. The wheelchair could be manhandled over these obstacles – in reverse when going up – but it was an uncomfortable and time-consuming business. Somebody produced many pairs of planks, which when not in use were left against the walls by each set of steps, and laid down in front of Nico's wheels whenever she approached. A large comic drama was often made of each ascent and descent, with trumpeters, outriders and cheering crowds.

Later in the term there was another student in a wheelchair, a boy with spina bifida studying engineering, a more experienced pilot than Nico but not as strong. They played polo on the tarmac forecourt of the college, using a football and proper polo sticks, the latter produced by Roddy Plumb. After a couple of impromptu games, Nico and the boy played exhibition matches in aid of Milchester Hospital. There were big crowds. The noise was so tremendous when Nico scored a goal that startled policemen appeared, prepared for the suppression of a student riot.

Life was not so bad.

Gerald Orchard continued as he had started; he remained the most assiduous of Nico's wheelchair pushers. He picked up things she had dropped, and changed books for her at the public library.

'Am I exploiting that odd young man?' said Nico to her mother.

'He seems to like it,' said Alice.

Once a week or so, all that autumn, Gerald Orchard bicycled to the gates of March Court. He stopped and looked up the drive at the house. With the change of the clocks and the earlier evenings, it was sometimes almost dark when he got there. Then he turned off the light of his bicycle, propped it against a tree out of sight, and prowled into the park.

He knew the Cavenhams kept no dogs, because they were away so often.

He could go right up to the house. He could look in,

until Pedro went round doing up the shutters of the downstairs windows. He had never been inside, but he was getting to know it well.

He felt like Moses.

Gerald Orchard asked Nico to his school's Christmas pantomime.

'It might give you a laugh,' he said.

As he asked Nico in the middle of October, and the pantomime was not until the very end of term, a few days only before Christmas, it was difficult to plead a previous engagement. In any case the pantomime was in the middle of the afternoon, unlikely to clash with anything.

'There's only two steps up into the hall,' said Gerald. 'There's dozens of boys to help with the chair.'

'Part of the rich tapestry,' said Felicity Peacock, when Nico told her about the pantomime. 'It'll make a paragraph in your memoirs.'

David Parkinson came more often to Turner's Cottage as the season wheeled into winter, as the estate went into the hibernation and gave him time to go visiting.

He was puzzled at the reception he got.

Not from Nico. She was, herself, his oldest and most beloved friend. But Alice? David was not given to fancies, to imagined slights, to terrible doubts about the effect he was having on people. He did not think he was unobservant, but he was certainly not hypersensitive. But Alice, without ever saying anything, seemed cool about his coming and glad when he left.

David searched his conscience, his memory, for his own words and actions. As far as the Maudes went, it seemed to him he was in the clear. He could honestly think of nothing he had done wrong – nothing to justify Alice's hostility.

It was not only inexplicable: it was, David thought, quite new. All David's life, he had been on terms of the most intimate friendship with the Maudes – with Barney while he lived, with Nico all her life, with Alice equally. There had been nothing assumed or false about Alice's greetings to him over the years. She had smiled and made him welcome; as she was transparently honest, he knew she had meant those smiles and welcomes. So it was through all the years of childhood and youth: so when Nico was abroad, and when she returned: so, certainly, when Nico was in hospital and David came with his hands empty or full, to be received in that little white room with love and gratitude ...

But since Nico had come home ... Why?

'Why?' said David to Nico, one afternoon when Alice was out.

'Oh, have you noticed, too?' said Nico. 'I wondered if I was imagining it. I don't know why. Is it something you've done?'

'Can you ask her?' said David. 'I don't think I can.'

Nico could, and did.

'You know, I suppose,' said her mother, looking away, 'that David has been seeing Felicity Peacock?'

'My God, I should hope so,' said Nico. 'They've been seeing one another at least once a week for the last twenty years.'

'Oh, don't pretend to misunderstand,' said Alice. She got up suddenly and walked out of the room. There was no kettle boiling or tap running, so Nico realized with dismay that her mother was too upset to talk about it. To talk about what? About David?

Nico wondered if she should tell David not to come and see her. She decided she was damned if she would.

Alice understood that she was upsetting both Nicola and David.

She did not know what she could do about it.

Nicola in those days was in great beauty, to Alice's eyes. The months in hospital had given her a sort of magical fragility. Her strange-coloured hair was thick and gleaming, and beautifully cut by a woman who came out from Milchester. She looked like a nymph, otherworldly, immortal. These were not Alice's words, but she accepted them. And out of this frail and fairy-like person came the humour, the robust commonsense, the irreverence and gutsiness of somebody whom anybody would choose as a companion. It was that combination, Alice thought, that made Nicola nowadays into a local heroine, something like a living legend. It was strange to be pretty ordinary, as Alice knew herself to be, and to have such a miraculous child.

How could such a girl not attract romantic devotion?

David might seem to a stranger completely the farmer, the bluff young squire, but he had a streak of idealism and poetry. He would cast himself as a true knight to Nicola's damsel. He would even glory in making the large, necessary sacrifices.

And Nicola? On such a rebound, what might she not allow herself to feel, especially for a friend so old and trusted?

So Alice should warn them . . .

Saying what?

Saying: I had a funny feeling as I was driving along . . .?

Saying: there's only one person who could have had any

motive for such an atrocity, and her motive was overwhelming, and it would be again, and history is repeating itself...

Alice was to talk like that, to Nicola and David?

She imagined the scene; in her mind's eye she saw them glance at one another, in pity and derision.

Tommy Johns reappeared in the normal world – Alice's world – in the middle of November.

He had been in his office when it was impossible not to be there; otherwise he had been at home. His wife had been at home. They had said, as they sometimes did, that she would benefit from a home environment, the challenge of daily life, the refreshing therapy of normal human encounters. Life became a nightmare, of unpredictable rages, orgies of destruction, incontinence and filth, the awful necessity of physical restraint, the temptation insidiously ever-present in the bottles of powerful sedatives...

Julia had been taken away at last, by a doctor and two nurses. They had looked reproachfully at Tommy, throwing his wife back into custody, washing his hands of her and getting on with his life. He had reappeared with a shattered face, like a man deprived for weeks of sleep and any tranquillity.

Alice wanted to talk about his troubles, not her own, but there was nothing to be said about them. There was no precaution to be taken, no direction in which to travel, not even any sense of guilt, of if-only or it-might-have-been. It was just pure bloody bad luck. Tommy had nothing to reproach himself with. He had nothing to look forward to except Julia's death. He was emotionally pulverized and physically exhausted. He did not want to talk about any of it, and there was nothing to say.

He saw that there was something on Alice's mind. There was that to talk about.

Alice was afraid of making a fool of herself, even to Tommy. She was afraid of dismissive mockery, even from him. She knew, from telling it to herself, how grotesque her story sounded. Tommy had twitted her before about jumping to conclusions, blowing suspicions into certainties: as when she said she 'knew' Nicola was going to bed with Hugh Jarvis. This was a rather larger business, and her 'evidence' even flimsier. It was no evidence. It was a sensation inside her own head. It was not even a vision or a visitation; simply a sick feeling. How could Tommy be expected to take that seriously?

But she was desperate to talk about it. She felt as though the knowledge, imprisoned in her head, was a lump of infection that needed to be lanced, released, or it would poison her brain, and send her mad. She *had* to talk to somebody about it, and now that Tommy had returned it had to be Tommy.

Tommy was not derisive, but he was not impressed either. He believed that *she* believed what she said. But he thought the 'accident' had been an accident, and the driver a drunken joyrider.

'I'm not neurotic or fanciful,' said Alice.

'That's true.'

'If I were given to voices, insights, any kind of psychic messages, if I was that sort of person, or ever had been—'

'Would I take you more seriously?'

'I might take myself less seriously. It's just because I'm so down-to-earth, boring, square, unimaginative, that this ... revelation is so shattering, so convincing.'

She meant it. But Tommy was totally unconvinced.

Tommy did not risk annoying Alice with his own

explanation of the 'revelation', which went like this: a by-product of tragedy could be anger – 'Why was this allowed to happen?' – and anger, emotionally, required a focus, someone to be angry with. Blame needed to be attached somewhere. Identified, the accused needed to be provided with a motive. Alice was arguing with the flawed logic of the appalled, in seeing the accident as a crime and in finding a villain.

Tommy liked Felicity Peacock, finding her amusing and responsive. This influenced his reaction to what Alice told him.

Alice had mentioned to Nicola that David was 'seeing' Felicity. Of course this continued to be true. How could they not see one another?

What did 'see' mean?

Never in her life had Alice felt more than a fleeting curiosity about other people's secrets, especially their emotional and sexual secrets. She was not one to pry. She had closed her mind, as far as she could, to speculation about Vi's long-ago goings-on, and Nicola's. But now, suddenly, shockingly, it was necessary for her to know.

How deeply involved was David with Felicity?

Putting it exactly, how angry was Felicity entitled to feel, if she once again found herself betrayed?

Feeling ashamed, almost defiled, Alice ever so casually elicited local gossip from Vi's daily cleaning women.

It was not very conclusive, but it was enough to make her sick with worry about the future.

Mary, the black nurse from Yorkshire, left at the end of October. She was sorry to go, and Nicola and Alice were sorry to see her go, but she was no longer needed on a full-time basis, and the expense (to Hilary Cavenham) could no longer be justified. She or another would return if there were any crisis, or if Alice were ill or needed a rest.

Mary's departure meant that Nicola was often alone in the house. That was all right. She always had a cordless telephone on her lap. Steps between rooms and in and out of the house had been eliminated. She was now an expert pilot of the wheelchair, profiting from the example of her friend with spina bifida.

David Parkinson or anybody else could now be alone with Nico, if they wanted to be, and if there was any point in it.

Of course, young men were not Nico's only visitors. Callers came in all kinds. Felicity Peacock came whenever she was at home. Felicity, like David, tended to come when Alice was out.

Alice would come back from the little school where she had resumed teaching, usually in time for tea. She would hear that David had come; that Felicity had come. She said nothing. There was nothing she could say, other than what she had said, which was already too much.

As Gerald Orchard had promised, a swarm of little boys, in high good humour, lifted Nico and her wheelchair up the two steps into the Assembly Hall of the Hardy House School in Milchester. The boys were excited with the end of term, with going home and the imminence of Christmas. The youngest ones were excited by the pantomime, too, though the bigger ones (as old as twelve) assumed a blasé air about it.

The hall was crowded with parents and friends of the school, as well as the hundred-odd boys who were not in the cast of the pantomime.

Nico was installed at the end of the front row, two chairs being removed to make room. There was a pretty good stage, with footlights and a curtain, given years before in memory of somebody. There was an upright piano. In summer, for the Speech Day in July, the hall would be stuffy; it was rather stuffy now, being so crowded, but also cold.

Nico had wondered how to get out of this. There was no way she could do so. Her father had sat through scores of awful evenings (village dramatic societies doing J.M. Barrie, local schools doing Gilbert and Sullivan) in order not to hurt people's feelings. Nico did not care about Gerald Orchard, but she was not prepared to hurt his pride, and this idiotic performance was strangely important to him.

It was hardly credible that a grown man should be so dim that a comic performance in a show put on for little boys was the high point of his year. But so it seemed to be. Nico consequently pinned a smile to her face, while the hall shrieked and giggled behind her, and the curtain bulged, and the music master took his seat at the upright piano.

The lights went down. The piano crashed into jolly melody. The curtain was jerkily hoisted.

Like most pantomimes, this one contained an element of time-honoured ritual, with heavy audience participation – the hero was cheered, the villain hissed, and so forth. Gerald Orchard got a pretty good hissing, as Blodwyn the Wicked Welsh Witch. He had a long wig made of grey string, and a steeple hat and a purple shawl and a broomstick. He sang a long, fierce song in his reedy tenor; he threatened all kinds of horrors to the pretty assistant matron who was playing the heroine.

It all did everybody credit, but it went on far too long.

There was screaming and thundering applause at the end, as the whole school saw the end of term rushing at it, and Christmas almost immediately after that. Gerald Orchard and the others, bowing as they took their curtain calls, were bathed in the joy of liberation.

Nico was committed to having tea with them all afterwards.

She thought she had done her bit, but she found she was expected for tea with the headmaster and the cast and the staff and some of the parents. She was lifted down the steps, and led by a dozen little boys across the yard. She was made welcome. The tea was disgusting, tasting of metal and iodine, but she ate a sardine sandwich with enjoyment.

The cast arrived in a jubilant body, having taken off their costumes and make-up. They were tremendously pleased with themselves: four masters, a woman teacher of languages, the young matron, two dozen boys. They all said it had seemed to go pretty well, talking to the air and waiting for compliments.

Gerald Orchard was trying to be modest, but he could not stop himself smiling. He was happier than Nico had ever seen him. He was wearing his coat over his shoulders in an actorish, sophisticated fashion. He was putting on another performance, just as self-conscious as the one he had been doing on the stage. He was acting an actor. Nico realized with a shock that she was the audience.

Why?

Nico thought she could understand the euphoria of somebody shining who had never had a chance to shine, somebody attracting applause who had never been noticed. Nowadays, more than ever before in her life, she faced the unfairness of the human condition: all her life, she had shone without trying to: she had drawn every eye in every room: she had attracted applause by accident. So Gerald Orchard was excited. Fair enough. He was extravagantly pleased with himself. Okay. It was fine for people to be happy, with or without sufficient reason. Nico had learned to value moments of happiness, having thought she would never again have any. She was glad for other people to have them. She was delighted for Gerald Orchard to have as many as he could. Nobody was thinking the worse of him for glorying in the moment.

But why was the glory beamed at herself?

Nico smiled and answered questions, and all the while a part of her mind was wondering what had got into Gerald Orchard.

The party ended rather abruptly, with electric bells ringing through the school. It was six o'clock – time for the boys' supper. Some of the teachers and all the boys left immediately. Even at the end of term, even just before Christmas, the timetable was immutable. The parents and the other visitors began to leave also, as though they, too, were subject to the school bell.

Gerald Orchard alone was independent of it. He was not on duty. Perhaps his success on the stage had relieved him of chores, of supervising supper or the tidying of classrooms.

The tea party had not been the most uproarious of celebrations, but Nico was sorry it ended when it did. Roddy Plumb was coming for her at six-thirty, after a meeting of his department at the Poly. Twenty minutes did not give time enough to embark on anything different, anything unplanned; but it was too much time to be killing in the front hall of the school, where Roddy was meeting her.

It seemed that Gerald Orchard was killing time with her. He came down from his cloud and offered to push her. There was no longer an army of little boys to swarm about the wheelchair as the Lilliputians overwhelmed Gulliver. But there was Gerald Orchard instead.

Grey ladies came and went, taking trays of cups and plates and the remains of the sandwiches; the departure of the tea-urn on a trolley reminded Nico of the hospital. She was left alone with Gerald Orchard.

Gerald Orchard was tousled and flushed; his hair was sticking up, now that it had been released from his wig; his jacket was still dashingly over his shoulders, as though he had been playing polo, or directing a film.

He pushed the wheelchair a few feet, and then stopped.

He said, 'You see, I'm not such a worm.'

'Not such a what?' said Nico, startled. She had heard, but she needed time to think of an answer to this strange remark.

'I don't make any large claims for myself as a Thespian,' said Gerald Orchard. 'The stage I fancy is politics, actually. My idea is ultimately to go into Parliament. Journalism and literature are subsumed. I think we can take that as read. What one needs is a companion. Somebody intelligent and warm. Intellectually aware. Somebody to bounce ideas off. To act as hostess. To have charge of administrative detail. Oh, heaps of things, a fascinating multiple role! And at the end of the day, the sense of achievement! Or there's farming. The rural life, made tolerable by cultural interests. Again, the pen is not excluded. What major rural novels have there been since Hardy? There's a gap which one despairs of seeing filled by the so-called intelligentsia of North London. I say, do I seem to you to be talking the most bloody awful rubbish? *For he on honeydew hath fed, and drunk the milk of Paradise.* I don't know if you know Coleridge? Not many people do, nowadays. I can show you all kinds of civilized delights, you know. By cripes, I feel inspired! And I want you to share my triumphs! With you beside me, by God, there's nothing I can't do! Nicola, let me push your chair down the long road of life, and you'll find we go between cheering crowds, and trophies will be strewn before your wheels!'

He was drunk. He was not drunk with drink but with applause.

Nico realized with a shock that this rambling rhetoric was a proposal. It came as an absolute surprise. She realized at the same moment that it should not have come as a surprise – that the strange, unexplained devotion he had been showing had been a courtship, had led up to this absurd and embarrassing moment.

Nico cleared her throat, because although she knew what to say, she did not know how to say it.

Gerald Orchard reached down over the back of the wheelchair, and grabbed one of Nico's hands, which was lying on the arm of the chair. He massaged Nico's hand, his own hands damp. He kissed it.

'What a couple we shall make,' he said, mumbling over Nico's hand as though scavenging for remnants of sandwiches. 'The house will be a Mecca!'

'What house?' said Nico, still making time.

'March Court, of course.'

Of course. The proposal was explained, sufficiently if not completely.

'We'll have a flat in London, too,' said Gerald Orchard.

'Oh shut up,' said Nico, aware that she had not found the right words.

Her message did not get through. He was still deafened by the cheers ringing in his head. He was a hero.

Nico was cold and tired. By now Roddy would be waiting for her. Roddy would be exhausted, after arguing with his colleagues. Roddy was infinitely patient and kind, but it was not reasonable that he should be kept waiting by this little man who was dribbling over Nico's fingers.

Nico was bored and uncomfortable; she was embarrassed by the exhibition Gerald Orchard was making of himself; she felt the beginnings of indigestion, from eating sandwiches made with damp new bread; she wanted to go home.

Gerald Orchard saw none of this. He went gabbling on, clutching her hand, ignoring her attempts to interrupt him politely.

'You're an impertinent little bore,' she said. 'You're a fortune-hunting creep.'

Nico was appalled by her own words. She had not intended to be so downright, so cruelly offensive. Cold and boredom and embarrassment and indigestion were talking. But she did not care terribly, if only she silenced Gerald Orchard, if only she got herself out of the place. It was not tolerable to sit there any longer and undergo this drooling. It was not tolerable to keep Roddy waiting.

Gerald Orchard did hear. He dropped her hand as though it had bitten him. He looked at Nico with a shocked, frozen face. He went bright red. He looked at that moment capable of anything, of suicide, of murder.

He ran out, leaving Nico alone with dozens of drawings by the little boys which had been tacked to the walls of the room.

★

Nico's Christmas, after this hiccup, was as good as loving kindness could make it. After the awkwardness of the previous year, the scratchiness between herself and her mother, it was a relief to feel united and relaxed.

There was a peculiar irony in that. The cause of the friction had been removed, as though by surgery. Nico was happier than she had been when she was happy, and she would never really be happy again. It was funny to live inside a tragedy, with the worse better than the best had been, with things easier because they were intolerable.

They went to the Cathedral as always on Christmas morning. There was a crowd of old and special friends, all the people Nico had known all her life, to surround the wheelchair in the special parking-space arranged for them by the Dean, to push the chair up the ramp beside the steps of the west door, to envelope and engulf Nico with Christmas cheer, good wishes, love, warmth, comfort, admiration. During the service, Nico felt, as always, eyes in the small of her back, but now the darts were not of admiration and envy but of pity and wonder. She had taken trouble with her hair, and put on lipstick. Somebody was heard to say that she had never looked more beautiful.

Under the tree at March Court, there were presents from everybody to everybody, but there were no presents from Hugh.

Inevitably, from the time she came out of hospital, Nico had been reliving scenes associated with Hugh (except the most important scenes associated with Hugh). With Hugh she had relived scenes associated with the whole of her previous life. It had to be so. She could not bar herself from the world she lived in, because Hugh had lived in it.

But there were scenes which were too much. The Boxing Day meet of the foxhounds was too much.

They were all a little too tactful, in understanding why she would not come. She supposed that this would be part of the pattern of her life – everybody being too tactful, when the reminders were extra strong. She thought the tact might be more difficult to bear than the reminders.

In the weeks after Christmas, David Parkinson's visits became more frequent, their purpose more apparent.

Nico was uneasy.

She loved and trusted David, but the memory of Hugh was fresh. And she herself ... she did not think she could ask such a sacrifice of her old friend, even though he might say he wanted to make it.

Nico saw that her mother, too, was uneasy at David's visits – more than uneasy; apparently sickened by David, frightened by him. How could that be? Alice could not or would not say why. Nico was completely puzzled. David could not have that effect on anybody, least of all anybody who knew him so well.

David saw it, of course – had seen it for months. He tentatively mentioned it to Nico. He was equally puzzled. He was hurt.

Alice repeated to Nico, in February and in March, that David was said to be seeing Felicity Peacock. To her this news seemed portentous; to Nico it was simply not news.

Miranda Jolly told Nico, as a joke, that Felicity had been seen with Gerald Orchard. They had an awful lot to say to one another, according to Miranda. This was surprising but not astonishing. They sang madrigals together; it was reasonable that they should have a drink together. What they discussed was anybody's guess. Nico wondered whether to tell Miranda, or Felicity herself, or anybody else, about Gerald Orchard's extraordinary outburst after the pantomime. She did not mention it. She was near to wondering if it had actually happened. She thought it would not happen again. It was not really a funny story; to tell it would simply be illnatured.

David Parkinson was seeing Felicity, and he was coming whenever he could to see Nico. As spring lengthened into summer, David was busier and busier; and the more so as his father increasingly handed over responsibility for the farm to him.

Nico sat in the sun. Her skin became pink-gold and her hair silver-gold; the one like a peach, the other like old polished pewter in firelight. David told her that she was more beautiful than she had ever been; towards the end of May he asked her to marry him. She did not say she would; she did not say she would not.

Alice had the sense that they were living on the lip of a volcano.

Nicola's safety lay in her not saying 'Yes' to David.

Nicola said 'Yes' to David.

They were in the garden of the cottage, under the walnut tree. Splashes of sunlight were spilled by the tree onto Nico's lovely hair.

'I still know I shouldn't do this to you,' said Nico. 'I was determined I wouldn't do this to you.'

'What changed your mind?'
'Funnily enough, my mother.'
'I thought she was against it.'
'She is.'

David digested this. He could make no sense of it.

David kissed Nico with passionate tenderness, leaning awkwardly over the wheelchair. He had never done so before: first, because it would have been premature; then, when it was no longer premature, because of Hugh; then, when Hugh was no longer there, because Nico was helpless, because it would have been unfair, taking an unfair advantage of her helplessness, a kind of rape. Now he drowned in the joy of kissing her at last, soft lips smiling under his lips, arms round his neck like steel bands.

Even as he kissed her, David was startled by the strength of Nico's arms. Then, even as he kissed her, he remembered that her arms were strong because she propelled herself in the wheelchair.

She said, into his cheek, 'My poor darling.'
'Poor is what I don't feel.'
'Saddled with a duvet or something. A useless doll. I feel selfish and guilty. I'm sacrificing your happiness to mine.'

David closed her mouth by kissing it.

'We must be very careful,' said Alice carefully.
'Why?'
'And say nothing about it, for the moment.'
'Why?'
'To please me. Is that a sufficient reason?'
'Yes, Mum. But why?'
'To please me,' said Alice again, with what could be seen as mulish and ill-tempered obstinacy, with what could be seen as terrified despair.

★

Alice and Nicola could say nothing about it; but they could not thereby keep it a secret.

David told his parents, because he would have exploded otherwise. His mother told a few old friends in her village and in Milchester, because she would have exploded otherwise. The Parkinsons saw no merit in secrecy; nor did anybody else.

'I expect you're quite right to do this,' said Felicity to David. 'You've thought about it and you know the score.'

David nodded and thanked her, as she wished him well. In his happiness he did not see the frozen misery of her smile.

Vi Cavenham recommenced planning Nico's wedding reception. It could not coincide with her twenty-second birthday, so Vi was planning that, too.

Nico never mentioned Hugh to David, nor to her mother, nor to Felicity.

But to Vi, Nico said, 'Now I have a feeling of coming home. Hugh was a journey to somewhere else, a lovely place but a strange one. I was emigrating. I wanted to then, but now I'm not sure I would have been happy so far away.'

'Hugh wasn't so bizarre,' said Vi.

'Compared to David, he was. I suppose at heart I'm just a cosy little homebody, happy playing safe. I never thought I was one of those, but I think I must be. Perhaps I wasn't one, and it's something I've become.'

As she went out of the house, she caught a glimpse of

herself in the Chippendale mirror in the hall. She looked beautiful. What they said to her was true. She looked happy.

A man was replacing one of the power-points, in the sitting room of Turner's Cottage. The switch on the wall was broken, Nico having sheered it off with the corner of her wheelchair. It was a simple job, but required a professional, an electrician who had come out from Milchester.
He had the cottage to himself. He was an old friend.
He answered the telephone three times, between 10.30 and 10.45. The callers all asked for Nico Maude. The electrician said that Miss Nicola had just gone off into Milchester, that she was shopping. Two of the callers were women, one a man. None left a message.

Who were those callers? Why did they want Nico? Why did none of them leave a name or any message?
Who else knew that Nico would be in the multi-storey car-park, just off the Buttermarket in the middle of Milchester, at eleven o'clock on Tuesday morning?
Besides the callers, three or four people. Three or four thousand people. Anybody who wanted to know. Nico's movements were no secret – could not have been, even if she had wanted. There had been no secrets about any bit of her life for fifteen months, since the February before last, since the accident. There had been secrets before that, right enough, but there was no place for that sort of secret in her life any more.
Eddie Datchett from the village helped her out of the car and into the wheelchair. Then it was plain sailing down successive ramps to the street.
How many people knew that she preferred the ramps

to the elevator? That she felt claustrophobic in the elevator, that she used it to go up but never to go down? Three or four people. Three or four thousand. The people she told, the people they told, anyone who saw her, anyone who asked, anyone in the world who wanted to know.

The place was dark, full of echoes, of distant noises amplified, the reverberation of a slammed door, the pulse of an engine four floors below. There was a smell of grease and exhaust fumes, of hot rubber and dust. There was nobody to be seen, just rank on rank of silent cars, and a forlorn little platoon of abandoned supermarket trolleys.

The wheelchair whispered over the concrete.

Eddie Datchett had disappeared on his own complicated errands. He would be back in two hours, punctual to the second. He often drove her and helped her. She liked that, because it was all he did. He did no more for her than she absolutely needed, knowing that that was what she wanted.

Was there somebody among the cars, a dark figure in the semi-darkness, dodging, bent, half seen? A sneak-thief trying the doors of the cars, looking for radios, purses, people's shopping? Cars were broken into in this place, as in many places. People knew that, and put valuables out of sight. Nico could hardly give chase to an active teenager, in her wheelchair among the parked cars. She stopped and looked and listened. There was nothing to be seen or heard, only the glint of chrome, the distant noises of the car-park and of the street outside and far below.

Eddie Datchett was out of sight and earshot. He would be in the fishing-tackle shop by now, picking over trays of dry-flies.

Nico gave a mental shrug, spun the wheelchair, and started to the top of the ramp. She paused on the very lip of the ramp, testing the brake.

She was aware of somebody immediately behind her, somebody who had materialized from hiding behind the cars, someone who moved silently and in a crouch. She felt a sudden huge shove, and the wheelchair began to fly down the ramp at a wild, sickening speed.

CHAPTER NINE

NICOLA HEARD A SCREAM WHICH was her scream. She saw the side of a parked van rushing towards her. There was an enormous clang; darkness and silence; voices; an overhead light in a calm white ceiling.

'A bit lucky,' said a man's voice which was not calm. 'A miracle.'

Nicola knew she had been pushed. This time she knew it was not an accident.

People heard the scream and clang. People gathered pretty quickly, and the ambulance was quick. Most of the dozen people who had been on various levels of the car-park gave their names to the police. Perhaps they all did. But perhaps one or more slipped away unnoticed, and got lost in the crowded streets.

The town was very crowded. Milchester was a place visited by coachloads of tourists in the summer, by Europeans and Americans and Japanese, as well as being the centre of a large rural population. Anybody could disappear into the throng, a local or a stranger. Anybody could be innocently in or out of the car-park. Ceaseless anonymous crowds brought their cars in, took their cars out, visited their cars to deposit bundles.

Anybody could go anywhere in the car-park, up and down and round, unseen, unchallenged, unrecorded.

Though Nicola was sure she had been pushed, a lot of people were sure she was wrong. By her own account, she had been poised just at the beginning of the slope. It was very foolish and thoughtless of her to adventure the wheelchair on those ramps. What were the elevators for? The people running the car-park should have a rule forbidding wheelchairs on the ramps. Probably there already was such a rule, and the girl had broken it. It did not make it any better that she was a local heroine. It made it worse, because she should have been setting a good example. There were people who talked like that, though not in the hearing of Nico's friends.

Alice asked the necessary questions, ever so casually. She did not want it known that she wanted to know. She did not want Felicity Peacock put on her guard.

She found out, and checked, and double-checked. There was no doubt. Felicity had been shopping that morning, somewhere among the shops of the town, in or near the Buttermarket, near the Cathedral, near the multi-storey car-park. She had come back to the Deanery with a basket of shopping, things from the chemist and the greengrocer, a couple of magazines, a book, a birthday present for somebody.

Nobody knew just when she had brought those things. How could anybody know? Nobody made a note of the time she picked up a magazine or paid for a lipstick.

Nobody could possibly know exactly where she had been, at the moment when Nicola was pushed. She said that she herself did not know where she had been, at that moment.

Alice was still the only person in the world who knew that it mattered where Felicity had been. And that it mattered where she would be in the future, every moment of the future, now that Nicola was going to marry David.

A miracle had happened. How many miracles could you expect?

Now what?

In the early hours of the morning, sleepless, Alice concluded that there were three options. David Parkinson could go right away and never come back. Nicola could go right away and never come back. Or they could mount a twenty-four-hour guard. None of these was possible. The third was the least impossible, the one that could be approximated.

Nicola told the police that nobody, as far as she knew, hated her enough to push her down the ramp of the carpark. She hoped she was right.

But she was not certain. She could not remember what she had said to Gerald Orchard, but she remembered his face when she had said it.

He was not adult; it was obvious from that proposal that he was not quite sane. He was idolized by his mother and ignored by the rest of the world. He had been brought up to believe that he was king, that he was entitled to everything; but the world had cheated, and given him a grubby little job teaching geography to small boys. And then Nico had cheated him. He was irresistible, but she had resisted. She had been dismissive, contemptuously rude. Nico was ashamed when she thought she remembered what she had said. It was unforgivable, and to a man like that it was dangerous.

This was all terribly unconvincing, but it was the nearest Nico could come to explaining the push.

She wanted some questions answered, but she was not in a good position for playing detective. She thought for a little, and then telephoned Felicity Peacock.

Felicity thought she was completely crazy.

'For one thing, people don't act like that,' said Felicity.

'Yes, they do.'

'Not in Milchester.'

'History's full of people like that, immature and unbalanced people driven mad by hurt pride.'

'Is he like that? I can't actually put a face to him. Are you sure I've met him? Anyway, if he's a master at that school, he must have been fulfilling his role as schoolmaster in the middle of a weekday morning.'

'Yes.'

'He was teaching away, filling their infant brains with wisdom.'

'Was he?'

'I'll find out.'

'Well, actually,' said Felicity later, 'he wasn't there. He had the day off. Nobody knows where he was.'

This was not for talking about. As an accusation it would be ridiculous, irresponsible, itself almost criminal. It was not a thing to joke about or speculate about or share with anybody, not her mother, not even David. What Nico had to do was keep quiet and be a bit sensible.

These were both boring prospects, but they were better than being murdered.

★

'Remember your telling me,' said Alice to Vi, 'that there was – that there had been – something between Hugh and Felicity Peacock?'

'Did I say that?' said Vi. 'How mischievous of me. I'm afraid it doesn't make much difference now, does it?'

'Yes it does,' said Alice. 'Felicity's origins ... Felicity comes from a ... as far as we know, she comes from a Southern background, doesn't she – Sicily, the Levant, somewhere like that? Where they have passionate resentments, jealousies, vendettas, a tradition of violence—'

'Does Felicity have a vendetta?' said Vi lightly. 'I would have thought she was too small.'

Vi began to talk about some changes they were planning in the garden.

Vi seemed not to hear what Alice was talking about, hinting at. It was strange. Vi was not usually dense. Alice was not usually mealy-mouthed, but she was held back from bluntness now by a sort of embarrassment. The problem had been there for fifteen months, ever since the revelation, because it was a revelation.

Yet, also, it was so obvious! The truth was in Vi's hands! She had not suffered the extra-sensory dart there at the bend in the road, but all the facts and all the logic were there in front of her. *Who else could it have been*?

And Vi knew that David Parkinson had taken up with Felicity Peacock. And that David was now engaged to be married to Nicola. That Felicity had been ditched twice. That Nicola was the reason both times. Vi knew all that as well as anybody – she knew everything locally as well as anybody, and she was better able than most to put two and two together. And she had never liked Felicity. And she knew Felicity had been 'shopping' somewhere near the multi-storey car-park. God Almighty, *who else could it have been*?

And Nicola had been saved by a miracle, and she was still going to marry David, and all the same motives held, the same hatred and bitterness and jealousy.

But Alice could not voice the new indictment as she could not the old one, over Vi's complete incredulity.

She could not voice it to Nicola.

Nicola's loyalty to her friends was absolute. It seemed to be typical of the young, her sort of young. The least breath of criticism was violently resented – some boy's manners, some girl's skirt; if they were your child's friends, you were best keeping your comments to yourself. All you did was drive a wedge between the generations. It was usual. Alice found that other parents said the same.

Probably all those kids defended, equally, their mothers against their friends. That was good, but it was no help just now.

Naturally Nicola was most defensive about her closest friends. Alice's cautious attempts to get her to be objective about Hugh Jarvis ... it was better to forget all that. Likewise it was no good Alice regretting out loud that Roddy Plumb wore odd socks, or complaining about the way Miranda Jolly ate the slice of lemon out of her gin and tonic. Nicola would not tolerate remarks like that about her friends.

Felicity? The very oldest and closest of all. Too close to see clearly. It was impossible that Nicola could draw back far enough from Felicity to see her properly. And if she had been able to do so, she would not have been objective. Loyalty would forbid that.

Loyalty was suicidal.

It would have been criminal folly, even so, not to have given the child some kind of warning. After what had happened, and what had nearly happened, she must be made to see that there was a threat.

To her mother's surprise, Nicola agreed immediately.

But she thought the threat came from another direction. Nothing would make her see where it really came from.

Nico agreed that there was a threat, that there had been, that there might be.

David said he believed Nico had been pushed, because she said she had. But it was obvious to Nico that he did not believe it. Even if he believed she had been pushed, he would not have believed it was Gerald Orchard. Nobody would. Flickie had refused to take the idea seriously for a second.

Gerald Orchard did seem an unlikely murderer. Nico thought that was exactly why he was a likely one. He was seen by everybody to be so pathetic, so inept, so harmless, so incapable of damaging anybody. Anybody perceived in those terms would want to prove himself different.

That face – that look in his face.

Nico said something about it to Vi, because she was used to confiding in her (some things). Vi did not know Gerald Orchard. If she had seen him, it was without knowing who he was or anything about him. It was therefore not as incredible to her, this theory of Nico's, as it would have been to the others.

That was odd – the person who did not know your suspect was the only one you could talk to about it.

Nico was a little embarrassed when she brought it out, partly because it was so very violent and medieval and melodramatic, and partly because the essence of the story was her own fatal attraction, together with that of the inheritance she would have, as they all supposed, when Hilary and Vi were dead.

Vi accepted that somebody could want Nico very badly, together with all Hilary's property. She listened seriously, which nobody else would.

But she did not actually believe, Nico thought, that Nico had been pushed.

It came from a familiar source, this new and peculiar item of information. It came from one of Vi's cleaning ladies, who went like Hoovers through the shops of the villages, picking up gossip like fluff, and emptying it at March Court in front of Vi and her visitors.

Felicity Peacock had been seen in a car in a car-park, with Gerald Orchard.

The story was told as scandalous. When couples sat in cars, everybody knew what they did, though not everybody understood how they did it. There were regular lovers' lanes just outside Milchester, which were places where couples sat in cars in the twilight.

Nico's reaction was one part indifference and two parts incredulity.

Milchester was the worst place in the world to be sitting with somebody in a car in a car-park, if it was meant to be a secret. Milchester was a village giving itself the airs of a city, and containing the worst of both. Felicity knew that better than anybody, having been a subject of discussion and speculation all her life. She would surely know better than to sit in the twilight in a car with a man, in the middle of the town, unless there was a completely boring explanation.

And if by chance Felicity did do anything so louche, it would not be Gerald Orchard she did it with ... would it?

It was known to the whole world that Felicity was the adopted daughter of a parson. She would be lucky to inherit £20,000. Gerald Orchard wanted more than that. The life he had designed for himself, politics and London flats and country estates, could not be bought for twenty times what Flickie would ever have.

She would not snuggle up to him, nor he to her.

Idly, with no more than mild curiosity, Nico asked Felicity about her mysterious assignation with Gerald Orchard.

'With who?' said Flickie blankly.

But of course she remembered after a moment who he was, because he sometimes sang with the *Cantatores*, and because Nico had been asking questions about him before.

'I haven't sat in a car with a man since I was sixteen,' said Felicity. 'And I didn't like it then, not in the front. And I had the sense not to get in the back.'

Felicity went away, as usual, before Alice got home from her school.

After the accident, during those months in hospital, they had given Nico sleeping pills. That was when the bones were being set and the rest stitched up. The pills were necessary. She could have continued taking them. Nobody would have disapproved. But she hated the idea. It was bad enough being dependent on people. It was odious to be dependent on little grey pills.

She had weaned herself off them, almost entirely, by Christmas. Now in midsummer she only took one when something told her, as it sometimes did, that she was in for a white night.

Time was, wide awake at three o'clock in the morning, Nico would have got out of bed and walked about the house. In this weather, she would have gone out into the garden, and sung very softly to the stars.

Wakefulness was all right, in those days, on those terms.

Now, again, she was sometimes caught unawares by sleeplessness. On these nights she tried to empty her mind, because of the midnight bitterness which knocked for entry into her skull. She tried not to think about horses in the dusk, on a bend of road under oak trees, or about naked bodies twined and writhing in a warm half-light in a secret place. She tried not to think about the sacrifice David was making for her, or all the ones her mother had made. She tried not to remember herself dancing and playing tennis.

She found herself wondering about Felicity Peacock and Gerald Orchard. She found herself frightened.

The house-hunting of David and Nico was greatly unlike that of Hugh and Nico.

It was accepted that Normandy would be most awkward for wheelchairs, elevators and such. Even if it were possible to flatten all the floors and abolish all the steps, the effort and expense were disproportionate. It was just not worth it. It would be better to find something suitable. When David eventually inherited Normandy, the question might arise again, but for the moment it could be put to one side. The thing was to find a house that could readily be made to suit Nico, and that was near enough to David's work.

David was trying to find time to do his own house-hunting, but Nico thought they could do with professional help. Tommy Johns was a friend of her mother's, and he was a local agent; his office knew about every property for miles round that was coming on the market, or might do so.

David and Tommy had barely met. David and his family had never in his lifetime wanted to buy or sell a property; and Tommy had almost no social life because of his wife. Tommy knew everything there was to be known about David, because Alice continued to use Tommy as a sounding-board for her hopes and fears (some of her fears). But to David, Tommy was no more than a face dimly familiar from meetings of the County Cricket Club and memorial services in the Cathedral, associated with tweeds and a Rifle Brigade tie and a look of patient exhaustion.

That Tommy was a friend of Alice was sufficient recommendation. It made it more surprising that they barely knew one another. David was impelled to wonder fleetingly what 'friend' meant. He thought it probably meant 'friend', but it was reasonable to hope not.

Tommy said, 'I know exactly what you want. I've been looking for weeks. I've found it. But I haven't yet persuaded them to sell.'

David was surprised at Tommy's exact knowledge of his needs and resources.

The property was unique. It was almost a joke.

In 1924 a man called Evelyn Dye came home from Australia very rich and with a passion for cricket and polo. He established himself on the edge of the village of East Brantham, six miles from Milchester, where he bought a cottage and some large, flat fields. In the midst of the fields he built a handsome pavilion, which was to serve both his sports. He installed himself in the cottage, quite snug, but he was more interested in amenities for his cricketers and polo-players than in comforts for himself.

The pavilion was capacious, sturdily built on one floor, somewhat Palladian in style, with a huge veranda and fine views and mains electricity, water and drainage.

The polo club was a casualty of the war, and the stables were converted for chickens and calf-rearing. One block was burned down by hippies in 1970. But the cricket survived in a scratchy, occasional form; caretakers camped in the pavilion, and opened it up for matches two or three weekends a year. Ownership by now resided with the Brantham Cricket Club, managed by elderly trustees who had retired to distant places. They were the ones Tommy had to persuade.

'It takes a bit of imagination,' said David, after half an hour prodding about in the pavilion under the incessant battering of the caretaker's wife's conversation.

'Use a bit of imagination,' said Tommy.

But David felt masculine and helpless, unable to visualize it as habitable, unable to tell which parts of the pavilion would become which rooms of a gentleman's house.

The caretakers used the kitchen, a bathroom, and one other room with two beds in it. There were eight other rooms under dust sheets; the air was musty and there were cobwebs over the windows. But the walls were dry and the rooms were full of sun.

Nico's special car at last arrived, a small grey automatic hatchback, the accelerator and brake on the dashboard. After a bit of practice, she could almost get out of the wheelchair and into the driving-seat unaided. Not quite. And, once in the car, she could not then fold and load the wheelchair into the back, or unfold it and get into it: so that either she was stuck in the car, or she needed a passenger, a helper; and if she needed a companion, what was the point of having her own car, of driving anywhere by herself?

Nico was the only person who thought on these lines, because she was the only one who truly faced how limited was the liberation given to her. She told Vi and Hilary, and everybody else, how marvellous it was, what a boost it gave her: what a psychological kick it gave her to buzz along a road under her own steam. It was partly true. And if she was going anywhere with help guaranteed when she arrived – any house of any friend, anywhere in the college, the bank, the museum, the village shop – she could turn up and toot the horn and wait to be rescued.

She went, and tooted, and waited to be rescued. Not long. They came running. They said they didn't mind, and it was obviously true, but Nico minded.

To Alice, it was easy to see what events had triggered the atrocities. Each was a milestone, the marking of a new phase. The sudden acts of terrorism were brought on by clear and obvious causes.

Nicola and Hugh had found a London flat, and they were on the point of signing the lease; the date of their wedding had meanwhile been fixed, and the place of the wedding reception. These things constituted an epoch, and they had caused the 'accident' at the bend in the road.

It all fitted, with everything Alice had heard and read about a psychotic personality, about the workings of a crazed resentment.

Sixteen months later, Nicola's engagement to David Parkinson was made known. This was another epoch. This was the salvage of a life, the miraculous recovery of a lost happiness. It caused the wheelchair to fly down the ramp of the multi-storey car-park.

And now Nicola and David had solved the problem that seemed so very difficult. They had found somewhere to live. It was odd but it would work. They were preparing to stamp that place with their combined personalities, call it home and their own, fly as a unit their flag over the roof.

It made an epoch, and the way ahead was a minefield. Alice did not want to let Nicola out of her sight.

But for hours of every day she had to; and now Nicola had a car. All day at school, Alice had one eye on the door of the classroom, waiting for a child or a teacher to come rushing in – 'Mrs Maude! Come quickly! Something terrible has happened!' ...

It came about, but not as Alice expected. No child ran into the classroom, no teacher; no cry was raised, no alarm; there had been no urgent message on the telephone, no policeman getting out of a car at the door.

Just a feeling.

It was only the second time in her life that Alice had had such an experience – a voice inside her skull that was no voice but only a kind of colour, a blood-red that was blacker than black, a deathly sickness, a certainty of evil.

This was new, this voiceless voice, because it was talking about the future instead of the past. It expressed the same hatred and terror as the voice at the bend in the road, but the terror was to come. It was immediate, close and rushing closer.

The voice said what Alice had been dreading to hear. It said that Nicola was in danger.

Alice was standing in front of a class of eight-year-old children, mostly girls, clean children with serious faces, one or two stupid, one or two naughty, two at least from broken homes and giving promise of neurosis – a normal mixture of the children of that age and place. Alice was telling them about the history of their own countryside, the valleys and villages they knew, the fields visible from the windows of the classroom.

'When the Romans came, this was all forest,' she said. 'Hardwood trees, the sort that lose their leaves in the autumn, oak trees and beeches and chestnuts. All the low ground was choked with great big ancient trees. If you'd been just here on the day that Julius Caesar came, and you'd looked out *there*, you'd have seen nothing but trees.'

All the children looked out of the classroom window. They saw a sweep of gravel with the teachers' cars, then a group of new pink houses; between the houses they could see a couple of sour paddocks, abandoned to rushes and thistles, a mixed hedge and a clump of hazels. It was a familiar view, uninteresting at the best of times, but the children stared at it because Alice was talking about it, because they liked her and often did what she asked, because looking anywhere was more fun than looking at the blank blackboard or the head of the child in front.

Alice looked out of the window, too, at the humdrum little houses and the glimpse of countryside; there was really nothing to look at, but with all the children looking out of the window it was impossible not to do so too.

'The people who lived here then,' said Alice, 'the Ancient British, hardly tried at all to cut down the trees and live in the ...'

Live in what?

What was she going to say? What was she talking

about? Who were these children? Why had they all turned away from the window to stare at her? What was this place with big windows and pale colours?

Alice was lanced by sick hatred and by terror.

Nicola.

Nicola was that morning going to the cricket pavilion in East Brantham. She was taking, or going with, her friend Miranda Jolly, in either her car or Miranda's; Miranda wanted to see the pavilion, and she was a very practical girl who understood about plumbing and wiring. Miranda was a useful friend to have. She was good at getting Nicola in and out of the car, in and out of the wheelchair, because she had done it many times. Miranda would look after Nicola as well as anybody could. Alice had come to school happy in the knowledge that nothing could happen to Nicola that morning.

What, then?

The car, they were in the car, they were going to East Brantham. Miranda beside Nicola in the car? No. Who, then?

Who was in that car with Nicola?

Absurdly, Alice looked out of the classroom window, as if on the gravel she would see Nicola's car and Nicola's companion. She saw the midsummer sun, the bland mid-morning sun, glaring off the roofs of the cars, off her own dusty car, glaring in the windows of the new little brick houses; she saw a great peace, no movement, no sign of life, at this moment when everyone was busy elsewhere...

Somewhere close by, outside the open window, there was the buzz and click of an insect. That was all. There was a rush of freezing air, of vaporized ice, through Alice's head, so that her hands trembled, and she felt that her face was trembling. The children were staring at her in silence, not understanding, perhaps frightened.

Alice told the children to be quiet, to wait for her, to read their books. She did not know what she said. They stared at her in frightened silence. She ran out of the room and out of the building. She ran to her car. Her hands were shaking so that she could not at once fit the key into the ignition. Somebody came running out of the building after her, a woman, a teacher, calling, asking what was the matter, asking if Alice had gone mad. That was unimportant. There was no time for any of that. Alice fitted the key into the slot in the dash and at last started the engine. She let the car too suddenly into gear, accelerated too hard, so that she started with a jerk, spinning gravel from the wheels and grazing a gatepost. Shouting followed her. She had no time to explain anything, and could not have done so. All of that could come later. The thing was to find out what was happening and stop it in time, to find out who was with Nicola and what they were doing and where, and stop them.

Miranda Jolly was not with Nicola. Somebody else was. That was what the voice inside her head had been telling her. Even as she drove madly to Turner's Cottage, Alice knew who was with Nicola.

The car screamed to a stop in the road outside the cottage. Alice jumped out. She left the engine running and the door open. She ran into the back gate of the garden. She saw that Nicola's car was not there, on the paved yard beside the cottage. Another car was there, some little foreign car of a make unfamiliar to Alice, not a car that she knew, not Miranda's car.

'Oh God,' said Alice aloud.

Old Herbert Miles was cutting the grass under the walnut tree, using the little electric rotary mower, which Alice had bought for herself to use, with the flex coming out of the kitchen window. Herbert had a key to the cottage, because he looked in if Alice was ever away. He came unpredictably to do the garden, and preferred cutting the grass with the little toy mower to other and more tiring jobs. He was a waste of money, but he was an old friend. He was a little brown man in heavy, baggy clothes, always the same clothes in all weathers, although he never showed any sign of being hot or cold, or being tired or in any hurry.

Seeing Herbert, Alice came to a sudden stop as she ran towards the house. She tripped and nearly fell over her own feet on the uneven brick-paved path.

She tried to speak, but for a moment no sound came.

'Miss Nico ben off in 'at foin new car,' said Herbert, speaking slowly, slowly, but answering Alice's question as though he had known she was trying to ask it. 'A-ben goen t' 'at new place, t' Brantham.'

'Who?'

'Miss Nico, 'course. 'Oom else?'

Alice stopped herself from screaming at him.

'Who was with Miss Nicola?'

'Um?'

'*Who was with Nicola?*'

'Oah! Along wi' 'oo 'at were ...'

Old Herbert frowned, a rearrangement of the thousand wrinkles on his face. He had never been much of a one for remembering folk's names, and now the system creaked worse than ever. Who was it with Miss Nico?

''At liddle maidie,' he said at last.

Alice again had to check herself. Only old Herbert would be able to tell her. He would only be able to do it in his own time. She struggled to keep her temper under control and her mouth shut; she prevented herself from dancing with agonized impatience.

"'At liddle missie,' the old man said slowly, slowly, 'd'be seemen furrin, loik.'

'Dark?'

'Ay!'

It was enough. It was the expected answer, and the worst.

Alice had heard Nicola on the telephone, telling Felicity about the pavilion, making it sound the biggest joke in the world that she should be planning to live in a cricket pavilion. Flickie must come and see it, said Nicola, immediately, at once, that very moment – or the following weekend, to be more exact—

Felicity, instead of Miranda Jolly.

'When?'

'*When?*'

'When did they go?' asked Alice, trying to speak gently, reasonably.

'Oah! What hour? Hoah! Mebbe a-ben hour sen.'

Oh my God. An hour. They had been at the pavilion for three-quarters of an hour, if they had reached the pavilion ...

It came to Alice suddenly that the caretakers were not there, that it was their day off – they would have driven to the coast, or to the other side of Milchester where their married daughter lived – that was why Nicola had made the plan with Miranda Jolly, to escape the conversation of the caretaker's wife ...

Nobody there. Nobody within miles.

Alice stood rooted, suddenly powerless, dithering, trying to think. What could Felicity do, after all? Her car was here, in full view – if not hers, a car that could be traced to her. Old Herbert had seen her go off with Nicola, just the two of them. If anything happened to Nicola ... But Felicity was insane, beside herself, betrayed and heartbroken – and she had already, with no more reason, with less reason—

Alice gave a single high, thin shout of fright, which took old Herbert by surprise and herself by surprise. She gasped some words of thanks to Herbert, and ran back to the car.

Even as she drove to East Brantham, too fast, dangerously fast, she thought that Felicity was cunning – she had inherited, perhaps, a streak of devious Levantine cunning, she had the cunning of the crazed, the obsessed, she would have the cunning of the cornered rat, every kind of vicious trick of self-preservation ...

Late morning now, noon, the midsummer sun glaring vertically down at the brambles of the roadside, the wild roses and the looping festoons of bindweed, the faraway downs beyond the river valley, blue in the distance – and now in the shade of the old cricket pavilion, the deep veranda and the dusty, deserted rooms—

Nicola helpless, imprisoned in that car or in the wheelchair ... Nicola entirely trusting her oldest friend—

For a moment, distracted by terrible thoughts, Alice seemed to have lost her way to East Brantham, to have gone wrong in the little blind lanes. The road she could see, the heavy trees, were totally unfamiliar. She slowed, uncertain, sick with anxiety. She had never before seen the road she was on. She rounded one sharp corner – there was another ahead – the brambles and bracken were piled high on high banks – nothing could be seen, no roof, no landmark – on or back? – she might be hurtling directly away from where she was desperately needed – but if she turned round, *that* might be directly away, and there was nowhere to turn in this horrible little ditch of a lane.

Turning. Signpost. Going too fast, she shot by it, missed the names, stopped, backed – then the names were strange, villages she had never heard of – she had overshot, by going too fast she had gone too far – there was no map in the car – oh God, which way—

The sun wheeled, the dust settled behind her, she drove on, round and round, utterly lost, seeing nobody, no house or farm, village, caught in an enchanted, accursed place with no signposts, landmarks, people, only the pitiless sun and the mocking flowers in the overgrown verges ...

Exhausted, sick with worry and with self-contempt, she turned a millionth corner and saw a remembered turning, and then the gate of the private road which led to the pavilion. The car bounced and juddered in the potholes; the big bullfinch hedge hid the pavilion until she turned the final corner—

There it sat like a toad, on the edge of the flat acres of grass, sun glaring on the slates of the roof, deep shadows under the eaves, no sign of the car, nobody here, silent and deserted: *where now?*

She had run the car almost dry. The red light was blinking, warning her.

Over her flooded a sense of despair and failure, a sickening sense of her own folly.

She had not saved Nicola.

God, perhaps, had given her full and adequate warning. She had been given every chance to save the child. But she was too late. They had come and gone. By folly, carelessness, crass stupidity, she had thrown the chance away, and Nicola was thrown away, and Felicity would get away with it.

Alice leaned her forehead on her arms on the steering-wheel of the car, and gave herself up to misery.

CHAPTER TEN

'THAT'S MY MUM'S CAR.'

'That's your Mum sitting in it.'

'So it is. Whatever is she doing?'

'Crying,' said Felicity Peacock.

'Hey, Mum!' called Nico from the driver's window of her own car, as she backed the car to park it beside her mother's.

Only then did Alice raise her tear-bedabbled face, and see a fathom away her daughter's beloved and beautiful smile.

Beyond Nicola was Felicity, in the passenger seat of Nicola's car. She also was staring at Alice. There was a strange expression on Felicity's face.

Alice was not concerned with Felicity's face, but only with Nicola's safety. She sat back in her seat feeling absolutely silly, and filled with such an explosion of happy relief that she was surprised to remain earthbound.

Of course they had not come straight to the pavilion. There had been a complicated detour, involving Miranda Jolly, and the reason for Miranda's absence, and the reason for Felicity's presence. The two girls explained, contrapuntally telling Alice how they had spent the previous ninety minutes. It was unimportant. Alice scarcely paid attention.

Miranda would come another time, to give her mind to the plumbing and wiring.

Felicity also would come another time, would be coming off and on for ever.

Alice had to get to a telephone, to apologize to her headmistress, to explain the inexplicable, probably to give some lame, invented reasons for her strange behaviour.

That was all right. It was not important. Nicola's safety was the only important thing in the world.

It was a weird thing to have happened. Admitted, described out loud, it would have been humiliating. It could not be described even to Tommy Johns: least of all to Nicola.

Alice was filled with a sense of her own idiocy, of the fool she had made of herself.

Wait, she thought. Wait a minute.

Those other things had happened. At the bend in the road something had truly happened, and in the multi-storey car-park. Alice had not invented them. There was nothing silly or fanciful about that death, those injuries, about the wheelchair flying down the ramp.

That motive was real. It was crazy but comprehensible. Alice had not invented that. She could not have done so. She could not have imagined such hatred unless she had in some telepathic way felt it, unless she had seen its effects.

And then there was Felicity's face, looking over Nicola's shoulder when Nicola stopped the car. Looking at Alice with an expression of . . . what?

The expression of somebody interrupted. Somebody thwarted in the middle of doing something.

★

Which still had to be done. Which she would do another time.

Alice had asked herself how the voice inside her head could be so wrong. But the voice had been right.

Alice's mental turmoil was bound to show itself a little. It was boiling so hard that it was bound to lift the lid of the pot, gush over the lip into view. She could not keep it bottled up, all this fright, all this certainty.

More or less involuntarily, she let something show to Vi. She always did; probably she always would. At least, she mentioned a name.

Vi did not seem to have the least idea what Alice was talking about. Rushed out of her classroom, jumped into the car? Voice? What voice? It was all far outside Vi's experience, Vi's imagining. Vi picked up a name, though. Vi had been hearing that name. What was it she had heard? Some scrap of local gossip . . .

'Oh yes,' said Vi, not really interested at all in what she was saying. 'The beady little number from the Deanery. My daily says she's hugger-mugger with—'

'Who?'

'Ah, who? Apparently it's been going on for ages, in a stealthy sort of way. A dim little man. Somebody astonishing, because she's such a dasher, if you like that sort of thing, which many do. Would he be called Gerald Apple?'

Alice took Nicola to March Court, to look with Vi through canteens of soup spoons and fish forks, shelves of surplus wine glasses, stacks of breakfast plates.

'They're only gathering dust,' said Vi. 'None of this stuff has been used in your lifetime. I daresay none of it's been used in my lifetime.'

Nico was embarrassed by the munificence of all this. She agreed to make a home for whatever Vi wanted to get rid of.

David came for Nico. They lifted her out of her new wheelchair, on the gravel in front of March Court, and into David's car. She took it calmly, hardly interrupting her discussion with Vi about the wedding. They were all used to it. By now it was nothing. Nico's face and forearms were brown and her hair was silver-gold in the sun. David treated her not like precious porcelain but like a girl he loved.

Vi watched, her face benign, her heart sick.

Nico had nothing, and she had too much. It was not fair. Vi had everything and she had never had anything. It was not her fault and it was not fair.

The leading personality of their lives that summer was the cricket pavilion. It was so absurd and so wonderful. Everybody talked about it that was involved. Everybody talked about it that was not involved at all.

The pavilion provided the scene, the reason, the mechanics of the new confrontation.

Vi's nose was rubbed in it.

Vi's nose was rubbed in other people's normalness, completeness; in her own misery and inadequacy, the half-life she had always lived.

It was past bearing. It was not fair.

To the pavilion Vi, that afternoon, brought Nico. It happened like that, as a matter of convenience. Tommy Johns came from his office in Milchester. David was later bringing Alice. There was to be a conference about the demolition of a party wall, the knocking of two rooms into one.

Vi, Nico and Tommy inspected the problem together,

and together suffered the amiable torrent of the caretaker's wife's conversation.

Vi had many times seen the pavilion before, but she had not often seen Tommy before. She had not more than met him, and that in company. She knew him to be an acquaintance of Alice's. She knew that he was respected professionally, and that he had had a tragedy in his life, and that he looked as though he needed a long holiday; nothing else. That day added nothing to that nothing. Tommy was there as a house-agent, and that was what he was being. He was advising about the structural implications of demolishing a wall. His voice droned pleasantly on under the yammer of the caretaker's wife.

Vi liked Tommy's style, neat but relaxed. He had the manners and appearance of a gentleman. He was exactly the same age as herself, she thought, just about fifty. She observed him closely without seeming to do so, under cover of inspecting the facilities of the ridiculous pavilion. He was compact, fit-looking; his clothes were inconspicuous but good; he had the kind of unconscious elegance that goes with an expensive education.

He was ten years younger than Hilary, two inches taller, two stone lighter, with more hair and a clearer skin and no bags under his eyes. He could obviously still do it. Vi wondered if he did do it, and if so with whom. He would be kind and patient, in the fashion of the very sexiest sort of man, the fashion which Vi had only imagined, which had dominated her daydreams all her life.

It came to Vi that she was in the presence of her last chance...

She became attentive to what Tommy said. She deferred to his opinion. She laughed mildly at his mild jokes. She was being kindly and sensible and unspoiled by wealth. Tommy's petals unfurled. Vi knew when somebody liked her, and she knew Tommy liked her.

He had very good hands, sensitive and capable. There was nothing those hands could not be imagined doing.

Vi asked herself why she allowed herself to be so attracted to a respectable stranger who was not in any way spectacular, whose magic was not obvious, who was not gifted or famous or even handsome.

The answer was obvious. Other people's love was being thrust under her nose. She wanted some herself. She had never had any and soon it would be too late. If shamelessness could have helped her, she would have been shameless, but she knew it was not the thing to be. She was doing all right as she was, being sensible and unspoiled and active and looking after the crippled niece.

Then Alice arrived with David Parkinson. Vi was expecting them, but she was not at all glad to see them.

Preternaturally alert to everything about Tommy Johns, Vi saw a change come over him. Nobody else would have seen it; he was probably not aware of it himself. He closed up. He became careful and distant. It was marginal – a tiny difference. There was no mistaking it. It was not David's doing, but Alice's.

Tommy disliked Alice?

On the contrary.

Tommy was hiding something because he had something to hide.

Vi clearly saw what was invisible, that Tommy and Alice had a special, close and secret relationship. What they did was not the point. What mattered was that Tommy felt for Alice what nobody had ever felt for Vi.

This, on top of everything.

Vi could not make out why she had known nothing of this. She had never seen Tommy and Alice together. Practically nobody, Vi supposed, had seen Tommy and Alice together. They were coy. How long had this been going on? Why were they so secret? Why had she never been told? Did Nicola know about it? Other people? A lot of other people? Everybody? Only Vi herself kept out, excluded, snubbed, not trusted? Was this another club that everybody in the world belonged to except herself?

'I asked you over,' said Vi, 'partly in order to talk about that cricket pavilion of yours.'

'Oh yes,' said Tommy Johns. 'I assumed Sir Hilary would be here.'

'Nobody's here.'

Tommy was a quiet man. He was not flamboyant, dominant, glamorous, a natural leader, a hero or jester, a demi-god or buffoon. He was shy and usually serious. He made a fair amount of money, but most of it went on his wife's nurses and hospitals. He entertained little and went out little. He was not a social lion or a wit or a celebrity. But nobody had ever thought him a fool.

This attractive, amusing Viola Cavenham was not grossly propositioning him, proclaiming her availability. She was putting out the most tentative feelers, no more than that. It was too much for Tommy.

Tommy was deeply concerned about Alice's daughter, although he knew her only slightly (the rarity of his meetings with Alice herself, their absolute apparent casualness, had prevented any closer relation). Had Vi Cavenham been necessary to Nicola at this moment of her life, in the finding and adapting of a house, Tommy would have felt obliged to think very carefully what he was at. Nicola's needs would have been his priority. But

Lady Cavenham was not at all required in the matter of the pavilion. Jacky Parkinson was not rich as Hilary Cavenham was rich, but he could certainly lend David enough money to buy the place. If David needed a mortgage, he could get one. It was quite a different ballgame from the Hugh Jarvis episode. There was thus no need for Tommy to use elaborate tact or double-talk. Good manners were necessary simply insofar as good manners were always necessary.

The decision that had to be taken, and that immediately, was how clearly his rejection should show. He would have liked time to consider this, but there was no time. He thought that Vi had better see and hear him say 'No'. Then there would be no more. That was important. There must be no more, or everybody would finish up embarrassed.

He said, 'I'm afraid there has been a misunderstanding. In the matter of the Brantham pavilion, there is nothing useful to be said at this juncture. I am in contact with the trustees and their lawyers, and nothing can fruitfully be discussed until we know if a sale is even possible.'

Tommy continued in this vein, at once gushing and repressive, until he got himself to the front door and out to his car.

His intention was to project layers of meaning. On top, he was saying that it was a waste of time talking as yet, because the terms of the trust might prevent the rump of the cricket club from selling. On the layer below the top, he was telling Vi Cavenham to mind her own business, because the Parkinson family were handling it and he was acting for them. Only at the layer below that was he telling Vi to belt up, saying that he did not want any part of what she was not yet suggesting.

★

Tommy was flattered, but he wished it had not happened. He was a little shocked, but only a little. He was surprised, but not astonished. It had happened before. He was not a great catch, but he was presentable, virile enough, and effectively unattached. The thing to do was what he had done – take evasive action immediately, unequivocally, as kindly as possible. There should be no misunderstanding, and nobody should be hurt.

Of all the presentable, unattached middle-aged men within reach of Milchester, why should Tommy Johns be the one Vi wanted?

Because he was Alice's. Alice had Tommy. Alice had everything. It was not fair.

Vi knew that Alice had grounds both logical and illogical for suspecting Felicity Peacock of acts of unthinkable ferocity. Her logical reasons were pretty good. Her illogical reasons were no good at all, but just as strong. Alice was not a fool, and she was completely convinced. As a result she was very frightened, not for herself but for the child.

Vi knew that Nico, for her part, had reasons for suspecting that Gerald Orchard had reacted with murderous violence to being rejected. This was partly as a result of a process of elimination – Nico reckoned that nobody else hated her. Vi knew it was amazing to Nico that Gerald Orchard hated her that much, but she was forced by logic into accepting that he did. It was not amazing to Vi. Vi knew about rejection. She knew about reacting with murderous violence.

Vi knew about unfairness, and what it made you do.

★

Vi imagined for most of her life that her infant experience was unique. She was very shocked to find that it was quite common. As to just how common, the newspapers reported violent disagreement – social workers, doctors, policemen, judges, child psychologists were all at one another's throats about it. Children were taken into care who should have been left at home, while children were left at home who were in the most acute moral or physical danger; everybody was right and everybody was wrong, and it all got a lot of publicity. Vi was appalled.

It was terrifying to think there were so many thousands of cases like hers.

Her mother might have saved her. But her mother was frightened. She was exhausted by her war work. She only knew about a little bit of it.

They lived in a room full of blue smoke that made Vi's mother cough. The furniture was upholstered in shining pink and green. It was hot. Nobody came into it except Father and Mother and herself. Outside the room was a passage with linoleum; outside again a street of small houses, with little sooty gardens and lace curtains in the windows. Some of the houses were missing, the bombsites like the missing teeth in Father's mouth. The war was still going on in her earliest memories, and everybody was involved in it except Father. He had nothing to do with it. His skin was yellow and his breath smelled, and he stayed in the room while Mother went off to work for the war. He stayed in the room with Vi, his little Vi, his rosebud, his consolation.

Vi could never thereafter feel, without wanting to scream, without wanting to be sick, a man's hand on her leg, a hand sliding up her thigh under her skirt, because her Father's hand had done that. It went with the smell of Father's breath, the smoke of his cigarettes, the colours of the chairs. Vi could never thereafter without nausea feel the tumescent pressure in the front of a man's trousers, because Father had made her feel the lump in his trousers. It gave her nightmares and stomach-aches. It was disgusting and frightening beyond anything else, beyond any sewage or disembowelled corpses.

Sometimes men in overalls came to see Father. They had kitbags or suitcases or cardboard boxes. Father sat with them in the kitchen, looking at the things they brought, in a cloud of blue smoke from their cigarettes. They never came when Mother was there, and she never saw them.

One day Mother took Vi out, all morning, to the place where she worked for the war. A lot of women looked at Vi and whispered. When Mother and Vi got home, Father had gone. There was a policeman in the room, who spoke to Mother. Whatever had happened, she had expected it. Vi never saw Father again.

They went away from the street of little houses, into a cream-coloured place called a hostel. It was very clean. There were other children, who did not talk to Vi. They were in the hostel when the war ended, when everybody went about with big grins, and Vi was allowed to stay up late. Peace was no better than war. Everything was still dirty except in the hostel, and there were not enough sweets.

Presently Mother said that Vi had a new father, and she must forget her first father, who had gone away and was now dead.

Vi's new father was not very nice, but he was better than the old one. His breath did not smell, and he did not do any of the secret things.

Vi had a little sister called Alice, who was scarlet and noisy and immediately the most important person in the world. Vi had never been very important, except to her first father, but now she did not matter at all. If she was noticed, it was because she was in the way. She was expected to knock things over, with the result that she did knock things over. Although it was not fair it was part of life, like sweet rationing and the smell of disinfectant in her new father's surgery.

When Vi was ten, people began telling her she was pretty. Mother and Father tried to stop them, but they went on doing it.

Vi was more and more often in trouble at home, from about this time, because everything she did was wrong while everything Alice did was right. Alice was a dainty little thing of about eight, tidy and polite and graceful, while Vi was becoming a teenager with a precocious bosom and clumsy, ill-coordinated movements and a kind of adolescent shyness that seemed rebellious. Even some of the teachers at school said it was not fair.

Boys began to want to feel parts of Vi's body. She felt sick, and sometimes burst into tears. The boys were cross and embarrassed, and told one another lies about her.

There were a couple of smashing girls who worked part-time at the grocer's, some years older than Vi, and they told her to keep at it. They said it was worth it. They said they hadn't liked it at first, but they'd got used to it and now they couldn't do without it. So she did try and it was still disgusting and it got her into worse trouble than ever.

Hands on her body smelled of Father's breath and his cigarettes.

It got to be war between Vi and her new father.

Mother had to take sides against Vi. It made Vi so edgy that she broke the cut-glass bowl which had been given to Alice as a christening present. It was a shame, and Vi was sorry, but it was only a bit of glass, not worth Mother's absolute fury.

Mother said, what did they expect? Vi was like her first father. He was a man who stayed out of the Forces with medical certificates, and never did a thing for the war effort. He made a dirty living when better men were being killed. He went to prison for receiving stolen goods. He committed suicide in prison. Good riddance.

It was the only time Mother ever mentioned Vi's first father, and she obviously regretted it the moment she'd done it, and she never did again, and refused to talk about it: except once, when she said she was forced into marrying him. Vi took this to mean that she had been pregnant, which, knowing her mother, was absolutely extraordinary.

She must have liked those things Vi hated.

Vi knew lots of girls at that time, in the middle and late fifties, when young girls were beginning to have a really good time. She had to keep up with them, and a bit over if possible. But there was that whole department of life she couldn't stomach. She knew that she was a freak, in that respect. In women's magazines and such, she had read enough amateur psychology to know why. It was not fair. In order to keep her end up, she put on a pretty good act of being fast and loose and liberated. It was the way to get asked to parties, the way to be admired and talked about. So a lot of boys were disappointed, and some of them said she was a fraud.

All this made life even more difficult at home. So as soon as Vi got adequate typing and shorthand speeds, she was off to London. Mother and new Father hardly pretended to be sorry to see her go.

She had a great time in London, exactly as she had expected. She was dark, with a high colour and a voluptuous figure. She may not have been fashionable, but she was desirable. She made the best of herself. She was a genuinely first-class secretary, which would have amazed them at home at Portsmouth, and she was soon earning plenty of money. She was popular in the office. She helped entertain clients. She dressed adventurously. She went to as many parties as she wanted. She had the knack of making people laugh. She had more admirers than most girls had hot dinners, and she laughed at them and teased them and fought them off when she had to.

As soon as she tried not fighting them off, as soon as she was lulled into intimacies, she felt terrified and sick and frigid.

She went home for Christmas. She still thought of it as home, and it was still the place to eat turkey and pull crackers. She saw that little Alice, now pretty well grown up, was a prisoner there, uncomplaining but exploited. Vi was truly sorry about that, but there was really nothing she could do.

She left for London feeling as though she had been let out of prison, and in that mood met Derek at an office function. He was really with it. He was getting his divorce. His company gave him a Jag. He was a man of the future, a meritocrat who was taking over the world, a man who had made it by ability and charm, without any advantages of birth or education; everybody said he was the man to watch, the tycoon of the future, the trail-blazer.

He suggested the trip to the Italian Lakes. He showed Vi the brochure, and it did look lovely. He introduced the other couple, who made it all respectable – Roland and Daphne, married, he an Account Manager at a big ad agency, she in fashion PR. They were fine. Roland made a bit of a pass at Vi the very first evening they met, but only as anybody might, not much more than instinct, just politeness; anyway Daphne never noticed.

Derek took too much for granted. He thought he was irresistible. He thought Vi was a pushover. He thought she had no pride, no dignity. He thought that because he was paying for the petrol he could undo her zips.

It seemed to Vi that Derek's breath smelled like Father's.

He sulked. He couldn't understand. He thought it was all an understood thing. Why the bloody hell had she come? Why did she think he'd asked her? What did she think they were there for, to eat spaghetti and look at the bloody view?

She tried getting drunk, but instead of making her amorous it made her vomit. That was really the end of the holiday, although it had another week to run.

Was it on the rebound from Derek, from the high-powered operator, that Vi found herself so drawn to Vernon Keegan? He was the first American she had properly known. He was the politest man she had ever known – so much so that he seemed to Vi the only polite man she had ever known. He was *not* high-powered. He was in public relations, but he was not at all like Vi's other friends in PR. He was more like a poet with clean fingernails, a nice priest of a gentle religion. He was old-fashioned, in a way Vi would never have excepted to admire. He was courteous to waiters, or would have been, if he could have afforded to go to places where there were waiters.

Vernon was rather a success in Portsmouth. The

family had never seen anything like him. Nobody had ever treated Mother with such stately gallantry. Vi was full of gratitude to Vernon, respect, admiration. She felt warm and welcoming to him. She thought her life was about to take a new and lovely turn.

They went for a country walk on a beautiful midsummer afternoon. And then he had to spoil everything. He was as crude as all the rest. He was a stinking, physical, greedy, slobbering, disgusting animal, with breath that smelled like Father's.

It was a shocking, a sickening disappointment.

That autumn, it was reported to Vi, little Alice had a follower. It was bound to happen. Alice was quite sweet, and getting pretty, much lighter than Vi, for men who liked the fragile look. And then, predictably, the monster of selfishness 'Father' sent the poor lad away. He needed Alice as a slave. Vi's heart bled. There was still nothing she could do about it.

She could do something about herself, and she did it in November of that same busy year: she got hold of the Honourable Colin Quin, the first Lord's son she had properly known, the first merchant banker, the first Old Etonian. He was adult, smoothly confident, sleek-haired. She knew that all his tastes were exactly right, in food and shoes and music, because they were his.

She was now, herself, in 1965, more unfashionable than ever, in that period of Twiggy and the rest, skinny little models with stick legs and no tits. Vi was a few years older than that, and she was no slimmer than she had been. She was a good armful; she was cuddly. She did not hide her curves (she could not have done so) nor her dimpled knees. There was very little she did hide. It did occur to her to wonder, fleetingly, if she were not sometimes a tiny bit vulgar for a gentleman like Colin

Quin, an aristocrat: but he seemed to like her just as she was.

She got it through to Colin, gently, insistently, that she was not the sort of person she might have seemed. She was fastidious. She was not one for sweaty clinches or gropes or familiarities. He was not to be misled by tight sweaters and mini-skirts. She was a lady, really, and he was to treat her with respect.

He did, and it was a great romance, and Vi gazed upon the Promised Land, and she was happy for the first time in her life, until he got drunk one lunchtime at a cricket match in the country, and pulled her behind a hedge on the boundary, and he was just as disgusting as the others, mumbling over her with wet lips, with breath that smelled like Father's ...

Little Alice about that time got herself attached to a little clergyman. As a matter of fact, the clergyman was worth a second look. Vi gave him a second look, but not a third. There was nothing there for her.

Vi had meanwhile buried her birth, her parentage, her name. None of it existed. She invented her origins. Since there was no other truth, her version was the truth. It was all ready in case anybody asked.

Vi played the field that year, after Colin had disqualified himself. She let nobody get close enough to do any of the things she hated. Men still asked her out to dinner, but not after the second or third time. They were not getting their money's worth. That was the year of her twenty-sixth birthday. One or two of her 'friends' teased her about being so very old. That may have contributed to the next event of her life, which took her by surprise, which she could not afterwards explain to herself – which was her marriage.

Charles swept her off her feet, but he did so respectfully. He had a bigger car than Derek's, and better manners than Vernon's; he was more aristocratic, properly speaking, than Colin. He took Vi to America. That was a good start. Because they were travelling, he was respectful all the time. There were always air hostesses hovering about. They went to Nevada, to Las Vegas. They were married there, in somebody's office. It was all quite legal, although it did not seem so. They went to a hotel in some mountains, into a honeymoon suite. There were flowers and baskets of fruit and champagne in a bucket. Vi rang the family in Portsmouth, to give them a surprise, to show off. They thought she would come to no good, and here she was. Charles was happy about paying for the call; he was still respectful up to that point and for another three or four minutes.

Vi had made a resolution that she would try. She gritted her teeth and tried. Other people could do it. But she could only try so far, submit to so much. More than that was still not very much, judging by things she had heard, but it was too much for her. What Charles demanded was obscene, impossible. He wanted to touch and to be touched. She had to run out of the room, to hang over the basin; she felt sick and terrified and the smell was the same.

Charles sent her back to England. He stayed in America. He was a bit sour about it. He thought he had been made a fool of. They were unmarried very quickly. Vi was still pure, in a technical sense. She always would be. It was a shame. It was a waste. It was not her fault. It was not fair.

And while Vi was getting unmarried, little Alice was marrying her little parson. He was made a Vicar, and they were given a Vicarage. It was all simply too twee and perfect, too good to be true. Vi made her London friends laugh when she talked about it.

Vi was busy picking up the threads of her life, and it was three months before she got down into the depths of the country to see the little bride and her parson.

She did not mean to pry or spy, or take anybody by surprise. She found the door open, and walked in. She found them together on a shabby sofa, pretty shabby themselves, holding hands. They were looking at one another, gazing, with expressions of the most unashamed and sickening naked lust. It was as though they were in bed, abandoned, giving an exhibition, doing all the things which people talked about, the thought of which made Vi sick. They were fully dressed and sitting on a sofa, but it was embarrassing and disgusting to see them looking at one another in that way.

It was all obvious. Alice could do it. Alice liked it. Alice had been doing it, and would be doing it again. For Alice it was successful, all that everybody said. Alice was a member of the club from which Vi was debarred. Alice was whole, Vi crippled. Alice was happy, Vi wretched. Alice had it, Vi hadn't. Alice could, Vi couldn't. It wasn't Vi's fault. It wasn't fair.

Marriage to old Hilary was all right, because he couldn't, and didn't want to.

Vi led a comfortable life, but it was only a bit of a life.

They found March Court. Why did they? Seeing Alice and her Barney together rubbed salt into Vi's wounds, but she could not stay away from them. She was fascinated by the sight of unmistakable sexual fulfilment. She was Tantalus transfixed by the jug of cool water. She got a kind of perverse kick out of seeing Alice's fingers tighten round Barney's, seeing Barney's quick, answering, understanding, loving, sexy smile.

It was natural that Vi should have ambivalent feelings about their child. She was a beautiful child, healthy and sweet-tempered.

Now Alice really had everything. The unfairness gripped Vi's bowels in the small hours of the morning, so that she lay rigid with her fingernails drilling her palms, so that she had to bite her pillow to stop herself screaming.

Alice had a full life. Alice and Nico. Alice had tenderness, and orgasms. Alice had everything. It was not fair.

Vi decided to take Barney away from Alice.

CHAPTER ELEVEN

VI DID NOT CLOSELY EXAMINE her own motives. She was not introspective, and being rich had got her out of the habit of self-doubt. It was enough that she knew that God had been unfair, and that she could put that right, and that it was high time she was given a little of what all the others had.

She devoted her mind more usefully to what she was good at: the practical aspect, ways and means.

What could she give the little man that Alice could not?

The obvious answer was money. That was a help, but only a bit of a help. Cash as such would buy nothing. Barncy was not for sale. He did not have enough sense for that.

What he would appreciate was single-minded devotion to something, to a cause – the giving of unlimited time and energy and concern and love and money.

Alice had some of those things, but not time or money. She had a big house – old, cold, difficult to keep clean – and very little help; she had an active five-year-old child; she had all those parochial carry-ons – Young Wives' Group and Girl Guides and Women's Institute and Bible Class and Red Cross and Church Coffee Mornings – and she could not focus on Third-World children (or whatever chose itself) as such a cause deserved. She could hardly focus on anything: she could hardly stand still long enough to hear the end of a sentence.

There must be times when a man wanted a companion who could stand still for a minute? A labourer in the vineyard who was also a listener?

Was it not almost a question of manners?

Would not more, honestly speaking, get done with less rushing about, a less frenzied display of non-stop activity? Was it not verging on the counter-productive, being so busy that everything was scamped? Was it not a case of visible effort being an end in itself? Might not a cause truly benefit more from a little concentration, a special devotion?

Not that there was any need to say anything negative. He would appreciate the contrast. He would not need it pointed out to him. At least, not much.

There was no tearing hurry. Vi was only thirty-four, Barney a year younger. Vi could take things gently, step by delicate step. It was not a grab she was planning, the snapping of steel jaws, but the spinning of an imperceptible web. He would be captive before he knew that anything was happening. He would be happy in his captivity. He would be dependent and grateful, and he would not want to go home again.

Vi took weeks finding her cause. She wanted one that was not quite obvious, not already represented in Milchester and the villages by the busy khaki-faced women who went round with collecting-boxes and organized jumble sales.

She fixed on an educational trust for the disadvantaged. It was a good cause, all right. Vi was shocked when she read about the levels of illiteracy, the reading problems of children from homes without books, from the one-room families with the TV on day and night. She allowed herself to be convinced about the need for remedial training outside the curricula of the comprehensives. Oh, there was much to do. The government should have been doing it, but it wasn't. Ill-trained teachers were only part of the problem, finance only part, inherent problems like dyslexia only a part. There was much to do, and Vi very quietly rolled up her sleeves to start helping to do it. She became a member of the organization, giving them a five-year covenant, putting herself on their mailing list. She asked for and got a catalogue of books on the subject, by educational psychologists, sociologists and such; she got reprints of articles in specialist periodicals, some of which were translated from German and other languages. She became an authentic expert in the field, though none of her knowledge was first-hand. She did all this silently and invisibly. Nobody knew that she was concerned in the matter, except a couple of unpaid secretaries in London.

She gave them more money. She went to London for meetings, saying she was shopping or having her hair done or lunching with a schoolfriend.

Hilary knew that she was concerned with a charity, but he was not surprised or curious. For him it was as natural as breathing. He had been closely involved with a number of charities all his adult life.

Vi assembled a shelf of books and a deskful of reports and papers. They were unobtrusive, unmentioned. She arranged for Barney to glimpse them. But she would not discuss them, changing the subject when he asked. She would not answer Alice's questions. She was doing good by stealth.

She was living the role.

She let all this sink in for many weeks.

Then she moved into a new phase. Without fuss or fanfare, she became County Secretary of the organization, in charge of fund-raising, publicity, arranging meetings, getting speakers. Only then did they all realize what she had been doing all those months.

Now, and only now, she recruited Barney.

Now, and only now, he became privy to the single-minded devotion with which she had become a key and caring pillar of the organization. He gave her some of his time – of course he did – contributing his expertise in communicating religion and morality to the young.

'You've got the sharp-end experience,' Vi said to him, and she got him to contribute an article on religious education to the newsletter. Hesitantly, apologetically, she asked more and more of him. He became ever more closely involved, over a further period of months. Often when they conferred there were other people present; often not. She was a different person at those times, a gentle and self-mocking humour not hiding her deep seriousness.

Alice, of course, was all this time cooking and cleaning the big cold Vicarage, and looking after Nicola and the Bible Class and the unmarried girls in the village, all whizz-bang-rush from one thing to another.

Barney never came out and said to Vi, 'I used to think you were selfish and frivolous, but now I see that I was wrong.' He did not say it quite like that, because he was too polite to admit that he had ever thought disparagingly of her. But he said enough to satisfy Vi that it was working; and his eyes said more than his voice did.

It was fascinating, the patient working out of her plan. It had the elegance of chess.

Even as County Secretary, Vi played down her role in

public. Even when she was taking the chair at meetings, she was unobtrusive as possible. In this she was in sharp contrast to all the other do-gooding important bossy committee ladies in and around Milchester, who had feuds and wrote to the newspapers and scrabbled for personal publicity. Vi never mentioned the difference. Barney could not fail to notice it.

It became part of Barney's routine to meet Vi, sometimes with her colleagues; in his frantically busy life it became a regular fixture no less important for being relaxing and enjoyable.

If a thing became habitual, it became a part of life. It became necessary.

Ever so gently the sticky gossamer was invisibly encircling Barney, round and round, and he liked it and valued it, and it was all in a good cause.

Vi was more than ever certain that if it was going to work with anybody, it was going to work with Barney. Take off the dog-collar and there was a breathing, warm-blooded physical man. She had always seen that this was so, from Alice's face, from a thousand signs. Now she felt it. She felt a responsive surge from her own blood, from her own secret and essential juices. The earth would move, the horizon lurch. She would come at last by the birthright of which she had been cheated.

And redress the unfairness that had embittered her life.

And all in a good cause.

She knew he knew.

She knew now that he was excited, that he was waiting as she was for the moment. They would know when the moment came, both of them at once. The spark would jump, the fingers meet and twine. She had read about that. Probably no words would be spoken.

Full understanding would flow between them, a hot two-way tide of desire.

Vi would do nothing to anticipate the moment, to hurry it roughly along. She would not jump the gun or startle him. She had waited and prepared for so long that she could wait a little longer. They would know.

They knew.

She knew, and it was obvious to her that he knew.

Extraordinarily enough, the occasion was a programme on the television, a serious documentary about the educational problems of the inner cities, classroom violence, ethnic minorities, the poverty trap. Their organization had been consulted by the producers, and was generously credited in the titles. The membership had been circularized abut the programme; everybody was to watch it. Vi and Barney watched it with Roland and Carola Berry and Joan Clapham in the Berrys' house in Milchester. They and Joan were great supporters of the cause and admirers of Vi; Roland had recently become Hon. Treasurer of the county branch. There was no particular merit in their watching it as a group, but they did so in a spirit of membership and togetherness. Roland and Carola provided drinks and smoked salmon sandwiches. It was July, a fine evening after a long hot day.

They sat in front of the Berrys' twenty-one-inch set, Vi and Barney by pure chance on a sofa which was a little behind the chairs of the others. It was a small sofa. There would not have been room for anybody else. They were not crushed together, but they were almost touching, their hands and knees and hips.

It was warm. The women wore cotton dresses and the men lightweight casual summer clothes. Barney was neat as always, but he was not dressed as a parson and did not look like one. It was beginning to get dark when the programme started, but Carola Berry had not turned any lights on, and did not do so.

There was a bowl of roses on a table beside the sofa, dark red turning to black in the dusk, and white blossoms which were almost luminous. Their scent filled the room like a blessing; it was the roses and their lovely perfume that made Vi realize what evening this was.

The screen flickered and yawped, and she pretended to pay attention. Her hand was on the cushion beside her. Against her finger she felt his finger, his living flesh. A bolt of electricity crashed from his hand to hers, up her arm and into her breast and belly, a surge of erotic tide which had been building for so long.

She did not move her hand, nor he his. She made no effort to grasp his fingers. She expected his fingers to move, but his hand, just touching hers, lay motionless on the cushion between them. He was right. There was no need of gesture, of the banality of hand-holding. The voltage slammed between them. She felt his vivid excitement in the motionless magnetic contact of one finger.

So they sat for three-quarters of an hour, the others' black heads silhouetted against the screen, the square blue eye blinking and flickering irrelevantly, the voices chirping and groaning unheard, the scent of the roses like an overwhelming canopy, like a command from God, the immediate future full of gold and scarlet.

Hilary was in London. The Portuguese were on holiday. There was nobody at March Court.

Vi had never felt this physical yearning, this mixture of intensity and relaxation, of excitement and a feeling of safety, this specific desire for the very things which had frightened and disgusted her, which now she wanted with sweet agony and urgency, because it was him, his hand, his body ...

It seemed to her that his motionless finger was vibrating, humming against her finger like a tuning-fork.

For the first time she understood that strange Biblical phrase, that someone yearned upon another with his bowels. She yearned upon Barney with her deep secret places. For the first time in her life she felt lust.

She thought his breathing was more rapid, his pulse racing. She could hardly restrain herself from grasping his hand. But he was right: for now, this touch was right.

The programme ended. Roland Berry and Joan Clapham immediately began to talk about it. Vi could not have spoken. Carola switched on the lights. Barney joined in the conversation about the programme. Vi glanced at him, astounded by the normal tone of his voice. His hands were in his lap. She had not touched him. She had been touching a rubber bone left on the sofa by the dog. It had not vibrated. His pulse and breathing were normal. He stood up. He had not noticed the scent of the roses. He had not noticed Vi. He was interested not in her but in the television programme, in Roland Berry's conversation and in a smoked salmon sandwich.

That night, at three o'clock in the morning, Vi made a different plan. She would put right the unfairness in a different way.

She was in no more hurry than before. The chance would come.

She watched the Maude family, which it was all too easy for her to do. She watched the fulfilled and tranquil love which flowed in an almost visible mutual beam between Barnabas and Alice, and dancing about them Nicola, evidence and trophy of their love. Her resolution hardened every time she saw them, and she watched and waited for the moment.

Vi felt no ill will towards her little sister Alice, towards the sweet child Nico. There was nothing personal about her plan. It was simply a question of fairness. Probably if it was put to them, they would agree that something had to be done to redress the balance.

The organization, the County Secretaryship, became useful in a new way. Vi was gently amused at this serendipity. She could go where she liked, when she liked, on 'business'. Often she told people exactly where she was going, and why. She made it all quite dull when she talked about it; her errands became a bore. Nobody asked about her 'business', in case they were told.

She proofed herself against curiosity.

It became a local proverb – nobody knew where Vi was, she was so footloose, so busy with the organization, rushing from one end of the county to the other, and often at meetings in London, about which everybody, once bitten, was twice shy of asking. People began to say, 'My dog's quite a Vi Caversham,' meaning that it strayed; they even came to say, 'My spectacles are regular Vi Cavershams,' meaning they were always losing them.

Through all this, Hilary smiled and mixed himself another drink.

Barney planned to do something which he never did: he was going to London. He was going to do something there which he never did, which was attend a jolly reunion of his schoolmates in the banqueting room of an hotel. It was a thing other men did every year, but Barney had never done it before. It was said that he was looking forward to it, that he was excited.

It was a date in the middle of November. He was going up and down by train. He would come home by the 11.46, the last train from Waterloo to Milchester. It was possible, but unlikely, that he would catch the train before, the 11.07. If thick fog was forecast, he might make arrangements to stay in London. If even worse problems looked like arising, he would probably not go at all.

Vi did not have to pry to find these things out. She simply waited for them to come up in conversation. They all did. Everybody for miles round knew in a general way that the Reverend Barnabas Maude, who never had time to go anywhere, was going up to London for a dinner; anybody interested, and many not interested, knew all the rest as well.

Vi knew that last train. She had many times taken it, after meetings or the theatre. When Hilary dined in London, he stayed at his club, but not Vi. She could easily arrange and afford a bed in London, but she liked waking up in the country; that in spite of the last train, which was pretty depressing. It was dirtier and colder than the trains of daylight, its lights dimmer, its rattles louder; it was always practically empty, hardly half a dozen people spread between its half-dozen carriages. It was a train they brought out only when nobody would use it or see it, a dingy, ramshackle old train fit only for the huddled travellers of midnight. It was still, Vi always said, preferable to the exhausting slog of driving all the way home in the dark, and that after the hassle of trying to park a car in London.

The Maudes knew that Vi sometimes took that last train; that although gloomy, grubby, noisy and ill lit it got you at last to Milchester safe and sound, three minutes after one in the morning, so that you woke up fresh as a daisy in your own bed, to the sound of birdsong instead of traffic. The Maudes knew about that, and it was more than likely that Vi's example was what Barney decided to follow.

That was a pretty irony. Vi liked that.

The great beauty of Vi's plan was that if it did not work it did not matter. Nothing was lost except time, and she had plenty of that. She had lived with injustice for thirty-five years. She could survive another few months. She did not want to, but she could; and she would, rather than take any avoidable risk.

Things that could go wrong: Barney, for any of ten thousand reasons, deciding not to go to London. Barney driving instead of going by train. Barney staying in London and coming back by daylight, on a crowded morning train. Barney with somebody else, accompanied, in convoy, involuntarily finding safety in numbers. Vi herself somehow prevented from getting to Waterloo, missing the train, missing Barney. Any of those things and a thousand others put the whole project in the pending tray.

Vi was pretty fit. She thought she was stronger than she had ever been. She had been swimming all summer, and playing golf and tennis.

More important than her physical strength was her moral determination. She could move mountains. All she had to move was Barney.

★

It was a classic English November day, mild, damp, misty, windless: a day of sodden yellow leaves plastering the ground, of cobwebs laden with translucent pearls, of smoke hanging in the air: a day of deadened sounds, of trees and buildings looming half visible, of air dense with moisture.

Barney was catching a mid-morning train, after having done two hours' work. Vi knew all about Barney's train. Everybody knew about it.

Vi went off early, with a bulging briefcase and a list of appointments. Hilary had no idea where she was going. She said she had practically no idea herself. This was all just as usual, what had become usual. She said she would probably not be home until after dinner. She said that nobody was to wait up for her. This was also usual for Vi, the new committed Vi of meetings and good works.

Vi drove to Bodhampton, an industrial town on the main line between Milchester and London. She put her car in the enormous car-park, paying cash as she went in. She left the briefcase in the car. She bought a second-class return ticket to Waterloo, and arrived in London just as Barney was setting off.

Vi was not crudely disguised, in the way of wearing a wig or a false nose, in case somebody she knew recognized her. A red wig would have been difficult to explain. She wore a large old mackintosh, and a plastic hood over the beret on her head. These things were in the back of the car. They were not her usual London wear, but they could be explained. She had decided to protect her coat and hat against weather worse than she had expected. A bit of absent-mindedness came into it – the case of a very busy person grabbing whatever came to hand, with more important things on her mind than what she looked like. And she was rich enough to be eccentric, in the matter of old raincoats.

But she hoped to evade notice entirely. Looking obscure, scruffy, self-effacing, a provincial dowd going to London to do some early Christmas shopping, she became part of a drab crowd on a drab, crowded train, and on the concourse at Waterloo, and on the Bakerloo line to nowhere in particular.

She pottered anonymously round a couple of unglamorous department stores, keeping in crowds, going nowhere where she would be isolated, or where she would be known.

In the early afternoon she telephoned the Vicarage, just to be sure, from a box in the Piccadilly underground. In the voice of one of her daily cleaners she asked for Reverend Maude. Alice said the Vicar was in London, could be reached in the morning, who was that ringing, was there a message? In a creamy Wessex voice Vi thanked her, and said that Josie Fox would be glad of of a word, and might be ringing the next day.

Barney was in London, or London-bound.

The streets darkened early, because of the heavy grey clouds which sat on the roofs of the buildings. Lights came on, reflected by streets which were wet although it was not quite raining. Veils of damp hung in front of the lights of the buses, and curtained the brilliant windows of the West End shops.

Vi took the day gently, keeping away from Fortnums and Harrods and places where she was known. It was sufficiently amusing and exciting to be doing what she was doing, to be carrying out this marvellously simple plan which had been prepared for so long.

It was only fair.

He had not rejected the glorious offer which she had

made him. He had not rejected it because he had not noticed it. It was too much. It was, in the most exact sense, adding insult to injury. It would be foolish to have qualms. Vi was not foolish, and had none.

Killing the time, all that damp and soothing day in London, Vi exulted in the awareness of righting a great wrong.

She went back to Waterloo early, far earlier than the last train, just in case he caught an earlier one.

There were other people waiting. She was inconspicuous. She waited for a long time. But it was not boring, because she was excited.

She felt strong and determined. She had right and fairness on her side.

At eleven o'clock the station was pretty quiet. Trains were still occasionally rattling in, but few people got off them. There were still a few people waiting like herself, and others not waiting for anything. The bars and bookstalls were shut, the music silenced.

The misty damp seeped into the huge interior of the station, so the lights were softened and the distances dimmed, footsteps and the rumble of wheels a little muffled, the vaulted ceilings invisibly high and the hands of the clock unbelievably slow.

He did not catch the 11.07. Few people did – not two dozen: damp and drab passengers who did not look at one another. Vi watched them without seeming to do so. Her evening newspaper had been gradually dampened by the air. She gripped it tightly as she watched the passengers through the barrier onto the platform, her own ticket ready, her mackintosh collar high round her neck and her plastic hood low over her face. Tension made her almost mash the damp newspaper in her fingers. She inspected the ruin with dismay. She was edgier than she had realized. She told herself to relax, or she would give herself nervous indigestion. At least, she thought whimsically, it showed that her hands were strong.

She had read all through the newspaper over and over again, without taking in a single word. There was only one more train. She would take the last train anyway. If he was not on it, if he had collapsed or decided to stay the night, it would be a dreadful anticlimax but not worse than that. But Vi thought she would see him within half an hour. She felt suffocated by suspense, but sustained by rage and by her sense of justice.

The great clock slowed so that twenty minutes took twenty hours, the next five minutes five days. Vi did not know whether to hold on to her newspaper, now a wet, crumpled ruin, or put it in a bin. The tiny dilemma loomed enormous. However disreputable, the newspaper was a kind of disguise, a *laissez-passer* in this place, a curtain to hide behind. On the other hand, it was covering her gloves with ink. She suffered her first attack of indecision, the newspaper shredding limply over the platform. She threw it away. Suddenly she felt naked, exposed, glaringly and guiltily visible. She retrieved the newspaper from the bin where she had dropped it. She saw a man looking at her oddly. She walked self-consciously away, and made a wide circuit round the station.

Eleven-thirty. The last train was there, silent and scruffy beside the interminable platform. It was only half the size of a daytime train. Solitary travellers, very few, were boarding the train almost furtively, as though expecting a hand on the shoulder.

Eleven-thirty-five. Barney was not coming. He was a

man who would leave an absurdly generous amount of time. Barney had never missed a train in his life, or any other appointment – he was the kind of well-organized prig who was always first in the queue. Vi would give him another eight minutes, and then get on the train herself.

They were crawling, week-long minutes, in that huge, dead place. The air was colder and damper. The station was still functioning, but reluctantly, as though the people were intruders, as though they were all too late.

Eleven-forty. Six minutes. There was no reason for the train to be delayed; there had been no announcement about that, no sign put up. It was not seriously foggy. It was not freezing. The train was going to leave on time. It was going to leave without Barney.

Vi suddenly felt tired, bottomlessly tired and enraged with the futility of the whole day. Why couldn't people do what they said they were going to do? It was bloody inconsiderate. Vi was betrayed again, by thoughtlessness, by selfishness. Her feet were sore and her legs aching, from all the walking and hanging around she had been doing. She could feel that the damp, polluted air had crept into her sinuses. The sandwich she had eaten for lunch had been compressed and ossified in her stomach by tension, by suspense and anger.

There was no need for any more concealment. He was not coming. He had made other arrangements. It did not matter who saw her. Vi pulled the ridiculous plastic hood off her head; she turned down the collar of her mackintosh, which had been making her look like a sleazy reporter in an old film. In a rage, but in her own person, she showed her ticket at the barrier, and started down the platform.

There was a small commotion behind her, of somebody trying to find a ticket. A soothing voice, a garbled apology. Vi stopped, turned, looked, and bolted into the train. Barney was walking unsteadily along the platform, a neat bald man holding his elbow.

Vi hid behind the messy remnants of her evening paper, and watched Barney walk by. He was frowning, making the gigantic effort to walk straight, to be dignified. He was wearing a dark overcoat, and a woollen scarf which fortunately covered his clerical collar. He was hatless and his hair was disordered.

It was astonishing. There was no doubt about it. Nobody had ever seen such a thing before. But then, Barney had never been to that sort of party before. Vi understood how it must have been – 'Here you are, old boy – nonsense, this is on me' – and probably Barney had drunk three or four martinis before he knew what had hit him, four or five glasses of wine, port ... At home, he might go for a week without having any alcohol at all; even at March Court he would have one small glass of sherry, perhaps, and one glass of wine. That was quite enough for him. But a mood of reunion, a press of familiar faces long unseen, a crowd of successful men delighted to buy one another drinks ...

It might make things easier or more difficult. Sometimes people became obstinate and surly. Possibly Vi ought to have predicted it, but she had not at all done so.

Someone at the dinner had known that Barney had to catch a train, had found out what train it was; the reliable bald man had helped him into a taxi and was now helping him into the train.

Travelling with him? If so, everything was again hanging in the balance.

Vi opened her window, and poked her head out. The train was due to go. Barney and the bald man were shaking hands, on and on, Barney probably apologizing at ridiculous length. His friend opened a door and pushed Barney towards the step. Barney climbed without mishap onto the train. The door slammed. It was the carriage next to Vi's. It was almost empty. Barney immediately leaned out of the window, to renew his thanks and apologies. Vi could not hear what he was saying, because the train had started to hum and shudder. The bald friend smiled and made deprecating gestures.

The train gave an electrical hiccup, and a groan, and started; it began to sway and rattle as it accelerated along the curve south-west of Waterloo.

South-west London rattled by in the dark – Vauxhall, Nine Elms, Clapham Junction – splashes and pinpoints and flares of light glimmering wetly through the mist.

Peering round the seats, Vi looked to see who else was in her carriage. There was an oldish, greyish man gustily asleep; a young couple with a gipsy look, the girl whispering furiously, the boy staring apathetically out of the window; another young man almost asleep, his head lolling, his mouth open. That was it.

Vi put her plastic hood on, and raised the collar of her mackintosh. She was still not really in disguise, but anybody who described her would describe somebody other than herself.

The train bounced and swung. Vi moved inconspicuously down the central corridor of the carriage, holding on to the backs of the seats as she passed them. The whispering girl might have seen her, but it was certain that none of the others did. It could be assumed that she was going to the loo, or looking for a part of the train in which she was allowed to smoke.

She stood for a moment on the bouncing platform

between coaches. It was dark. The noise of the train was louder. She looked through the grimy window into the next carriage. She seemed as she stood on the bridging platform to be in the opposite mode to the next carriage – she swung to the left when it swung to the right, so that each swing seemed twice as violent and the train likely to sway off the lines.

Three yards away a fat woman sat with a fat leather bag on her lap, the bag and the woman's knees and chins all swaying and bouncing with the train. Her eyes were shut, but little convulsive movements, clutching at the bag in her lap, showed that she was not asleep. She was facing down the central aisle, facing directly at the door behind which Vi stood.

Two seats beyond the fat woman was Barney. He had his back to Vi. All that was visible was his right arm, lying along the arm of his seat. His sleeve was not so very distinctive, but there was no doubt that it was his arm. He was probably dozing; perhaps deeply asleep.

There were other people beyond, but well beyond. They were invisible to Vi, but could be located by coats and cases in the racks over their heads. There were four people, maybe five, all at the far end of the carriage.

Vi twisted the knob of the door immediately outside the carriage. It should not have been possible to open the door when the train was moving, but it was. To make it impossible was a safety precaution not yet general, an expense not yet everywhere undertaken by British Rail. This dirty, sub-standard late-night train had doors that could easily be opened even when it was going its fastest.

Vi opened the door a crack, to make sure that it was possible, that it could be done quickly and with one hand. She shut it again at once. The wind of the train's motion tried to wrench the door out of her fingers, to slap it open against the side of the carriage. The action of the handle was smooth and easy. Somebody had been oiling the lock. That was very good.

It was dark now outside the window, the outer suburbs here and there showing the flare of an office-block or supermarket, the beam of a headlight on a wall. Buildings and bridges rattled past the window, black on black.

Vi went on into the carriage, and gently past the fat woman.

She came to Barney's seat. His arm was no longer lying along the arm of the seat, but limply hanging over it, wagging from the elbow with the bouncing of the train as though he were a dummy or a dead man.

It was funny that such an appearance could anticipate reality.

Barney's mouth was open. His face looked yellowish and damp, as though the clammy mist outside the train had come in and settled on his skin. He looked strangely raffish, his scarf rucked round his ears, his hair on end. He was breathing noisily.

Vi thought he would have a headache in the morning. She corrected herself with an inward snort of laughter. Barney would not have a headache in the morning.

She took off her plastic hood and pulled down her collar, so that for Barney's benefit she resumed her normal personality. She sat down beside Barney. They were not visible to anybody else in the carriage. She shook Barney by the shoulder.

He surfaced slowly, from the depths of his boozy sleep. He focused with a frown, gradually.

'Vi,' he said at last, not very surprised, not so very drunk.

'Alice is in the next carriage,' said Vi. She spoke

softly, so that the others would not hear. She spoke too softly: Barney did not hear. She raised her voice, unhappy to be shouting over the rattle of the train. She said that Alice was further along, that she was waiting for him.

'Alice,' said Barney thickly. 'Home.'

'Here,' said Vi. 'Next door. Come along.'

'Come along,' agreed Barney, blinking and swallowing, and looking in a puzzled way about him, as though perplexed by this strange upholstery, these unfamiliar windows.

Vi stood, and helped Barney to stand.

With her free hand, Vi pulled up once again the collar of her raincoat, and pulled the plastic hood once more over her head. Since Barney had seen and accepted her, she could resume her anonymity. Barney looked surprised at her new appearance. Vi moved out into the aisle, and pulled Barney with her. He came docilely, not apparently wondering why Alice did not join him, not understanding why she was on the train but not incredulous, probably not remembering why he himself was on the train.

Vi did not know if the fat woman saw them. She could not have seen Vi clearly. The person she saw, if her eyes were open, was huddled in a big scruffy mackintosh, and crowned with a cheap plastic hood. That was not Vi. It was somebody quite different. It did not matter if the woman's eyes were open or closed.

They went into the rackety, rocking space between the carriages, and to the door Vi had tried. There was more noise here. It was dark. The black countryside rushed invisibly by. The train was going fast, through unrelieved blackness, through the valley of the shadow of death.

'Come on,' said Vi.

She opened the door and pushed Barney out of the train.

She tidied herself, and went back to her seat. The gipsy girl might have noticed her return, but nobody else had seen her at all.

CHAPTER TWELVE

SITTING DOWN, VI FOUND THAT her hands were shaking. That was bad. She deplored her own weakness. It was to be ascribed to physical effort rather than to nerves. She clasped her hands in her lap to keep them still.

That was where Barney's hands had been, when he sat beside her on the sofa. She did not like hands in laps.

Vi took her hands from her lap; she sat on them, to stop them from shaking.

She got off the train at Bodhampton, with four or five other people from various parts of the train. The gipsy girl perhaps saw her get out. Nobody else looked at her. The man who took her ticket did not look at her.

She found the car and started it and drove home.

There was a light in the hall, and in the drawing room. The house was infinitely welcoming. The warm colours and the warm air seemed to cosset and congratulate her. There were drinks on a tray. She did not usually have a nightcap, but this time she thought she deserved a little whisky.

Now that things had been squared off, it was Vi's duty and pleasure to do everything in her power for little Alice.

Hilary helped also.

Alice had joined the lost legion, the sisterhood of the loveless, the company of the unaroused, the women who slept alone. She qualified for kindness.

The illiterate children had lost their relevance. Vi eased herself out of that situation, pleading the needs of Hilary, Alice, Nicola, the village, her own health. It was better so. The children needed more attention than she could give them. Vi's charity began at home; there she was unstinting, as her nature was.

Mother and daughter grew up together in Turner's Cottage, in which Vi had installed them. They lived dependent on Vi for everything that mattered, for comforts and social opportunities, for glimpses of the larger world.

All those years, Vi watched Alice. Alice was not getting it. Vi would have known. The light was gone from her eyes, the unfair, intolerable light which had driven Vi half-mad. Vi was content.

Vi watched Nicola, too, as soon as she entered adolescence. They all said what a beautiful girl she was. Was anybody chaste any more, any teenager? Nicola was. She was protected, fenced, kept under lock and key. There was one dangerous influence – that little wog tart adopted by the Dean of Milchester – but in spite of her, Nicola lived in virtuous solitude. She had better go on doing so.

There were parties in Milchester. Everyone was a risk. Vi searched the child's face. No flame was lit.

Italy was a risk. Vi searched Nicola's face and her conversation when she came back, and she was satisfied that no flame had been lit. There was no knowing what she had allowed herself, but no great bomb had been exploded.

Then came the man Hugh Jarvis.

Vi had met him – seen him – while Nicola was abroad. She understood that he would be a man for the girls. He was tall and sleek. He was like an otter; he was like the Russian sables which Vi nowadays kept in store, dark and luxurious and beautifully understated. Vi did not then speculate about the effect of Jarvis on Nicola, since she was a thousand miles away.

But when she returned, so did Jarvis. It was inevitable that they would coincide; with hindsight, the result was pretty well inevitable. The child was looking wonderful, better than ever; he was undoubtedly a dish. They met at some kind of typical Milchester function, something arty, at which it was probably a relief to find a distraction. They both found one, all right. Somebody who was there described their meeting to somebody in a shop, who reported it to one of Vi's cleaning ladies, since it concerned, so to say, one of the family, who naturally reported the news to Vi. Vi could visualize the meeting, unfortunately, as clearly as though she had been there. Dark and fair. Both slim, elegant, simply but excellently turned out (Vi was a judge of that); both intelligent and amusing. For her, he would have had the fascination of his worldliness, his high metropolitan gloss. For him, she would have had the charm of innocence.

Nicola was confused, embarrassed, not displeased to be teased about Jarvis, after that single meeting.

And then.

Vi saw. Even Alice could see. A mole would have seen, a blind creature blinking in unaccustomed sunlight. The girl had a silly grin and a constant blush. Her expression was a mixture of guilt and pride. She was almost blatant about it.

This little chit, hardly out of her teens, had already graduated.

They had done it and it had worked. That sudden, involuntary, remembering smile was the ultimate give-away, and it caused a lump of sick envy to rise like a jellyfish in Vi's throat.

Disgusting, abandoned slut.

It was not fair.

There was the chance that the affair might end in tears, without anybody taking a hand. First love, so intense, such a revelation, was apt to burn itself out when grown-up realities were faced. It had not, admittedly, happened to Alice; but there was always hope. Vi would certainly have preferred not to take action again.

Hope evaporated. The bond grew visibly stronger over the weeks. Nicola looked just as happy, as brilliantly illuminated by an internal sun, only less self-conscious, and hardly guilty at all. There was a delay, caused apparently by Alice, so that the birthday party was not after all the expected milestone. They were reprieved. Misery was still possible, and would have changed the sentence.

But no, they went ahead, they announced the engagement, they found a flat, they raised finance from old Hilary, they were still screwing like stoats and loving it; and Vi, with an effort only she knew about, hid her sick and resentful anger, her just and righteous rage – and waited in the certain knowledge that she would once again be given the chance to right this wrong.

The weeks slid by, no obvious opportunity arising; and they were talking about curtain materials, loose covers, wallpapers.

Months before marriage, they were showing a sort of tranquil stability which they should not have felt until months after the marriage; they were no longer surprised at themselves, at one another; they were still excited but no longer astonished. They were used to one another but not bored with one another. It was all very sweet and very sickening.

They had better enjoy it while they could.

They enjoyed it while they could, resuming at full speed after a brief Christmas break (scratchy moments there between mother and daughter, as though Alice had forgotten her own outrageous luck). They enjoyed it under sentence. Vi saw them as mice caressing one another's whiskers on the very lip of the trap. But Vi did not really enjoy the situation. She was in a way sorry for them.

The ingredients came together on a February day – an evening so early that there was scarcely a day at all, the horses coming back from a local expedition, the route exactly known, the time pretty well known, the massive old Volvo parked outside the Village Hall, not five minutes' walk from March Court...

Only her outraged sense of justice could have driven Vi to drive the car as she did.

Behind that weight of solid Swedish metal, she ran no personal risk. She could not afford the luxury of worrying about the horses. She told herself not to consider that aspect, and did not. She was in position in the car twenty-five minutes before they came by, in a farm track off the road, well enough hidden in the half-light. She heard the horses before she saw them. She waited until they were nearly at the next corner, then started the car, switched on the lights, gritted her teeth, and did her little bit for fair play.

She was a bit bruised and shaken when she got out of the car. She had an eight-minute walk, which was probably good for her. Nobody even noticed that she had been out. Nobody, in the general consternation, noticed that she, too, was a casualty. This would have been a little hurting, but on balance it was a good thing that nobody noticed anything about her.

Neither of them thereafter would flaunt their sexual gratification. Justice was done.

A few weeks later, Alice claimed to have received an extraordinary message. An angel appeared to her in a dream, except that it was not exactly an angel, and she was driving her car at the time.

She thought the little wog tart had done it out of jealousy. It was an awfully good theory.

It became quite a hobby of Vi's, fixing up little Alice's cottage for the wheelchair. She threw herself into it. She was determined that the two of them should be as happy and comfortable as could be, now that things had been straightened up. Vi was magnanimous in victory. She could afford to be generous, because things were fair after all.

Alice said history was repeating itself. She did not know how right she was.

Alice thought it was only happening in one way. She thought it was just that another young man was in love with Nicola, that Nicola was going to be married. She was frightened for Nicola, of a new threat to Nicola. She was right, but she did not know the half of it.

She was right to be frightened for Nicola because of Nicola's blatant, tacit boast. Vi saw the look in her face. Everybody saw it. It was as though she had come straight from his bed. Behind her eyes was that internal lamp which had been lit by Hugh Jarvis, in his bed.

The child was happy. Sex made her happy. *Even*

without a body she was fulfilled. How could that be?

Nicola knew self-forgetting bliss. She had experienced it, it had become part of her; she could relive it. As a useless cripple she had a sex life denied to Vi.

It was not to be borne.

Now, on top of this, the man Tommy Johns. It was strange that in all those years Vi had never really noticed him. Indeed she had hardly met him. It was as though he had been kept from her. Perhaps he had. In a qualified sense, he was a replay of Barney. He was another gentle, unassertive man with hidden strength: a man with sex appeal the greater for being almost entirely hidden. Of course there were differences – Tommy Johns was much more worldly, a successful operator in a tough profession, and with it much less happy owing to personal tragedy (a potent combination). To the imperceptive, the two would have seemed sharply different, but to Vi's special eye and special needs the similarity was overwhelming.

They were men who could make it work for her.

They could, but they wouldn't.

They were Alice's property.

Alice had all the luck. All along, all their lives. It was not fair. So that now, in front of Vi's eyes, there was not just one monstrous inequity but two. Mother and daughter both. Not one wrong but two screamed to be put right.

How could that mother best be punished? By way of the daughter. The daughter? By way of herself. Two birds.

The chance came far quicker than before, perhaps because she was more confident, readier to improvise. A shopping expedition to Milchester was all it took: the wheelchair in the multi-storey car-park. If there were other people about, she would wait until another time, some different opportunity.

It was a fine moment. Clang! It was a fine noise. She felt once again that surge of triumph, in making herself mistress of her own fate and that of others. She felt strong and clever.

But all the child got was a black eye.

Yes, she was safely out of the car-park and into the supermarket, one of the crowd, anonymous as one of the trolleys.
 Yes, but something was hooked like a burr in the corner of her memory, something seen only at the very edge of vision, a glimpse, a face.
 Sixteen years on. Could it be the same? Why should it? How? If it was the same, then this must surely be the purest chance, the most harmless coincidence.
 It did not register at the time, at that moment of excitement. It did not register for many days. Then it came back to her, not easy to see, no nearer than the corner of the mind's eye, difficult to concentrate on, difficult to distinguish.
 Could it be the same? If it was the same, how could it possibly be coincidence?
 The gipsy-looking girl, on the last train out of Waterloo that misty November night in 1975. No longer a girl. Could it be the same? Standing this time by the back door of the supermarket, the way in from the car-park, standing waiting, waiting for somebody. Waiting for Vi?
 At midday Vi was sensible about it, logical. Suppose it was the same. The girl had been on the train to

Milchester. Right, she lived in Milchester. She went shopping in the supermarket. Vi might have seen her once a week for the past twenty years, without noticing. Why notice this time? Obviously because she had been excited, on edge, unusually alert. It was not even, properly considered, much of a coincidence – two people living in the same area might be expected, every once in a while, to see one another ...

Yes, supposing it was the same girl, it was actually surprising that Vi had not seen her before.

This line of thought worked at midday, but not at three o'clock in the morning.

In the streets and shops of Milchester and the surrounding villages, Vi found herself searching for the dark, intense face of the girl on the last train from Waterloo.

She saw the girl. She almost saw her. She sort of saw her.

Could it be the same? Of course it could. Why else was the girl on the train to Milchester, if she was not a Milchester girl?

Sixteen years ago. So now she was in her middle thirties. That would be right. That was what she looked. A youngish, slim, gipsy-looking woman of about thirty-five. Plenty of those in Milchester, in any place in the South-West of England.

Nothing to worry about. Nothing to be surprised at.

Now that she was aware of the girl, Vi quite often saw her. That was not strange. But it was strange that she was always to be glimpsed only at the corner of the eye. Look directly at her, and she was gone. Still nothing that could not be more or less explained. Vi saw her, as it happened, in crowded places, busy streets, the bus-stop, the station platform, at the end of an aisle in the supermarket – places where people were all the time moving, where things intervened – cars, buses, trolleys – places where nobody stood still. The girl wouldn't stand there waiting to be stared at. But still it was odd that she was never in the centre of Vi's field of vision, always in a moving blur at the edge . . .

Vi had never been one for lying awake in the small hours. Now she was.

The time came for Nico's final examinations. She steered herself daily into the main hall of the college, and sat at a table with the others under the eye of the invigilator. She was marked not only on those papers but also on her work throughout the course, on her dissertations and on the reports she had brought back from Italy.

No allowances were made for her disability. She needed none. The examiners who marked her papers had never heard of her.

She got an excellent degree, and the offer of the job was confirmed.

She would start the job when she came back from her honeymoon. That would not be before everything was ready at the pavilion. In any case, David could not get away before the finish of the harvest.

Everything was going well, too well.

Everything for Vi was going badly, as badly as ever. All the injustice was still there, all the disgusting unfairness. It was all waiting for another stroke, another push to redress the balance. It was all up to her. She knew what had to be done.

But she was scared.

For the first time, she knew she was observed.

The gipsy girl was watching her.

Wherever Vi went nowadays, she looked for that dark young woman. Often enough she saw her. She would glance in Vi's direction, no more than that. That was enough, more than enough. She was checking up.

Week followed peaceful week, and Alice allowed herself to mock herself. The term ended at her school, and high summer stretched ahead. No voices came, no colours of blood or of death inside her skull. Premonition left her alone, and disaster left Nicola alone.

Everybody was away. Felicity Peacock was away. Nicola saw a great deal of David, although he was very busy. Great things were being done at the pavilion. The wedding was still two months off.

Nicola's life was incomplete, as it always would be, but within the bounds of the possible it was as good as could be.

Alice allowed herself to relax.

Old Matt Norman came that August to stay at March Court; he had been in the Coldstreams with Hilary, in North Africa at the end of the war. He was an undemanding guest, requiring only to be topped up once an hour. He and Hilary were deep in one another's confidence, but as far as Vi could hear, neither had anything of interest to confide. Their lives were blameless. They were law-abiding and charitable. At worst, they told stories revealing ancient brother-officers as being snobbish, of having had one too many at a regimental dinner, of making a pass at a nurse in a military hospital. These long, long reminiscences were like some pleasantly monotonous rural sound – bees in fruit blossom, distant cows lowing at milking time, a ripple of water over sandy shallows.

Even Vi's ceaseless bitterness was lulled by the soporific drone of Matt and Hilary. It blanketed the ulcerous sense of unfairness. She thought less often about her sister and niece. When she did, a sleepy voice at the edge of her mind said, 'The hell with it.' It was too hot to worry about other people's sex lives. It was too peaceful. The conversation of the two old men was like Mogadon, like Pentothal.

Then there was that Sunday afternoon, the fourth day of Matt's visit. Sunday was often a day of champagne cocktails and the braying of voices over the lawns, but not this time. Everybody was away. A great peace had descended on the neighbourhood, disturbed only by the distant bells of the Cathedral, by the creaking of deck-chairs as the old men uncrossed and recrossed their legs. There were no swimmers breaking the surface of the pool, no trout that of the river. The birds had fallen silent. The very air was deep in siesta.

Vi wandered indoors from the terrace to get more coffee. She knew that Hilary would have done so if she had asked, but he was happy and deep in conversation. She was not interested in anything the Sunday papers had to tell her, in reviews of books she was never going to read or music she was never going to hear. She was content to stroll as far as the kitchen.

She came back onto the terrace six minutes later, back through the French windows of the drawing room, back from the honey-coloured shade indoors to the green shade out of doors.

She heard Hilary sleepily say, 'Oh yes, Vi's quite a good old thing. Good housekeeper. Reliable. We rub along pretty well.'

261

'Bit of a half-life, eh?' said Matt after a pause.

'It would be, without Alice and the girl.'

'Nicola? Is that what she's called?'

'My little Nico.'

'They're good news, those two,' said Matt. 'I like those two.'

'Why do you think I bought a house here?'

'I thought ... the way I heard it ... I thought it was so that Vi would be near her sister.'

'Everybody thought that. Vi thought that. Vi didn't make the decision. She didn't buy this house. It wasn't her money. It was my money and my decision. I came here so that I could be near Vi's sister.'

Vi went softly away. She took the coffee-pot back to the kitchen. She emptied the coffee into the sink. She sat slowly down on a stool by the kitchen table.

On the table was a chopping block, used by Maria for vegetables, with a heavy knife and a couple of scrubbed carrots. Without knowing what she was doing, Vi began to chop up a carrot, very slowly, into tiny pieces.

The corn silvered, and fell to the blades of the combine. The fruit swelled and reddened. Gradually the world reassembled, with sunburned noses and sheaves of holiday photographs.

Felicity Peacock came back, pale as a midwinter snowdrop. It was one of her ways of being different.

Gerald Orchard came back, but nobody knew what colour he had become, because nobody looked at him.

The cricket pavilion was inching towards completion. It was going to be handsome as well as practical. Nico became intimately friendly with bricklayer, plasterer, plumber and electrician, and they became her slaves. The plasterer and the electrician nearly came to blows about the colour of the dining room. Tommy Johns was happy to have been so useful.

Nico's marriage to David was thus brought daily nearer. It could happen at short notice, because no fuss was to be made. This was Nico's decision. The other one would have been large and glamorous, and the thought of that too painfully reverberated. A romantic wedding dress, a veil and tiara, did not go in a wheelchair: so Nico thought. Hilary was disappointed.

The autumn term approached for Alice, and the need for leaving Nicola for hours of every day. David told Alice that he would look after Nicola, but he was still very busy, and he meant something different.

The evenings began to draw in. Earlier shadows crossed all those peaceful lawns.

Everybody's local hero and heroine, David and Nico, faced at best a good second-best, and they both knew they were lucky to expect so much.

It was a far cry, for Nico, from the almost unbearable happiness of two years earlier. They had been too confident then, too blatantly happy. They had tempted Providence. Never again, for any of them, that intensity of magic, that first-time miracle. What she had now was a serene contentment.

It was not a bad thing to have.

It was safer.

When Vi was an important secretary in an important advertising agency, all those years before in the hectic sixties, she had been a very good organizer. It was one of the things she was paid for – setting up meetings with people who did not expect to be at any meeting, who did not expect to be sold a new television commercial. She had to juggle dates and times and engagement books, and get people thinking they were going where they chose, when really they were going where Vi and her boss chose . . .

It was an administrative skill, and a diplomatic one. Vi had not lost it. Her popularity as a hostess, as a social queen in the town and its countryside, had not come about by accident – purely by the opening of bottles. Some people had to be kept apart, others pushed together; some chemical reactions worked in large parties, some in small, some at noon and some at midnight, some in full dress and formal circumstances, some in towels by the pool. Vi had made and unmade matches without number, not by accident. She had made and unmade friendships; created and destroyed loyalties. It kept her busy, at times when she had very little else to do. She was not slapdash in her arrangements, not absent-minded, not in too much of a hurry. She had brought all her skills from Mayfair to Milchester.

She remained what she had always been, like all good confidential secretaries: particularly good on the telephone. Once she had extracted her boss from untold complications, latterly herself. She had cajoled and blustered, persuaded and bullied, given imitations of anger and apology, and told the most convincing lies you ever heard – like all good confidential secretaries, like all successful social manipulators.

So that when now she made her plan, she went very gently and deliberately about carrying it out; and although it was complex, and involved several people, it was nothing special compared to some of the arrangements of the ad-men in the old days. You drew up a timetable, and you sat down at a telephone. It was something she knew how to do.

You had to be a choreographer. A puppet-master. And a psychologist. You had to be prepared to take pains.

You had to be very certain that what you were doing was right.

She waited until the school term began. That meant that she knew where some of her puppets were in a general way, and could find out where they were going to be with great exactness. They would be held in suspension in classrooms until she needed them. The movements of the others could be predicted only roughly, but they could be influenced. In the end they would all do exactly as they were told.

Vi posed as a silly parent, on the telephone to the office of the Hardy House School in Milchester. She spoke to a grim secretary, a woman unlike herself as a secretary. She could tell that the creature despised her, probably despised all the parents of all the boys at the school. Nevertheless she gave Vi the information she said she wanted, as well as much information which she actually wanted. Vi learned the exact hours during which Gerald Orchard could be expected to be taking a class, and those in which the duty roster had him tied to study periods and prep; she learned what afternoons in the week he would be supervising games, and when he was free. The secretary was not really aware that she was giving Vi these details. But she was not betraying any confidences. None of it was secret. There was no harm in anybody knowing Gerald Orchard's timetable; at least, there had never previously been.

Vi spoke to another secretary in a school office, the little school where Alice taught young children. Vi knew the ancient spinster who had that job three days a week, knew her to be intelligent and suspicious-minded. If Vi asked about Alice, even in the most roundabout way, her questions would be reported to Alice. The source of the questions must therefore be precisely defined but obscurely remote, so that nobody could check up even if they wanted to. Vi became the elderly widow of an American Archdeacon who had once known Barnabas Maude.

Nobody at the school would check up on a long-dead American person. They would not bother; they would not know how to go about it. Vi did not know if there was such a thing as an American Archdeacon. The secretary accepted with some astonishment that old Mrs Marcia Hogwood had found among her late husband's papers a note in glowing terms about Barnabas Maude, and finding herself, on a visit to Britain, in the neighbourhood of Milchester . . .

Mrs Hogwood gave the secretary a number on which she could be reached, the telephone of the friends where she was staying. She found out, while she was at it, at what times Mrs Maude might be available to call, and also when she might, during the day, have an hour or more free.

Alice would ring the number, which would turn out to be a wrong number, the number of no matter whom in the Milchester area, an old woman from far away having made a mistake, perhaps through not understanding the English system of telephone numbers. Alice would be curious, no doubt, and the secretary also, but there would be nothing they could do about it. Alice would wait for Marcia Hogwood to call again, and leave messages in case she did.

She might ultimately wonder if Marcia Hogwood was genuine, but there would still be nothing she could do about it.

Vi put Alice's and Gerald Orchard's timetables together. She moved them backwards and forwards until vacant spaces coincided.

She rang up the Deanery in Milchester, in the knowledge (from Nico) that Felicity Peacock was in London.

The Dean answered, which made things easy for Vi. He boomed with magisterial friendliness down the wire, unsuspecting, communicative, unusually well informed, as it happened, about his adopted daughter's plans, since he had dealt with a number of calls similar to Vi's over the previous couple of days. Felicity's engagement book, left by the telephone in the hall of the Deanery, was peppered with job interviews.

Vi, on hearing this, became the secretary of a prospective employer. She made an appointment for Miss Peacock to see Mr Scudder, Personnel Director of a firm of management consultants. Vi did not have to give a performance, this time, but only to remember her own manner in another epoch.

Felicity would be disappointed that Mr Scudder and his company did not exist. That did not worry Vi. By the time the appointment was supposed to happen, Felicity would have other things on her mind, such as being accused of murder.

Vi laid Felicity's timetable alongside the others.

Hilary appeared, saying that it was time for a drinkie. Vi had tried to get him out of the way of saying 'drinkie', which she thought he had adopted for her sake, as belonging to the world to which she had belonged. But she had given up bothering about it. Hilary was one of the ones who was going to be punished.

Vi abandoned the telephone until she could be left alone with it again. But if her voice was idle her brain was busy.

When she could, she rang up the Normandy estate office. She spoke to the answering machine. She was yet another secretary, making the call on behalf of an insurance company. She was soliciting business in a manner that conferred a favour. She did not leave a number, but called again, and again, until she spoke to the part-time farm secretary. She found out when it would be fruitless for her boss to come to Normandy, when Mr David Parkinson would be at Milchester Market or in London or Bristol, or had an appointment with a buyer or seller or contractor. There were great blocks of time when David Parkinson was away or tied up. That was very good.

Vi did not want David available. She wanted him far away and otherwise engaged.

She put David's timetable beside the others.

Vi put aside the telephone. She went to Turner's Cottage, and found out from Nico what Nico's engagements were. Nico had plenty of engagements, especially with the people working at the pavilion. Vi made a note of the times without seeming to do so.

Vi said, 'Speaking of the pavilion, I gather you're pleased with that funny little man who's been doing your plastering.'

'He's amazing,' said Nico. 'I've wasted hours watching him. He seems to be crawling, taking the most tremendous pains, being absurdly meticulous, and then you suddenly realize he's done yards and yards.'

'Would you mind if I went and had a word with him? I don't want to distract him from the pavilion, but we're going to need some high-class patching on one of the cornices.'

'He's your man. I should think he's pretty booked up. Yes, of course, go and talk to him. If you like, I can find out when he's going to be there. He seems to have about eight jobs going at once.'

'That could be a bit of a bore.'

'Yes, but he's worth bearing with.'

Vi learned, in this conversation and another with the men at the pavilion, when the place would be occupied and when deserted.

She was travelling back from the pavilion to March Court, driving her BMW slowly along the edge of Calloway's Wood, enjoying the golden evening and the music of Richard Strauss, when she saw the woman.

She looked more than ever a gipsy, in a long red skirt and a bright shawl over her head and shoulders in the manner of the Balkans. She was beside the road, on the verge, amongst bracken and rough grass, under the trees at the edge of the wood, the overspreading branches of mixed oak trees and pines; she was in the shadow of the dense branches, so that her face under the shawl was hardly visible. But Vi saw that she was looking intently at the car, at herself. It was as though she had been waiting for that car, that driver: as though she was checking up.

Vi had the feeling that the gipsy woman was making a note of the number of the car: that she would remember it and write it down.

Vi told herself that she was allowed to drive her own car down a public highway, without feeling guilty and frightened.

The woman lived in or near Milchester. She was going for a walk in Calloway's Wood. Probably her bicycle was propped against a tree somewhere out of sight.

If she wanted the number of the car, she was welcome to it.

Vi was now in a position to select a day and time when the pavilion would be empty; Alice, Nico, Felicity Peacock, Gerald Orchard and Vi herself all available; David Parkinson away, and Hilary and others out of the way.

There was more to it than that.

Vi needed a time shortly before which her people would not be available to answer the telephone. But they must become available very soon afterwards. They would be given messages. They would get their messages, but they would not hear the voice that had made the call.

It was all pretty tricky. It might not work the first time. It was fun meanwhile. It was what Vi was good at. It took her back twenty-five years.

There was a bit more preparation to be done, the issuing of what Hilary called 'warning orders', a phrase Vi supposed he remembered from the Army. These had to come as messages, too – messages for Felicity Peacock and Gerald Orchard. The warning orders were that some time in the near future there would be a request to come immediately to the pavilion.

This would not seem extraordinary. Nico and Felicity were accustomed to sending for one another at short notice. Gerald Orchard would manage to believe that Nico wanted him.

Alice and Nico herself would not need warning orders. Alice need only be told that Nicola wanted her. Any of a thousand emergencies at the pavilion would bring Nico. There had to be someone to help her into her car, who would not then come with her in the car. That would have to be fixed. Vi set herself to fix it.

The day established itself as the following Thursday,

the second in October; the time as three in the afternoon.

Vi hoped it would be fine for the murder, but it was not really important.

CHAPTER THIRTEEN

THAT FIRST DATE WAS ABORTED, that Thursday afternoon, because Felicity Peacock disappeared somewhere, and David Parkinson cancelled an appointment so that he could go with Nico to the pavilion.

The next opportunity was late morning on the following Tuesday, but it was possible that at short notice, on a weekday morning, either of the schoolteachers might be needed, might become unavailable to Vi.

Besides, it was raining; a miserable morning.

Time was slipping by. The people were picking mushrooms in the fields and blackberries in the hedges. Farmers were seeing the end of the worst of their working year. The pavilion was almost ready for occupation, even by Nico, and although the date remained a secret, it was whispered among the villages that the marriage was fixed.

Another reason for haste was that, pretty soon, the pavilion would be on the telephone. At the moment anybody who went there dropped like Robinson Crusoe out of human ken.

Another Thursday came, with a gentle autumn sun dispersing a golden morning mist from the watermeadows, with brilliant colours spangling the hedgerows, scarlet hips and haws among the silvery drifts of old man's beard, with drops of water kindled to fiery diamonds, beading the cobwebs between twigs, with Nico's hair its strange silver-gold in that sunshine, and the golden blush of her cheek remembering the stronger suns of midsummer.

Vi saw Hilary off in his Mercedes, drew up her mental checklist, and sat down to the telephone in her sitting room, out of earshot of the servants.

At the Hardy House School, a message was left by telephone with the secretary in the office for Mr Gerald Orchard, who was taking a class at the time, saying that he was needed by Miss Maude at the cricket pavilion in East Brantham. She would be there about three. It could be assumed, though it was not stated, that Miss Maude herself was telephoning with this request.

Gerald Orchard was a weedy but valuable red herring. It was known to a few people that Nico had turned him down the previous Christmas, more or less brusquely; it had been said that he harboured extreme resentment on that score, little as he was entitled to any such thing; it was said that he had been in contact, in some sense, with that dangerous Felicity Peacock, who had reason to hate and envy Nicola. All this might not be widely known now, but it would be widely known after the tragedy. It was just the sort of thing that came out.

Felicity Peacock had an appointment with a dental hygienist at noon; she was then meeting a friend for a semi-business lunch at a pub called the Bunch of Sparrowgrass. She planned (said the Dean) to spend the afternoon at home, recasting and retyping her CV. A message was left with the dentist's receptionist that Nicola Maude wanted Felicity at the pavilion at three. She was not to ring in the meantime, for unstated reasons, but simply to turn up. It was a question of the position of wall-lights, which had to be decided immediately because of the plastering. The dentist's receptionist assumed that the caller was Miss Maude herself, and would probably tell Felicity so when the latter emerged from the chair.

Felicity was another and still more potent distraction. Her position in successive triangles was already known exactly to a few, and guessed by many; it would be seen universally, after the tragedy, as a more than sufficient motive. Alice's view, in other words, would be shared by almost everybody.

It would be on record that Felicity had been sent for, to the cricket pavilion. The dentist's receptionist would say so even if Felicity did not.

People would be hard put to it to choose which was the murderer. A lot of people would think that the two of them planned it together. 'In cahoots,' said Vi to herself. More and more people would think like that.

Vi felt powerful, organizing public opinion in advance.

She was getting her own back at last.

Alice was teaching until 12.45, then supervising the children's lunch. Just before lunch she would be given a message by the school secretary, who would have taken it a few minutes previously on the telephone: Nicola needed her at the pavilion at four. Never mind why. That was enough.

In transmitting this message to the old secretary, Vi did not try to pretend to be Nicola, who was well known to the people there. She was somebody in a great hurry, in too much of a hurry to explain who was speaking and why Nicola herself was not speaking. The secretary was puzzled but not suspicious.

Nobody would ever have the faintest idea who made that call or why. Obviously it was not the murderer, if they decided there was a murderer. Alice's presence at the scene of the action was in practical terms unnecessary. But morally it was necessary to Vi. Poetically it was necessary.

Nico was at home, in the garden. She was pruning an escallonia which had at last finished flowering, much of which she could reach from her wheelchair.

She had the cordless telephone.

She had nothing particular to do that afternoon. David was away. There was nobody working at the pavilion. She was at Vi's disposal.

She was indeed.

Vi packed a holdall with the necessary things. She knew exactly what she needed, because she had thought about it carefully and made a list, as she had done in the days when she was a secretary. She had examined Nicola's car, and made measurements, so she knew the things she had were the right size.

Eddie Datchett came round to put Nico into her car and the wheelchair into the back. Eddie was disappointed that this was all that was required of him. Driving Nico had been the high point of his life. He did not allow this to show, but with silent efficiency tucked her into the driving seat, and stowed the chair behind her so that it would not rattle.

To most people, Nico would have said where she was going, if only by way of making conversation. You did not make conversation with Eddie. He never asked a question, and seldom even answered one. He was almost too restful a companion.

Nico drove to East Brantham, wondering what was on Vi's mind. It was a lovely afternoon, and she was more or less happy.

She expected Vi to be waiting at the pavilion, with her car. Vi was there, but the car not. Nico wondered how Vi had come. She had certainly not walked, not Vi. Somebody had presumably given her a lift, and she was relying on Nico for a lift home.

'Hello, darling,' said Vi. 'I've been stranded here, like somebody on a desert island. I couldn't even get in.'

'I should hope not,' said Nico, laughing.

It was four minutes to three.

'Just at this moment, and before we get down to the business of the afternoon—' began Vi.

'What is the business of the afternoon?'

'We haven't got down to it yet. Before we do, will you very kindly take me along the back drive?'

'Yes, of course. Why?'

'There's a fungus I want to look at.'

This was ridiculous. Vi was not a person who looked at fungi. She had never been known to spare a glance at a wildflower or a bird. It was so ridiculous that Nico simply nodded, and Vi got into the little car beside her. Vi was carrying a canvas bag with a zipped top, the bag distorted by something inside it which did not easily fit into it. Nico supposed it was something for the pavilion or its not-yet-created garden. She thought Vi would have left this awkward little burden on the veranda of the pavilion, but it came with Vi in the car, under her feet in the passenger seat.

Nico started the car. She drove round to the back of the pavilion, and along a track which went through a belt of pine trees. The track crossed a narrow strip of waste scrub, once pheasant preserve, and went through a small, dense wood before joining the road. Probably it had once been used as the back drive of the pavilion, in the high days of polo and smart club cricket matches, but it no longer deserved such a title. It was sometimes used by the builders.

Vi asked Nico to stop in the middle of the wood. It was only as she did so that Nico saw that Vi's car was there, backed into a clearing beside the track. The car was pretty well invisible from anywhere except the track.

'Can you park beside mine?' said Vi.

'I thought you'd been abandoned.'

'No. Somebody else is going to be abandoned.'

Nico parked beside Vi's car. Her car was also now hidden.

'That's it,' said Vi.

'I expect you'll explain in the end.'

'I shouldn't think so,' said Vi. 'There won't really be time.'

Vi got out of the car. She picked up the canvas bag and put it on the ground between the cars. She busied herself with the bag, with something in the bag, but Nico could not see what she was doing. Vi was preparing some kind of surprise. Presently Nico would know what this was all about.

Vi opened the back door of Nico's car, on Nico's side. She climbed half into the car, behind Nico, pushing the folded wheelchair along the back seat to make room for herself. Nico saw in the rear mirror that she was wearing cotton gloves, which she must have taken out of the bag. They were gloves she used for light and dainty jobs in the garden, which were the only sort of jobs she did in the garden. What gardening was she going to do in the wood behind the pavilion?

Vi had taken something else out of the holdall – a length of broad webbing with leather straps at the ends and a buckle on one of these. Nico saw that it was a surcingle, used over a New Zealand rug on a horse put out in the winter. Suddenly the surcingle was over Nico's head and her shoulders and arms, and round her chest below her breasts and just above her waist, round her upper arms, holding her body and arms into the driving seat of the car. It was pulled tight, very tight. Nico heard the little squeak and click of the buckle as the strap was secured behind the driving seat.

Nico could move her head and shoulders, and her forearms and hands and fingers. But nothing else. Above the waist she was imprisoned and below it paralysed. She could not reach the door-handle or the handle of the window, or the ignition key or the controls of the car. With her fingertips she could reach the traffic-indicator lever and the lights and the windscreen-wipers. She could reach the horn-button, but it did not work unless the ignition was switched on.

She could shout, but with the windows of the car shut she would be heard only at a short distance. Her car was surrounded by a thick wood. The road was fifty yards away, and the only things on the road were vehicles going by, and few of them. There was no chance of Nico's voice reaching anybody at the pavilion, even if there was anybody at the pavilion.

'Why are you killing me?' asked Nico.

'I'm not,' said Vi. 'Your car is.'

Vi was busy with her bag on the ground, and then with something out of Nico's sight at the back of the car. She slightly opened one of the rear windows. She put the end of a hosepipe through the window from outside. It was the rolled hosepipe which had distorted the canvas bag, pushing outwards from tight coils. No doubt the other end was attached to the exhaust-pipe of the car, Vi having previously prepared some kind of linkage.

Vi's face had an expression Nico had never seen on it before, a kind of grim satisfaction. It might be the expression of somebody taking a dead rat out of a trap, or squeezing the trigger of a rifle aimed at some vexatious predator.

Vi opened the front door of the car, and leaned in. She was still wearing the cotton gloves. She kept her hands out of reach of Nico's hands. She turned the key in the dash and started the engine of Nico's car.

'This is all,' said Vi, 'for the sake of fairness.'

Nico had nothing to say. She did not feel like pleading, and it would have been useless. As well as satisfaction, there was absolute determination in Vi's face. She knew exactly what she was doing, and she thought it a good thing to do.

Nico felt desperately sorry for her mother and David and Felicity and other people who loved her, but for herself she did not so greatly mind. She would never have killed herself – she did not think suicide was necessarily a sin, but for her it would have been cowardly, selfish, ungrateful and immoral. It was not an option. But the life that stretched ahead of her was not so very wonderful. To go to sleep painlessly, on a fine autumn afternoon, was not so bad.

'I don't really mind, you know,' she said to Vi's retreating back; but the doors and windows of the car were shut, and the engine was running, so it was doubtful if Vi heard.

Vi strolled back towards the pavilion. There was no hurry. It was necessary to go delicately. She did not want to be heard or seen. She did not want to get flushed and untidy.

It was lucky that the trees behind the pavilion were pines. She could go under them with only the whispered crunch of her footsteps on the carpet of dead pine needles, and there was no undergrowth to crackle and grab.

Felicity Peacock's car was there, a vehicle well known locally, an ancient Beetle.

A bicycle was there, propped on the railing of the veranda. Vi did not know one bicycle from another, but she thought there were no prizes for guessing whose bicycle this was.

They would be nonplussed.

Both would be sure that Nico had asked them to be there. Each would be much surprised to see the other. Each would be annoyed that Nico had asked the other. They would be suspicious and guarded. They would be possessive about Nico.

Did they know one another beyond the barest acquaintance? Vi was not sure, but she thought not. Their close relationship was, as far as she knew, entirely her own invention, designed to get everybody looking in the wrong direction. Certainly they would have recognized one another, and certainly with surprise and displeasure. They had arrived separately. They would leave separately. Each would think the other had killed Nico.

It would be impossible to prove that either had, but it might be very difficult to prove that they had not.

Another small car mumbled up the drive to the pavilion.

Alice.

Alice would send them both packing. She was already

violently suspicious of Felicity, and she knew what Nico thought about Gerald Orchard. The stage was set for a good row. Vi wished she had been within earshot. She watched Alice get out of her car, look round for Nico's, see Felicity's, advance towards the veranda.

Vi was hugging herself when she saw that somebody else was watching; standing in the cover of the pine trees, like herself, and watching the drama at the pavilion.

A thin, dark woman of about thirty-five, with a long, gaudy skirt and a gipsy shawl over her head and shoulders.

She was not watching the pavilion. She was watching Vi. She had been doing so all along.

She had known where to come and when to come, and she had been waiting in the wood. She had seen Vi and the surcingle, Vi and the hosepipe.

And she knew about the last train from Milchester, sixteen years before, and she knew about the ramp in the multi-storey car-park.

It came to Vi, like a blow on the back of the head, that she had tried once too often. Hilary had tipped her into this one, Hilary's confidence to Matt Norman.

And Tommy Johns.

And this pavilion, which might have been designed by Providence specially for Nico.

And Nico, looking happy when she had no right to be happy.

Vi saw that it had all been too much for her, that she had been pushed too far, beyond prudence.

It was simply another thing that was unfair, but now she had overdone it and she was found out and destroyed.

Vi found herself creeping back out of the pine trees,

and across the belt of scrub. She was in the wood. She did not look round, but she knew very well that the gipsy girl was following her, moving stealthily, watching everything. Vi knew what the gipsy girl expected of her, demanded of her. She knew she must do what she was told, or it would be worse, much worse, the police, the courtroom, the newspapers—

She would get Alice's pity, but at least she would not see it.

Here were the cars, the hum of Nico's engine. Nico was slumped back in her seat, looking as though deeply and peacefully asleep.

The child was happy and fortunate even in death.

Vi opened the door of Nico's car. She switched off the engine. She detached one end of the hosepipe from the exhaust, and pulled the other out of the window.

'All right, all right,' she said to the gipsy girl, who was watching from the wood.

Vi attached the hosepipe to her own exhaust, and put the other end through the window behind the driver's seat. Once again she was unhurried and definite in her movements.

She strapped herself into the car.

She said aloud, 'I don't know why I did that.'

But since she was buckled in, she let it be.

She turned the key and started the engine.

She could just see the gipsy girl in the tangle of trees, looking at her intently, making sure that she did what she was told.

'She's perfectly all right. They say it would have taken at least another half hour.'

The three of them stood under the walnut tree outside Turner's Cottage.

David Parkinson said, 'What made you go down that track? What made you think they were there?'

'I don't know,' said Alice.

'I think God made you go,' said Felicity Peacock. 'Can I see Nico now?'

'Yes, she's expecting you.'

After Felicity had gone indoors, David said, 'Was your sister completely crazy? Is that what it was?'

'I hope so,' said Alice. 'I do hope so.'